Small Victories

Books by Sallie Bingham

Passion and Prejudice
The Way it is Now
The Touching Hand
After Such Knowledge

Small Victories

a novel by

Sallie Bingham

𝒵

ZOLAND BOOKS

Cambridge, Massachusetts

First published in 1992 by
Zoland Books, Inc.,
384 Huron Avenue, Cambridge, MA 02138

PUBLISHER'S NOTE:
This book is a work of fiction. Names, characters,
places, and incidents are either the product of the
author's imagination or are used fictitiously. Any
resemblance to actual events or locales or persons,
living or dead, is entirely coincidental.

ISBN 0-944072-20-8 (cloth)
ISBN 0-944072-25-9 (paperback)

Printed in the United States of America
Book design by Boskydell Studio

Library of Congress Cataloging-in-Publication Data

Bingham, Sallie.
Small victories : a novel / by Sallie Bingham. — 1st ed.
p. cm.
ISBN 0-944072-20-8
ISBN 0-944072-25-9 (pbk.)
I. Title.
PS3552.I5S62   1992   91-66474
813'.54—dc20   CIP

IN MEMORY
JWB

Small Victories

North Carolina
1958

Chapter One

L ouise had been awake since five, waiting for the alarm to go off. When it did, she snatched the clock from the nightstand, snagging a doily, and squeezed its face before she remembered to push down the alarm button. Then she rested for a while, holding the clock, in the high old bed that had belonged to her father. The room had not been changed since his death, fifteen years before. The armoire still held his clothes, and under the bed his boots lay side by side, the mud from his last barracks inspection lining the cracks. Louise sat for a while, remembering him, quite calmly, as though he had shrunk to match the dark portrait over her desk. Paying bills, she often stopped to stare at it, thinking of nights when she had prayed for him: Oh Daddy, be safe. She had carried on even more than her sister, Shelby, when he died.

Across the hall, in their mother's room, Shelby turned and groaned. Louise listened. Everything depended on Shelby's mood. If she got out of bed on the wrong side, the whole day would go badly. Louise listened for several minutes. Impossible to tell from the thrashing whether

Shelby was lost in another nightmare or only trying to get out of the sheets. Finally Louise slid out of bed—she was light and thin as a child—and padded across the hall.

"Good morning, merry sunshine," she said.

Shelby had the pillow over her head.

"It's time to get up." Louise took the pillow by the corner and tossed it on the floor. Shelby's face looked like a stone in the wild swirls of her hair. She was lightly and freshly sweating; moisture beaded her pink face. Louise looked at her left hand, arranged on the turned-down sheet, and saw that she had put back the ring.

"Get up so we can get started," she said. "You know they're coming at ten." At the same time, she reached for her sister's squat hand. Quickly she let it fall. She did not mind anything about Shelby except her dampness, the perpetual moistness of a large woman in a warm climate. Taking her hand again, she began gently turning the ring on her fourth finger.

Shelby opened her eyes and stared at Louise.

"You know you can't wear that ring to the station," Louise said, trying to ease it over the swollen joint.

Shelby snatched her hand away and hid it under the sheet. Louise considered. Shelby, aroused, was a good deal stronger than she was.

"I laid out your new yellow dress," she said at last, turning away from the bed. "And I'm going to let you have sugar cereal if you get yourself downstairs fast." She tried to tune her voice to the exact pitch of careless insistence: too careless, and Shelby would not get up; too insistent, and she might begin to cry. "I'll wait for you downstairs," Louise said.

As she left the room, Louise heard the bed creak and knew that her sister was putting out her feet.

She smiled. The first step was taken. Now they would have plenty of time to get to the train. She pursed her lips and whistled a few bars of "Rock of Ages," running her hand down the skin-smooth mahogany stair rail. This is what nobody in the wide world understands, she thought. This happiness. Small victories! She thought of Big Tom, her cousin, riding the train, and wondered if he had ever had that feeling.

He was a big man, from the Big World—they had called it that in all seriousness when they were children—and he thought that her life was drudgery. "Louise, Louise, you were not made to wash bathroom floors," he had said once, patting the shining flank of the claw-footed bathtub. She had shaken her head then, too, commiserating with the frail spinster he saw, wondering how she stood it, wondering whether she was going to be a martyr for life. Then, when he had left and she was wiping out the toilet, she had dropped her head almost to her hands and laughed, "like water running down a drain," he would have said. He had slid his hand down the stair rail a million times, but he had never felt it, smooth as the inside of an elbow, as she felt it while Shelby was getting out of bed.

Still, she would have to think of a way to get that ring off.

She went down to the kitchen and lighted the stove. It was damp in the basement room, and she shivered, then took her mother's shawl off the hook behind the door and draped it over her shoulders. Standing on tiptoe, she smiled at herself in the triangular piece of mirror stuck up next to the fireplace. She knew that the verdict had never been rescinded: she was the plain one of the two sisters, fits or no fits, and it would always be that way. Her parents had both told her—her mother gently, her father with sharp concern—that she would have to make her way in the world on sheer strength of character, since she had neither looks nor charm. Stubborn rudeness had never done Shelby any harm; she had been a blond, curly-headed child whose emotional storms, it was thought, would pass. Louise, however, had needed to cultivate a precise mixture of humility and wit. Her father had predicted she would never leave home.

He would have taken Shelby by the hair of her head and pulled that ring off, Louise thought, then rapidly she prayed, Oh Daddy, be safe, as she had always prayed when he was in a rage. It had seemed to her that he might burst, purple and swollen with the words he hardly dared to utter. When she was grown, she had learned to manage him: she would shriek at him, like her mother, "Now you stop that!" Then she would sit back to watch him run down, fuming and rumbling, enjoying it, as though she had fanned the blaze.

She would have to magic that ring off.

She filled the old tin pot with water and measured some coffee out of the can. It was nearly empty, which meant she would need to drive to the supermarket. The supermarket delighted her; she could lose herself forever in the aisles. The brightness of everything they sold there—even the plastic cereal dishes came in brilliant pinks and blues— pleased and appalled her about equally.

When she was younger, she had tended to dress herself in grays and whites and avoid the newer parts of town, but now that she was forty-five and "out of the woods," as Big Tom called it, she could afford to indulge herself. Nobody would ever misunderstand. Also, she had the money to spend now on cereal dishes or a plastic purse with enormous daisies on it or red shoes with green plastic heels—all inappropriate and thrilling. Big Tom had started to send the money after he told her not to wash any bathroom floors. The check came every month now, with a letter from the bank. Before, they had been getting by on Papa's meager leavings.

Big Tom had also hired her a maid. No; you could not

even as a joke call Bella a maid. She was the niece or more likely the out-of-wedlock daughter of old Herman down at the store, and she had always been in the habit of coming up to help when she needed ready cash. Now she was on a regular schedule—Tom had typed it himself and taped it next to the stove—and she had had the nerve to go out and buy herself a white plastic apron. Still, she didn't do much and never would, as long as Louise had the say-so. The house, after all, was hers, and she had always attended to it.

"Shelby!" she called up the stairs, sweetly, and wondered if her sister had gone back to bed.

There was no use in looking yet. She put the sugar-cereal box on the kitchen table, wondering if everything Tom did for them was free. That did not seem likely, from what she knew of human nature, but then Tom was a special case. He would have been able—at least in the years when she had known him best—to make a pure gesture, a wave of his hand, causing flowers to sprout on a barren plain, water to gush from a stone, beauty and pleasure and sweetness to spring out of the dry dust. He had been that kind of boy, that kind of young man—generous, shining, with his long, pale fairness and his blue eyes. He had changed, of course, had grown important, and thick and older; she had been shocked to see the size of his stomach the last time they went swimming. But she knew she had kept a corner of his boyishness; he was still young with her. That was something neither his wife nor his son could properly understand.

She put the place mat with the cardinals on it—another gift from Tom—on the kitchen table and poured the sugar cereal into Shelby's bowl. It had long ago become apparent that Shelby, when faced with the simplest decision, would fly into a whirlwind rage. So Louise decided for her. Not only about the small things, such as buying her clothes—which was not such a small thing, since Shelby loved dresses and would brood over the selection—but about the large things as well, such as where they would go for the two-week vacation Big Tom gave them every summer, and what they would send him for Christmas. The year before, Shelby had knitted him an orange muffler; she was quite good with her hands. But when Louise had gone out, on behalf of them both, and bought a silver pen-and-pencil set for Tom's desk, Shelby had sulked for days.

As for this summer's vacation, Louise had to smile when she thought about that. For the first time since Papa's death, they had gone to the beach. They took a room in a quiet motel near the water, and Louise found a stand where for a dollar they could buy fruit for lunch. She had not realized that their beach happened to be the one patronized by the state football team, which was in training nearby. Shelby stayed out from morning until night, turning bright red in the sun; mostly she just watched the boys prancing back and forth. Towards the end Louise took her, for a special treat, to one of the practice games, but that was a mistake. Shelby got completely out of hand. She jumped up and down, waving her arms and shouting, until the people in the seats behind them started to complain. Louise gave them some acid looks, but by then the situation was beyond mending. After the final whistle, Louise tried to keep Shelby from racing out onto the field, and Shelby, carried away, scratched Louise's arm. Louise was furious, but underneath she felt her old sharp smile, buried, like a seed. "You little wildcat," she said. Shelby spent every evening for the rest of the vacation sitting in the car, waiting to be driven to a game. It was around then that she had commenced wearing the gold ring; Louise had not yet discovered where it had come from.

She went out into the hall again to call Shelby, using the

same kitten-sweet voice her mother had used nearly forty years before to wake them up. Then Shelby had been in a crib, and Louise, who had graduated to an iron cot, had helped her fat little sister over the rails.

Shelby was already coming down the stairs. She was wearing her blue bathrobe and her pink bunny slippers, and to Louise she looked good enough to eat. Shelby was, of course, much too heavy, but in spite of that she managed to look doll-like, with her hand poised daintily on the mahogany rail. Louise had always been proud of Shelby's hands; she cut her nails every Friday and applied two coats of clear polish. Shelby's hands would never be spoiled by dishwashing.

Louise waited at the bottom while Shelby came down, one step at a time. She slid her hand carefully along the rail. At the bottom she lifted her hand off as though it were made out of glass and placed it in the crook of Louise's arm. Louise guided her down the hall, past the sharp angles of the hall tree, and on into the kitchen. Shelby sighed with pleasure when she saw her cereal, and dropped her hand from Louise's arm. She hurried to the table, then waited for Louise to pull her chair out. "My, we are good this morning," Louise said. Then she pulled out the heavy, dark-colored chair with the dingy needlepoint seat her mother had made. Shelby settled into it, as lightly as a balloon, and Louise, too, sighed: the second trip of the day had been accomplished.

Going to the icebox, she took out the glass she had prepared the night before: Shelby's pink medicine, mixed with milk and strawberry syrup. "Here's your cocktail," she said, placing it near Shelby's hand.

She put on a pair of rubber gloves and began to polish the silver teaspoons she would use for the company. From the sink, she looked out over the old parade grounds, now heavily grown up with kudzu vines. The town was hidden below the bluff, beyond the railroad tracks. "They'll be here in an hour," she told Shelby.

Shelby chewed.

"I want you ready to leave in forty-five minutes. I don't want to keep them waiting."

"Milk," Shelby said peevishly.

Louise turned to look at her. "You haven't touched your cocktail."

Shelby banged her hand on the table.

Taking her time, Louise went to the icebox and got out the bottle of milk. Shelby watched her pour it into a glass, then snatched the glass from her and threw the milk down her throat, gurgling and staring at Louise with satisfaction. Louise leaned down to wipe the white mustache off Shelby's upper lip. She would never drink her medicine now.

Sometimes it was worth trying to make Shelby do something she didn't want to do, but usually it only aroused her powerful stubbornness. Louise looked down at the ring, tight on her sister's stubby finger. Swiftly she shifted her goal. The ring, after all, was more obvious and more embarrassing than the mere possibility, the faint forward echo, of a fit. Louise thought briefly she might be able to wrench the ring off. She was really afraid to try; and today, she knew, it would be especially difficult to take Shelby by surprise. Her blue eyes, lashless and pale, were fixed intently on Louise. The only way to do it would be to persuade Shelby to take the ring off herself.

Suddenly she felt annoyed. What did it matter, after all, whether or not Shelby wore the ring to the station? A little imagination had never hurt anyone. But it would startle Big Tom. He would be afraid that someone might notice the ring and ask about it—would think, even, that a squib might appear in the evening *Herald*, as indeed it might have years before: "Miss Shelby Macelvene was seen yesterday lunching at the Pine Grove, wearing a yellow linen afternoon dress and a gold wedding ring." No, she would have to think of something.

Speaking in a monotone, as though she were reading aloud from one of Shelby's fairy-tale books, Louise began to talk. "Dear, he called last night, after you had gone to sleep. He asked if he might speak to you, but I told him you were exhausted."

Shelby, still chewing, gave a low grunt of surprise.

"He said he would call back in the morning, unless they had to leave before nine o'clock." She glanced pointedly at the kitchen clock. "He didn't want to call any earlier, for fear of waking you up."

Shelby had stopped eating now. She laid the spoon down on the plastic mat.

"He asked me to give you the message, if he wasn't able to reach you this morning," Louise went on. She could imagine him now—Shelby's beau—a blond boy in an open shirt, a "slumberous strength" in his overdeveloped shoulders and arms. The kind who would call Shelby Little Lady. "He asked me to take your ring down to Marchand's and have your initials engraved inside."

Shelby stared. Her face grew pleased and calm, as it did when Louise was giving her a facial with baby oil warmed in a pan on the stove.

"If we get an early start, we can take it by on our way to the station," Louise said. She added, "He said it would make the ring more personal."

Shelby got up from the table with airy swiftness. She moved quickly to Louise and held out her hand; the ring was in her palm.

Picking it up, Louise felt that it was still damp, and in a spasm of fastidiousness she wiped it on her skirt.

"Thank you, dear," she said, and she dropped the ring into her pocket.

Then she turned Shelby towards the stairs. It was time to get her dressed, which promised to be something of a chore.

Upstairs, Shelby sat on the side of her bed, flimsy and drooping, reminding Louise of the way she had behaved when they were both young girls, moping and dreaming through the long afternoons while the distant sounds of the school—a cadet shouting, Tish rolling the garbage pails up the ramp from the cellar—bricked them up together. There were certain times—Sunday service, evening parades—when they were allowed to participate in school activities, but for the rest, they had been ordered by their father to keep to the house and garden. They sometimes managed to see the boys—or at least Shelby did. Louise remembered hearing her laughing in the garden, remembered running down with her heart in her mouth to see a boy sitting in the grape arbor, as comfortable as a monkey.

She had been beaten for that; and Shelby, too.

"Here, dearest, put on your shoes," Louise said. She held out the big white pumps, which she had cleaned the evening before. Shelby started to cry.

Holding her in her arms, Louise tried to comfort her. "It's all right, dearest, they'll have it done by tomorrow; I'll tell them they simply must. Tomorrow evening at the latest you'll have it back again." Shelby was gasping and snorting; her hot tears soaked through Louise's sleeve. Louise felt a pain in her chest, as though a sob had caught there, beneath her breastbone. It had been years since she had cried last—since the closing of the school and their father's death. "There, now," she said, patting Shelby's broad back. "There, dearest," hearing in her own voice her mother's tender formulas, her mother, who had seldom had time for them. Why is the world so hard? Louise thought. Why is the world so hard even when we expect so little? At the same time, she eased herself away from her sister.

She got her dressed finally and started her down the stairs. Talking all the time in her calm, pleasant way, she helped Shelby out the door and into the car. She talked partly to prepare her, though she never knew whether her sister heard her or not.

"Tom and the family have been to the Cape," she began, thinking that Shelby might be startled to see their tans. "Tom said they had a very good time. He called last week, you remember, in the middle of that cloudburst, and I was afraid to stay on the telephone." She shook her head, recalling the bitterness of that disappointment: she had hardly heard him say ten words when a violent thunderclap forced her to hang up, for fear of being electrocuted. And he had not called back. "They had clam chowder every day," she went on. "It'll be their last trip together for a while, I guess; Young Tom is going back to college the middle of next month."

Shelby reached for the key, which was dangling from Louise's hand—it was an old game—then giggled when Louise snatched it away and pushed it into the ignition. She did not feel like playing with Shelby now. The jolt of the engine starting frightened Shelby, and she gave a mewing cry. "It's all right," Louise said, reaching over to pat her knee. Shelby's yellow dress was already drenched under the arms and across her back. Well, Louise thought, there was no help for that, in this heat; Mugsie would be sure to notice, but then Mugsie was always dry and neat. She thought with some distaste of Tom's pretty wife. Now why in the world she should always look like she'd just stepped out of a bandbox . . . Louise stopped herself. Mugsie had her feelings, too. Louise remembered how after Young Tom was born Mugsie had had to stay in bed for a month with a bad case of nerves.

She steered the car slowly down the gravel drive, bumping dreamily over potholes. They passed the round brick guardhouse, almost destroyed by vandals the winter before, and Bella's handwritten signs—Keep Out Keep Out—and the long wall of the west barracks. The soft clay-colored bricks were still solid, but the green wooden window frames were buckling; almost all the glass was out. A thick hedge of goldenrod and milkweed, its pods full to bursting, had grown up to hide the tumbled wooden stairs. On the other side of the drive, a flock of Queen Anne's lace hid the long flight of stone steps that led down to the river. The growing things were all a help, Louise thought; in winter, when the place was bare, she was forced to face the decay.

Shelby settled back with a happy sigh as they drove out through the wooden gates, which hung from their top hinges like half-torn-out pages of a giant book. Then they went down the county road that edged the bluff and dipped abruptly into the valley. A bridge crossed the French Broad River and the railroad tracks. After the dry summer, the Broad was low; Louise saw turtles sunning themselves on the sandy shoals. A hot smell rose from the low water. Louise stopped at the other side of the river and watched for a gap in the traffic on the highway into town. "We have plenty of time to drop off your ring," she told Shelby.

Once on the highway, Louise drove reasonably fast. They passed the old brickyard, now unused, and the new cement plant, where Bella's brother worked. It was a long building, gleaming white, with blackberry bushes at the edge of the parking lot. What industry there was in the area had moved onto the edge of the Broad. Louise was glad her father had not lived to see that. He had always said that growth would come to their side of town, but he had meant handsome houses, green lawns, not cement light industry. In fact, the new houses had all grown up on the eastern side of town, where there was a better view of the mountains.

She drove uphill into town, through streets lined with frame houses; the double-decker porches looked cool and sleepy in the hot morning sun. Mrs. Grant, out weeding tomatoes, waved and watched the car go by—hands on her hips and speculating, Louise knew. They passed the gate to the graveyard where everybody was buried, and Shelby said something under her breath. Then they turned left on Main and stopped in front of the office building—fifteen stories high—that Big Tom had helped to finance. The old square, open on three sides where buildings had been torn down, humped and waved under the boiling sun. "I won't be gone a minute," Louise said, parking under the only tree and getting out of the car. She remembered in time and turned back to take the key out of the ignition. Shelby had her eyes closed, but Louise saw her gape of displeasure when she heard the key click out of its hole.

If Louise had had only herself to contend with, she would have left the key. The last time she had done that, though, a crowd of people had gathered to watch Shelby run the windshield wipers and blare the radio. One busybody had even told her it was a crime for her to leave Shelby alone in the car with the key: "Why, you never know when she might get it started." Louise had saved her breath, knowing nothing she could say would mean a thing. Years ago she had often tried to explain, "Shelby's just a child," but people had not wanted to take that; they had looked at Shelby's bust development (she had had to wear a brassiere since she was twelve) as though it proved something. Louise never tried to explain anymore.

It was only a few steps to Marchand's. The dark windows were crowded with wedding-present silver. She remembered motoring in with her father to place the order for graduation prizes; old Mr. Marchand was alive then, and he had always said the same thing when he saw them coming: "Fine weather, for this time of year." Like most people, he was afraid of her father, who had no charm. Once when Louise went in with her mother to place the order, she saw that the old man was disappointed. Her mother, who hated the town—"Why, it's just a boom town like those places out West, only it's built on TB patients instead of gold"—always had time to say the right kind of things, but she had no dash, no flair. The Colonel made you feel like dirt, with his abrupt silences and his forbidding stares, but people would have paid real money for the honor.

Secretly, Louise had always liked the town. As a child she had admired the TB people she saw promenading the streets, the ladies with their parasols and embroidered linen dresses, the gentlemen so spick-and-span, even if they were dying. She had liked it even better in the off season, when the hospitals in the hills were shuttered and the streets were empty and the bars were full. Then it was small and crowded and low: a hill town, plain as plain.

She did not have her mother's standards to go by. Her mother had grown up in the Tidewater, and that was a place with a past, whereas this town had sprung up around the turn of the century like a mushroom after too much rain. Now, of course, nobody came to the mountains anymore for their health—that had all been discredited—and the hospitals and half the town had been pulled down. She went into Marchand's, gasping at the sudden cool.

Young Toby Marchand did not bother to get out of his chair when he saw her. She said good morning and then bowed her head to look into a case of watches. It hurt her still that she could not command respect from the townspeople; she hoped it was mainly because in the old days she had never had much spending money. Catching a glimpse of her face in the glass-topped case, she saw that her mouth was pursed—like a turtle's mouth, she thought. She licked her lips and carefully applied a smile, then turned to young Mr. Toby. "If you please, I have a ring here that needs engraving." She felt for it in her pocket.

He lifted himself up by slow degrees, revealing an enormous belly. She passed him the thick gold ring without comment; he studied it cautiously. "This looks like eighteen carat," he said.

"I'm not here for an appraisal, thank you. The initials are SLM."

"Miss Shelby?"

"No other," she said, knowing it would be all over town by the end of the day. She added, "It's a keepsake from one of the aunts."

Toby did not comment. He handed the ring to his assistant, who disappeared into the back of the shop.

"How long will that be?"

"Well, if you can wait five minutes. . . ." He smiled at her, and she saw his teeth, neat and sharp as a field mouse's. She was startled. Staring at him, she tried to think of the right thing to say, but memory failed her. She was imagining how it might have felt if he had smiled at her in the other way, the way the construction workers on the other side of the square smiled at the secretaries in their short skirts. A smile that was like a brand. She had always wanted to feel that.

He has a belly, a beer belly, she thought, but it did not signify.

"Miss Shelby still about the same?" he asked carelessly, subsiding into his chair.

"She's had a good summer," Louise told him. "You know we were at the beach."

"I know she ate that up. You, too."

"Yes, it was a wonderful change."

After that there was really nothing at all to say. Louise staved off her panic. Toby whistled and glanced around the shop. Finally Louise went over to the window and looked out at her car; she could see Shelby's lap and one of her arms. She was sitting very still.

The assistant came out with the ring, and Louise inspected the initials. She paid, then waited impatiently while Toby polished the ring with his chamois. At last she dropped the ring back into her pocket and hurried out to the car.

Shelby was sitting straight up, staring straight ahead.

Sliding into the car, Louise glanced at Shelby. Her broad, soft mouth twitched, as though Louise's glance had settled on her lips. Otherwise she was as still as a stone.

"They'll have it ready tomorrow," Louise said.

Then she drove down the hill to the station, past the dusty florist where she always bought Shelby's Easter lily, and the dry cleaner that had ruined Shelby's new print silk.

The station parking lot was almost empty, and Louise was able to bring the car up to the front. She turned off the motor and stared at Shelby again. Her sister's silence awed her; she remembered the way she had felt when she let Shelby fall down the stairs, so many years ago. She had stood on the landing, watching the little girl tumbling lightly head over heels, and it was not until she heard her mother screaming

"Louise! Louise!" that she realized she had been irresponsible.

"You stay in the car, it's too hot to get out," Louise said. Sliding out of the car, she straightened her dark-blue skirt. She and Tom had bought the suit together, five years before. Tom had made her try on a lot of suits, all in various shades of blue, before they decided on this one. It had been the most expensive of all. Louise, concentrating on that memory, hurried out onto the platform.

The train was late. She stood with three other people, under the glass dome. Once it had been cleaned every week, but it was blind with smoke and dirt now. She tried to recall what she had been able to see through it before; possibly the tops of trees. She could smell the river, stagnant beyond the tracks. Most other things about the station had changed, too. The luggage wagons, parked at the end of the plat-form, had no use now; she remembered them piled high with the cadets' footlockers at the start of the term, with three or four sweating colored porters pushing them along. Just about this time of year: it was always hot in September.

She had never had any friends among the cadets, lacking Shelby's daring, and the girls at Miss Wimple's in town had seemed drab, not worth knowing. Besides, they had made Shelby's life a torment, and Louise had never been able to forgive them for that, even after Shelby was allowed to stay home from school. So the only other child she had really known was her cousin Tom.

Because of a weak chest, he had been sent when he was twelve to spend a year at the school. He held a special position there as the nephew of the Colonel. She remem-bered that he only spent one night in the barracks before being moved to the guest room in her parents' house. Tom was a frail boy, white and quiet, with a persistent hacking cough; Louise came to know him well during that first winter, when he was kept in bed with colds. It was her job to bring him meals on trays, usually steaming bowls of soup, which he detested; he told her about the syllabub his mother fixed, but Louise did not dare to ask for so many eggs. However, she learned to make his trays look more attractive, cutting out paper doilies to go under those soup bowls, or arranging pipe-cleaner flowers in an empty jar. In the spring he grew stronger and began to go to class again.

She had never seen the school uniform worn the way he wore it—quietly, but with dash, the long blue stripe down the side of the trousers scarcely narrower than his leg. The uniform collar, high enough to choke the other boys, fitted like a gold band under his chin. He was still excused from drills, though she knew, with regret, that he was no longer "delicate." But he had trouble sleeping and was often frightened by nightmares. One night when he could not sleep, he called her name, and she heard him in the room she shared with Shelby, at the top of the stairs. She could not recall that he had ever used her name before. He called again, softly, insistently, his voice carried on waves of darkness in the sleeping house. Snatching up her robe, she went to see what he wanted. He rambled on about his mother, whom he called his Irish Rose—about how she would come to sit with him when he couldn't sleep, and hold his hand. Louise did not know her aunt Rose; the family was not given to visiting. She had seen her once, at a Christmas party, where she had scandalized everyone with her high, shrill laugh and her girlish manner. Louise did not like to listen to Tom's descriptions, but she sat stolidly by his bed, a hand on each knee, through them all. After all, the only thing that mattered was the he needed her; the words rang like bells. And she was not in the habit of questioning miracles.

He had called to her often at night, in the dead hours

between midnight and three. She learned to sleep thinly, fragilely, so that she would hear the first syllable of her name. Then she would pad barefoot down the hall to his room. Turning on a lamp and shading it with a towel, she would listen to his long stories, about picnics and outings, birthdays, weddings, all the confetti of his life, lightly stirred by his love for his mother. Louise's disapproval did not block her gradual understanding of the woman he called his Rose: Rose cried when she was happy, and laughed at the same time, and had a way of swooping down on those she loved with exclamations of joy and relief. Every morning was a new awakening for Rose. Louise felt that it was a question of taste; she did not think she could comfortably countenance such displays. It did not matter; it did not matter at all. Louise was content to sit, half listening, half dreaming, until Tom turned onto his side and fell asleep.

Tom, growing stronger, had become quite spirited, entertaining Louise with a language he had made up in his head. He had all kinds of phrases for things that were not ordinarily discussed—chamber pots, for instance. He even had a special name for her father: Blackmoreland, he called him. Tom never liked her father; he made no bones about that. Once they had an argument over the suitability of a gentleman wearing a sword to a dinner party, and Tom rushed out of the room.

Louise had never seen her father angrier than he was the night he found her sitting with her cousin. He loomed in the doorway suddenly, tall as a column in his white nightshirt. "What is the meaning of this?" he shouted. The question caught in her mind, making a greater impression than her father's hand across her face. What is the meaning of this? She never knew for sure. She was such a plain little drone, in her long, limp dresses, spending her days chasing after Shelby, quieting her down by brushing her hair or trying to amuse her with riddles or silly games. The nights were the dream, the nights were the part she knew she would not be able to keep. She was really no match for Tom as he grew stronger. Still, they stayed together—mostly, she thought, because of the secret language Tom had invented. At that time, she was the only one who understood.

One rainy spring day when they were playing sardines, she had ended up hiding with him under her father's bed. He whispered new words to her, from his language. She laughed until she nearly choked, though all the words Tom taught her represented things she already knew about, or at least had guessed at. She had learned enough from the rooster and his hens that lived at the bottom of the back stairs, enough to feel hot, and queasy, when Tom told her what those things were called. She was thirteen then—a year older than her cousin—and inexplicably, she had gained a little weight, which padded her straight, brittle child's body. She had grown a belly, like a bunch of grapes. Putting her hands on her belly, pressing, she thought of Tom's language, and the silly words. This would be in the evening, after she had spent the day helping her mother put up tomatoes, or persuading Shelby to let her wash her hair. In the evening, in the half-light, when the catalpa tree outside her window sieved the setting sun, she would press her round belly with her hands and feel the words warm against her skin. Of course, she knew that she could not keep that; in the fall, after Tom went back to Kentucky, she grew quite thin.

They had never lost touch with each other. Even when Tom went to college in the North, he wrote to her every week; she kept his letters with the others in a shoe box, arranged chronologically. When he got married, she went to the wedding; Tom sent her money for the train trip and a new suit. She wondered whether Mugsie knew the secret language, and at the bridal dinner, she almost asked her, so painful was her need to know. Somehow she avoided it. Then, after Young Tom was born, she was invited to the baptism. Even during the war, even later, when he was getting into politics, even during campaigns when he could hardly stop to eat, Tom never failed to write her every week. She always knew that on Tuesday she would find his letter, in the mailbox with the circulars and the bills.

Now, standing on the train platform, with her feet together and her hands tightly folded, she began to repeat his name: Tom, Tom, Tom. He had carved it on the Chinese cherry tree, in back of the guardhouse.

A slight stiffening and rearrangement on the platform alerted her to the train's arrival. It crawled into the station, a dispirited beast. She hurried to the door of the Pullman and saw that the steel step was missing; Jimmy, the porter, was helping people out by hand. How the railroads have gone down, she said to herself, straining for a glimpse of her cousin. Mugsie came down first, clutching a carryall and staring over Louise's head. Louise went to her and kissed her cheek. "Where's Shelby?" Mugsie asked.

"She was feeling the heat, so I let her sit in the car," Louise said quickly, twittering as she sometimes did when Mugsie studied her. Mugsie laid her hand, in its fresh white cotton glove, on Louise's arm. She was a pretty woman, and her lips on Louise's cheek felt deliciously cool, like a sliver of cucumber.

Young Tom, behind his mother, bobbed his head at Louise, and she was astonished to see how thin he had grown. She held out her hand, sorry for her lack of interest; she had hardly thought of him all summer. Paul had been her favorite. Somehow, growing up, Tom had eluded her.

He looked brown and parched as an Indian fakir, she thought, in spite of his neat seersucker suit. When he took her hand, he squeezed her fingers steadily, and she was surprised to feel that his skin was dry and tough.

She started to tell him how glad she was that he had come, but she was distracted by Big Tom's halloo.

Last as always, best as always, he covered the distance between them with big steps. Louise swooped into his arms, light as a milkweed parachute, her recklessness excused by her laughter. He held her for a moment, then asked, "Where is Shelby?" Cocking her cheek to receive his kiss, she began to explain, then stepped back to see him. It had been four and a half months since she saw him last, and she noticed that he had lost weight and seemed pouched and tired. It had nearly killed her when his face finally lost its blond-boy radiance, and that had not been so long ago. She had gone to hear his acceptance speech, and watching him on the platform, she had thought, It's gone, it's gone. "My, it's grand to see you," she said, and slid her hand into his crooked arm. He held out his other arm for Mugsie, and they turned towards the parking lot. Over his shoulder, Big Tom asked his son to round up the luggage.

They chattered together on the way to the car, trading bits and pieces of conversations that were always the same, at each meeting and even over the telephone. "Such weather." "The garden is ruined." "They say the worst harvest in years." "Everything just burnt up." "How are your tomatoes?" It did not seem to matter who said what, as long as all the lines were spoken. Later, after a meal together and a few glasses of wine, she and Tom would leave the subject of the drought. He enjoyed filling her in on his life; he stored up jokes and anecdotes that he knew she would particularly appreciate because of their homely sharpness. In three campaigns, he had never failed to describe his opponents in words that had special meaning for her. Louise was already smiling, prepared.

Coming out into the hot sun, she saw a crowd gathered beside her car. She was suddenly tempted to turn and run in the opposite direction, up the hill behind the station and into the trees.

"What is it?" Mugsie asked, jerked along by her husband's arm.

Nobody answered. Still linked, they ran awkwardly, bumping each other's elbows and hips. Young Tom, behind them, said something, and then they were on the edge of the crowd.

"She'll choke," someone said. "Get her tongue out."

"Let me through," Louise ordered. Dropping her cousin's arm, she began brusquely to part the bystanders. From then on, she forgot about Tom completely. She had heard Shelby gagging.

Forcing her way through, she came to the center of the circle and saw her sister lying on her back on the ground. She was flinging herself violently from side to side. Her face was wet and livid, and her yellow dress was up to her hips.

Louise knelt down beside her, opened her purse, and snatched out a wooden ruler. Catching hold of Shelby's head, she smelled her sister's hair, rank and hot, and another stench that confirmed her worst fears. Shelby had lost control of herself. Her eyes were rolled back, and she was moaning. Louise pried her teeth apart with the corner of the ruler and then slipped it back between her molars. Shelby's jaws snapped on the ruler. "All right, now," Louise said, trying with her free hand to pull down Shelby's dress.

Someone tapped her shoulder, speaking, but Louise twitched the hand off. Rapt, she was watching Shelby's face. Fixing her eyes on her sister's rolled-back eyes, she began to count, by twos, to cut the time, knowing that each second meant a renewed assault on Shelby's brain.

She kept counting by twos, slowly and steadily, and as always, the magic worked. Shelby's body tossed more slowly, and the arc of her thrashing shrank. Finally her knees fell heavily together and she turned onto her side. Her eyes closed, and her whole body, with a jerk, relaxed. She was asleep.

Louise pulled the ruler out of Shelby's mouth. She put it back into her purse and then slowly looked up. She could see legs and feet but not faces; the faces were far away, blurred. She knew they were staring at her, then turning to leave. One man said something, but she neither heard nor replied. She was searching for Big Tom.

All along she had felt him beside her, right at hand. Now she knew he had left her. She began to feel pain, and fear. He had never left her before when this happened. He had crouched beside her, scowling, his fair face drawn and contorted. But this time, she realized, there had been a crowd.

Hastily she began to explain it away, to ward off panic. Why, of course, yes, what would have been the use of his staying? What could he have done? It was not the peach-colored spare bedroom in Kentucky with the rug as thick as moss, and it was not the living room at home, where Shelby struck her head, falling, on their mother's rocker. It was not the garden when it started to rain and it was not the car the time they were on their way to the drive-in. It was a public parking lot, plain cement, with people.

That was our luxury, she thought.

Then she saw Young Tom. He was standing beside her, as though he had dropped from the air. "Father's calling an ambulance," he said.

Louise jumped up, snatching his arm. "Go back and tell

him no. No! Shelby's fine now, it's all over; it's just one of those things, it passes. Help me get her into the car!" she cried, for she had heard the siren.

She pulled Young Tom over to Shelby. "How can we lift her?" he asked, perplexed. Louise looked over his shoulder at the ambulance, which had turned into the parking lot. She saw Big Tom and Mugsie start towards it from the station.

"You take her feet," she told Young Tom, and she crouched down and put her hands under Shelby's shoulders and began trying to lift her. Straining, she dragged her sister to the side of the car and then knelt to get her hands under her buttocks. Young Tom hovered over her. "It's no use," he said, but he leaned down and tried to push Shelby up into the car. "Push, push," Louise begged, but Shelby was too heavy. Young Tom stepped back, wiping off his hands. Shelby, her back against the car, began to slide sideways towards the pavement. "It's no use," he said again.

Louise shrieked at him, "What's the matter with you, can't you lift?" Sweat ran into her eyes, stinging more than tears.

Tom knelt on the pavement and tried once more to heave Shelby up into the car.

There was a light aluminum clatter as two men in white dropped a stretcher in front of them.

Louise stood up and shouted, "Tom! Tom!"

He appeared behind the ambulance men. He was telling them something. When Louise shouted his name, he looked at her and spread out his hands, palms up.

Mugsie came quickly to stand beside Louise. "Louise, get a hold of yourself, darling," she murmured.

Louise pushed past her and ran to Big Tom, grabbing his arm so suddenly that he was nearly thrown off balance. She began to speak to him in a hoarse whisper. "It's over now. It only happened because I forgot her medicine. There is nothing to do now but take her home."

Tom did not answer. He turned to read a piece of paper that one of the ambulance men was holding.

"What's that?" Louise snatched at the paper, tearing a corner.

"It's a form, a piece of paper," Tom said. He began to fumble in his pocket, and one of the ambulance men handed him a pen.

"You're signing the commitment," Louise said. She tried to snatch the paper away from him, but Tom held it out of her reach.

"It's just for a few days," he said. "That's all. Just for a few days, to have her checked."

"I take her to Dr. Harris every month!"

Tom said something to the two men, and they turned towards the stretcher.

Her voice sank to a whisper. "Don't let them take her, Tom. Not now. Let me take her home first and change her and give her a bath."

"Honey, she's sick. You know she's sick. She needs treatment. More than you can give her. And you've got to have a rest."

"We all noticed how tired you look," Mugsie said.

"I want her at home," Louise said. Her voice was barely audible. She heard one of the men gasp as he tried to lift her sister. Then the stretcher clashed into the rear of the ambulance, and the doors closed.

"It's all right, Louise," Tom said, patting her shoulder, waiting for the moment when he could tell her that it was finished. "She'll be comfortable. This is a private place. Dr. Harris told me it's the best place in the state."

"You spoke to him?"

"You know I call him from time to time, to see how Shelby's getting along."

"What did he say about her? Did he say she's worse?"

"Oh, honey, you know this condition deteriorates."

"He told me two weeks ago she was doing fine." She tried to assemble her anger, to shield herself with it, but when she saw that Tom had turned his face away, she began to whimper. "How long?"

"Why, just a little while." He would not look at her. Louise fixed her eyes on the point of his chin. She wanted to remind him of the secret language and the sardine games, but she was afraid it would not make any difference.

Mugsie began to explain. "On the train we were talking it over. You know how Tom worries about what might happen. I mean, anything might happen to Shelby, you never know when she will just . . . it's happened before," she said hurriedly. "Tom felt it would be best, at the next opportunity, to get her extended care. Of course, we didn't expect the opportunity to come so soon."

"Dr. Harris suggested it," Tom said.

Behind them, Young Tom said, "Here, they've dropped her shoe." Louise saw him bend down and pick up one of Shelby's white pumps. He went around to the front of the ambulance and handed it to an attendant.

The doors slammed, and Louise heard the engine start. She put her hands up to her face. "They won't know anything about her strawberry cocktail. They won't know anything about her ring." She put her hand in her pocket and pulled out the gold band. "She ought to have her ring," she told Big Tom. "At least she ought to have that."

He was looking at her indistinctly, strangely.

"Let's get in the car, Louise," Mugsie said.

Chapter Two

Young Tom climbed into the backseat beside her. When she felt the upholstery give, Louise looked up. He held out his hand, palm up, fingers shaking, and she caught hold and squeezed, while the smile she had lost came back again. "My," Louise gasped, reaching for her purse with her other hand, "I have got to get a hold of myself!"

Tom, startled by the strength of her hand, did not answer.

His mother, watching from the front seat, offered her handkerchief, and Young Tom saw that she was trembling and fading into a replica of Louise's distress. "Louise, I believe, I truly believe, it's for the best," Mugsie said.

Louise did not say anything. She looked at Tom's hand, which she was still holding, then patted it gently and returned it to his knee.

Big Tom asked for the key, and Louise felt for it in her purse. Rapidly she began to describe Shelby's adventures with that key: "She was so quick at finding it, it didn't seem to matter where I hid it."

"Now, that's just what I mean," Mugsie said. "Supposing she did find it one day? What then?"

"Why, she'd start the windshield wipers," Louise said, looking bright and quick, Young Tom thought. And stubborn: she was staring at his mother. Cousin Louise, the old lady whose affection had once meant something to him, seemed to be emerging from his forgetfulness like a mule out of a honeysuckle thicket. Stubborn as a mule, instead of the neuter canary bird he remembered.

During his summer at home, Tom had lapsed back into his habit of translating his family into animals. Not the wild beasts of the wider world or even the scraggly squirrels and rabbits of their suburban woods, but the daffy-eyed, big-eared darlings of the Walt Disney books that still lay on the shelf by his bed. He was not afraid of his father or his mother, but he found them incomprehensible. The luminous cartoon creatures were incomprehensible, too; where did their good humor come from, and their charm?

Big Tom was backing the car out. "What do you say to going to the Pine Grove?" Tom knew it was not really a question.

"Oh, yes," Mugsie said.

"But I'm not dressed," Louise said. "I thought we were going home first."

Mugsie was smiling at her. "Honey, we're not worrying about the way you're dressed. What we all need is restoration. A drink and a good meal." She rubbed her palm in circles on her round stomach, which she had kept after her two pregnancies, like a talisman.

Louise looked at Tom, and he saw, before he transformed her into a cartoon squirrel chattering on a tree branch, a witch of a woman, frightened, maybe angry. "Tom, do you want to go there?" she asked. "Or would that just be a big bore for you?"

Tom knew too well what his father wanted. "Maybe we can go out to your place afterward."

"Why yes, for tea," she said, and he could tell he had disappointed her.

"That's settled, then," Big Tom said, relieved.

They drove in silence through the streets. Louise had quieted down; she stared out the window almost as though she were being taken on one of their regular drives, to Chimney Rock or along the Blue Ridge Parkway. Now and then she pressed one finger firmly to her lips. Tom looked past her narrow profile, trying to see what she saw. The mean little town had always depressed him. Once, trying to find the charm his father seemed to take for granted, he had walked for a while around the main square. Going into a storefront that advertised fortune-telling, he had realized after a while that it was in fact a whorehouse, and had gone out again, feeling too young to laugh.

"How we used to love the gardens at the Pine Grove," his father said. "Do you remember? Those salmon-colored tea roses by the tennis courts. Of course, they'll be past their peak now."

Since Louise did not say anything, Mugsie quickly took up her part of the conversation. "And that iced tea with fresh mint they used to serve every afternoon, when people would sit down in the shade to cool off before going up to dress for supper. That was when I first came here," she added. "I'd bought myself a tennis racket—"

"They manage now with conventions," Big Tom said.

"Oh yes, the hungry hordes," Mugsie agreed.

"Louise, you can have your favorite chicken livers," Big Tom said, speaking directly into the rearview mirror.

Assembling herself out of her silence, Louise answered, "Why yes: chicken livers with rice."

"You always used to love that. It always used used to be your favorite thing. And then afterward, lemon sherbet."

"They make it themselves," Louise said.

"Some things don't change." Mugsie sighed with relief, sinking back and relaxing now that Louise was taking her part in the conversation.

"I wonder what the food will be like at that place," Louise said. When no one answered, she went on, "Shelby always has had a picky appetite. Why, there's only one green vegetable she'll have anything to do with." After another silence, she asked Young Tom, "Do you know which one that is?"

He gestured his ignorance with open hands.

"Chard. With bacon grease. Mama used to call it nigger food."

"I'm sure they'll have plenty of that," Mugsie said quickly.

"Mama didn't say that to be racial," Louise was explaining to Young Tom. "She always said she preferred the colored people to the poor white trash around here. She never was resigned to this place."

"She was a Southern belle," Big Tom said with a laugh. "The prettiest girl east of the Mississippi. She never could get used to ordinary life after that."

"That was where Shelby got some of her ways." Louise followed his lead. "To this day, when she shakes her hair back, I see Mama, standing in front of the pier glass trying different ways."

She noticed that Young Tom seemed baffled. "I mean, different ways of shaking her hair back. It's a kind of language, you know. There's an angry way and a saucy way and a way that's just to lift it off the back of your neck."

Mugsie said, "Look at the view." They were winding up into the foothills, with the town spread out below them, twinkling and glittering in the sun. Beyond, the low rim of the hills was already purple.

"My," Louise said, vaguely. "Looks like rain coming over the hills."

They turned into the cobblestone courtyard in front of the hotel. Built out of local boulders, it was sand-colored and immense, with ground-floor windows that opened onto the shady lawn. A procession of cars passed under the porte cochere, and a Negro in a cockaded hat helped people out. "Hello, Martin," Big Tom said when it was their turn. "How's your mother feeling?" He stood for a moment, listening intently, while the man bent forward to tell him the latest disaster. Then, shaking his head, he hurried on to join the rest of the family at the revolving door.

Louise, nervous, was swiping at her skirt, but Mugsie had settled her face for a good time. Standing beside his cousin, Tom saw the girl she had once been, translucent, blond, gleaming—all caught in the perfect angle of her cheek and chin. Seen full-faced, she had aged in the appropriate way. But her deceitful profile preserved the prettiness that had caused him, as a boy, to sigh when she bent down to kiss him good night.

As they passed into the hotel, Young Tom dropped back to find his place behind the other three. By an accident of the revolving door, Louise, too, was left behind, and as he helped her into the triangular glass chamber and set her spinning, she looked back at him with an expression he had seen, a couple of times, on a shot rabbit. "Oh God," he said, under his breath.

She was smiling by the time they were reunited under the gold chandelier. Big Tom was looking around eagerly,

turning on his toes to catch the eye of the headwaiter, who
hurried towards them, saying, in a breathless undertone,
"Oh, Senator. . . ." Big Tom was a regional favorite, and
headwaiters and most other people were in awe of him.
Fifteen years in the state legislature had done nothing to
besmirch or even affect his character, Young Tom thought,
and if in the early days his father had excited envy because
of his money, his good looks, and his charm, his recent
misfortune had changed all that, making it hard for people
to decide whether he was more to be admired or pitied. In
that way, Young Tom thought, the balance had been
righted, for too much good luck would have spoiled his
good luck, and envy, in the end, might have brought him
down. Young Tom was not usually able to be so objective
about his father, but at that moment, insulated by Louise, he
looked at Big Tom as long ago he had looked at him when
he was taking up the collection at church.

From a distance: it was the only way to deal with his
potent charm. Usually Young Tom was dazed by it. He
remembered waiting for his father to come home in the
evening, standing by the curtain in his blue and white
playroom (which had been solely his until his brother, Paul,
was born), his hand on a blue tassel that he folded and
unfolded until his father's car slid around the corner of the
drive and pulled into its usual place, about a foot from the
front porch. The driver, jumping out like a jack-in-the-box,
would hasten around to open the rear door. Most of the
time the door would already have been opened from the
inside, and Tom's father would be springing out, swinging
his briefcase and striding into the house, where, Tom knew,
his mother would be waiting in her white silk lounging
pajamas (or her flowered chiffon hostess dress or her red
velvet robe) for the kiss and the long look which caused Tom

to remain a minute longer at his post by the window—a full minute, which he had heavily and heartily begrudged. Finally he would hear his father's rapid footsteps in the hall and would turn towards the door, knowing that for this he had set up his lead soldiers at ten o'clock in the morning and pasted fall leaves on sheets of colored paper and eaten his chicken croquette at lunch and lain uncomplaining in his darkened bedroom for an hour afterward and gone out with Bessie in the afternoon and asked her only once to push him on the swing and kissed his mother when she held out her cheek and climbed into his bath without dawdling and brushed his hair by himself and gone down on time to eat his supper in the kitchen and said nothing when, again, it was a chicken croquette . . . for this. For his father's face, in the opening door.

The headwaiter was waving them on, and they went, in a line, Big Tom at the head, to a table in the corner. A palm drooped close by; its leaves brushed Mugsie's face as she took her seat. Big Tom placed the two women on either side of him; Young Tom, undirected, pulled back the chair opposite his father. Louise was still scrubbing at her skirt.

"Now," Big Tom said with a sigh of anticipation as the waiter handed him the menu.

"Oh, these descriptions," Mugsie groaned after they had all studied the pages for several minutes. "'Roast duck with a skin crisp and crunchy, honey-dunked before it is roasted to a turn on the eighteenth-century spit in our kitchen.'"

"I remember when no matter what meal it was, it was grits," Louise said.

"Louise, dear, you'll have the chicken livers, won't you?" Big Tom asked. "So, Mugsie, you have the duckling, and Tom, will you go along with that? Then I'll have the livers with Louise, and we can order white wine." He folded his menu and laid it aside, and the women did the same.

Tom, staring at the printed page, put the words carefully out of focus and felt the familiar burn, the long, slow burn, crawl up the side of his face. YOU HAVEN'T SPOKEN TO ME ONCE SINCE WE GOT OFF THE TRAIN. "I haven't decided yet, Father," he said.

His father put his hands in his lap, pressing his fingers tightly together. "What do you find appealing? The chicken divan, I believe, is quite good. Or you could try the frogs' legs."

"You always used to love frogs' legs," Mugsie said.

The headwaiter stood above him, pad in hand.

"I think I'll have a steak," Tom said.

"But honey, we're having white wine," his mother reminded him.

"Well, I'll have a beer, then," Tom said, closing his menu.

Big Tom held up his hand. "Are you sure you don't want to have something more festive? I mean, something that's a specialty here? You can have steak anywhere."

"I think I'll have a steak, rare," Tom repeated, looking at the headwaiter. The headwaiter was watching his father.

"What about the chicken livers?" Big Tom asked. "They're very fine here."

"I don't like chicken livers," Tom said, looking at his father, and the burning flush spread from his left jaw across his cheek. His nose began to run, as it always did when he was angry. "I'd like the steak, please, Father," he said.

"Very well, then," Big Tom said. "Steak for the young gentleman."

Softly, at his elbow, Louise said, "I believe I'll have the steak, too."

Young Tom stared at her. Discreetly, she unfolded her napkin and laid it across her knees.

"But Louise, darling, you never have liked red meat," Mugsie said.

"I haven't had a steak in a dog's age," Louise said. "Shelby has to have a turkey for Christmas, you know. It wouldn't be Christmas for Shelby without a turkey. I tried to give her a chicken once—with turkey you go on forever—but she knew right away, and she wouldn't touch it."

"Honey, you have what you want. Anything you want at all," Big Tom said.

"I'll have a steak, rare," Louise said.

Big Tom shook out his napkin and covered his knee. "We had a bad trip over the mountains," he began, and Tom heard the strain salting his voice and tried to guess its source. "The Pullman was unbelievable. I really think we're going to have to try flying."

"The filth," Mugsie explained. "I don't believe they've cleaned that Pullman car in ten years."

"Windows so begrimed you couldn't see out of them. And a sulky porter I'd never seen before; I had to ring three times before he would come and make down the berths. Not like dear old Ripley, who always called this town the garden city of the universe."

"Of course, the food was unspeakable," Mugsie took up the story. "And when I think there used to be a rose on every table!"

"Remember that, Tom?" Big Tom looked at his son. "When you were small and we made the autumn trip? A rose on every table in the dining car, and the chef would come out and pat you on the head?"

"I remember," Tom said. "Also that time we got stuck in the tunnel."

"Yes, there was an early snow that year, and we couldn't get through until the tracks were cleared."

"How long did we spend in that tunnel?" Tom asked, touching the memory carefully, like a sore. "It seems to me we stayed there for hours."

"Oh, it was only a few minutes," Mugsie said. "Darling, do you think I could have a drink?"

"We don't want to keep the meal waiting," Big Tom said, giving Louise a significant look.

"Well, I thought since it will take some time to prepare the duckling . . ."

"No," Big Tom said.

Tom looked at his mother. She lifted her hand and felt her short blond hair, carefully arranging a curl over her ear. "Iced tea?" she asked.

"We're having wine," Tom's father said.

"But I'm thirsty." Mugsie smiled at him.

"Then have a glass of water." With a brusqueness Tom had never seen in him before, he motioned to the waiter to fill his wife's glass.

"Thank you," Mugsie said.

Tom, separating the strands of her clear, childish voice, tried to find a thread of irony. There was none. "Your father is the best man in the world," his mother had told him several times. She had not elaborated; he had not asked her to. From other people—servants, strangers—he had already collected his father's attributes: generosity, public-spiritedness, a courageous championing of every liberal cause. Once, when Tom was crying for some forgotten reason outside of church, a man he'd never seen before had suddenly come up to him and said, "A boy like you, with a father like yours, has no business crying."

Louise made a little scuffling sound, and he looked over

at her. She had dropped her napkin and was attempting to retrieve it with her foot. Bending down to get it for her, Tom bumped his forehead against hers, and they stared at each other, stunned. *Her head is as hard as a rock,* he thought ruefully, rubbing his forehead. Then Louise began to laugh.

"What is it?" Big Tom asked, prepared to smile.

Louise still laughed, silently, gripping her stomach.

"Louise bumped into my head. She has a head like a rock," Tom said.

Big Tom laughed once.

A waiter appeared and hovered questioningly. "Where's that bottle of wine?" Big Tom asked, and the waiter scurried off.

Mugsie said, "I don't know where they get all these young boys to wait on tables. I suppose they try, but their manners are not up to scratch. Remember Archie, in the old days?"

"How proud he used to be of his red jacket!" Big Tom recalled. "You remember the time he spilled the mint sauce on it, and he said his pride hurt?" Big Tom glanced at Louise. "You must remember that, Louise."

"Why, yes. That was the autumn we had the floods. The last autumn Papa was alive."

She fell silent. Then, when Young Tom thought the opportunity had passed, she said, "Things do stick in my head, for no sort of reason: it was August eighth, last summer, when I made my cucumber pickles. A terrible hot day. I took Shelby down to the river afterward. You know she can swim, or float, I should say, like a rubber ball. Fearless as a baby. Or are babies fearless?" She looked at each one of them in turn, seeking an answer.

Mugsie said, briskly, "In California they've made some studies about that. I forget the conclusions."

Louise went on, softly, "Anyway, that's the way she was. If I woke up at night and heard a noise, I'd go to Shelby and see if she was scared. Not a word of it! Not a word. She was as brave as a lion."

"Here comes that wine," Mugsie said with a girlish hand-clap. She pushed her wineglass forward as the waiter slowly drew the cork, and Tom saw that she was beaming with anticipation. She had often told him that he needed to learn to enjoy life, and he knew that she had learned to appreciate each of its details. He watched his father as the waiter filled the glass, slopping the wine. Big Tom held the glass by its stem and turned it slowly to catch a ray of light; the wine glittered and tipped like an enclosed sea, and when he brought it to his lips at last, it seemed to Tom to quiver. His father took a sip and rolled it slowly on his tongue, depositing it at last in the back of his mouth. "Fine, fine, absolutely first rate," he told the waiter benignly, waving him on towards the ladies. When he came to Young Tom, the waiter hesitated; he had turned his wineglass upside down.

"I'd like a beer, please," Tom said, his voice roughening, like a child acting the part of a man in a play. His father gave him a long stare. "Is that what they drink now at college? German beer?"

"Any kind of beer they can get a hold of," Tom said. He was trying to keep his father's eye. Those eyes were blue and dense and beautiful, semiprecious stones, their whites as bland as a baby's. His father continued to stare at him, but his eyes, which had been peaceful and indefinite before, changed suddenly; there was a tiny squirt of anger in back of the irises, and Big Tom looked away. "A Löwenbräu, please, waiter," he said.

Mugsie began to talk in her light voice. "Don't you miss

those times in Cambridge? I mean, getting together with your friends?"

"Yes," Tom said.

"I mean, the studying can't be all of it," Mugsie went on thoughtfully. "Not these days. The studying was all I cared about, but I went to college out of an intellectual bayou. I know you don't need to work all the time. Your roommate and the people you had in your classes, you must have gotten together a lot."

"Yes," Tom said. "Well, not a lot. Now and then."

"And now this summer, at home, all your friends seemed to be away."

"Never mind that," Big Tom said quickly. "He'll see them all at Christmas."

"Or at Thanksgiving," Mugsie said. "Won't you be coming home for Thanksgiving?"

"I don't know. I guess so," Tom said.

"How did you like it up there?" Louise asked.

"Oh, it was all right," Tom said.

"Of course freshman year is always difficult. A lot of strain," his mother said.

"It wasn't the strain." Tom turned towards Louise. "It was just—last spring—I started feeling I wasn't getting any-where . . . drifting. . . ." His hands made one of the old gestures; he knotted them quickly together. "I thought the summer might give me some time to think."

"Of course," his father agreed. "You'll find your perspec-tive is entirely changed when you go back next week."

Cambridge in the autumn. Tom had been through it once before. He had not been used to the early winter, and the first snow, falling through the arcs of light from the street lamps, had excited him and made him run and leap. But later, after the snow turned to iron and filth, the cold itself began to numb him; coming back from classes, he would stand in his entry, stamping his feet and rubbing his hands together, and as his ears started to tingle, he would feel his brain turning and thawing inside his head. "Why don't you get yourself an overcoat?" his freshman adviser asked him, but he had no intention of doing that. That would mean he had accepted the place.

During midterms, when he had been studying, Tom would go out sometimes at midnight to get a cup of coffee, and he would see the lights in other students' rooms and occasionally catch the sound of phonograph music. He began to love Cambridge in the winter, finding his place in the silent crowds where no one criticized or questioned or even seemed to notice him; he invented all kinds of lives for the students who sat beside him in class. He thought he loved Cambridge in winter more than any other place he had ever been in his life, more even than the hill where he had grown up, in spring, when the lily of the valley whitened the spaces under the ragged pines, when the ants on the peony buds went wild on clear sap, when he and Paul rolled down the pasture hill. Cambridge was the real world, the place where his father had shone for four years, the place that issued its graduates passes, good for a lifetime, into the realm of understanding.

In the spring, he had begun to doubt all that, because he saw couples on the riverbank, and in the library, and intercepted, unwittingly, their words and looks. He realized, suddenly, that he was alone. But if that was not its meaning, Cambridge's meaning, then what was the use? He was spending four hours a day then on his history review, and sometimes the pages of his notebook would rise and fall under his eyes and he would hear his own words repeated again and again, into incomprehensibility, as once when he was five or six he had repeated the Lord's Prayer until the blessed words, his mother's words, guaranteed to keep him from harm, had lost sense and shape and sagged like overblown peonies, toppled by their own weight, bent all the way to the ground.

"Have you thought any more about law school?" his father asked.

"Not since the last time I talked to you," Tom said.

"I'm not putting pressure on you to decide at this point. I'm only hoping you'll keep all your options open."

"I know. I'm thinking about it."

He wondered what his father would think or even feel if he told him that for the last month at college he had not been able to read anything at all; even the front page of the Boston newspaper had bent and waved in front of his eyes. His mind was perpetually distracted, torn, by images, vivid and unmeaning: a girl he had seen asleep on the riverbank, her mouth open and dry, his English professor catching up his little son in his arms.

"It must be hard to make friends, in the beginning," his mother was saying, in her soothing voice. "I remember when I first went, I was afraid to ask the way to the dining hall. But you'll find your own people, in the end."

"I guess I get more work done this way," Tom said mildly.

"Well, of course." His mother looked at him with a faint smile. "You certainly have always had the right attitude. I remember even in nursery school, Miss Nelson said your attitude was beyond reproach."

Louise had been following the conversation, her pale eyes gliding rapidly from face to face. At last she said, in her mild way, "Tom, you're so bright, you always were the bright one—" She stopped abruptly.

"That's right," Tom said. "Paul had the charm, but I had the brains." He smiled.

Then he waited for their silence to envelop him, soft and cottony, a nest into which he could plunge and disappear. No one talked about his younger brother, who had died less than a year before.

"Paul was a nice boy," Louise said judiciously, as though she were delivering a final verdict. "He was always so easygoing. He reminded me of one of Papa's younger brothers, the one we always called Little Billy; he never was much taller than a child. But full of jokes and fun! You never would have known, from looking at him, that his spine was all out of whack. That was what kept him from growing to his full height. Paul was like that."

"Paul was six feet tall," Mugsie said.

"I don't mean the height. I mean the cheerful disposition. The last time I saw him, when he must have been feeling pretty poorly, you never would have known it; he always had a joke of some kind on his lips. 'Why does the chicken cross the road?' he asked me when we were driving home from the station. Of course, I knew the answer to that. But it wasn't the answer he wanted. 'In hopes of a speedy driver,' he said."

"Here comes the food," Big Tom said. "The steak is for the young gentleman, and the lady. My wife is having the duckling."

Louise cut a piece of her steak and put it in her mouth. She closed her eyes and chewed rapidly. Young Tom could tell from her rapt expression that the steak was the best thing she had put in her mouth in a long time. She wiped her lips delicately and looked around at the rest of them. Then she began to talk. "You know, Shelby is so stubborn about taking her medicine. I found a way to make it taste better by mixing it with milk and strawberry syrup, but she knows from the way I keep after her to take it that it isn't just a treat. Oh, she is a devil!" she exclaimed delightedly, her light eyes moving back and forth. "She could always wrap me around her little finger! She got it fixed in her mind last June that she wanted an evening dress, though what in the name she would do with it . . ." She gasped, and smiled. "An evening dress, to the floor. She tore a picture out of the paper and followed me around with that picture in her hand. Finally we went downtown—I gave in—we went downtown, it was a warm day, a Friday . . ." The smile appeared and disappeared for the last time, and Louise put her hands to her lips. "The trouble is, I don't want to be alone in the mornings," she whispered, and tears began, for the first time, to run down her cheeks. "I won't be able to get up and fix breakfast just for myself. Forty years—I've always made her breakfast, even when she was little; I was the only one who knew how to get her to eat. I still sing her that song, that 'Jolly Old Sow' song, when she's having one of her moods. . . . They won't know what to give her to eat, in that place."

Big Tom reached out and touched the back of her hand, which was still pressed against her lips. "Louise, honey, the time has come. She has to be taken care of."

"I've taken care of her for forty years, all except for that last time you put her in, and what good did that do?"

Mugsie said hastily, "Yes, of course you did, darling. But as you know, her condition is likely to deteriorate."

"Last time it was because I forgot to make her take her medicine, too," Louise said. "I swore I would never forget it again. I swore it. And then today—I don't know what happened—I was so excited about you coming . . ." For the first time she looked straight at Big Tom. "Don't take her away from me again, Tom. I don't have anybody else. I know she's a trial to everyone, frightening to people, even, because they never know what she might do, but at home with me she's gentle as a lamb. Stubborn sometimes, but that's all."

"Louise, you have to think about about her, too," Big Tom said. "What's best for her, you know. She'll be very well taken care of where she's going. I talked to Dr. Harris, and he said this was the place he would recommend."

"We didn't have his recommendation last time," Mugsie added.

"It seemed to me that Shelby was not making any progress," Big Tom explained.

"'Progress'?" The word, so light and neutral for the others, seemed to have a special meaning for Louise. "I don't know what you mean. Shelby's been taking her medicine, she hasn't had a bad time since last Christmas."

"When she fell down the stairs and broke her arm," Big Tom reminded her. "She didn't get out of that cast until the end of January."

"There was insurance," Louise said faintly.

"It's not the expense. I wish there were more I could do in that line. What I remember is how happy she was in the other place. I know you never liked it, but it seemed to me she was happier in that hospital, with all those friendly people around her, than I'd ever seen her before."

"She used to cry when I left," Louise said.

"Oh, I don't mean she didn't miss you. Of course she did. You've been her whole life," Big Tom said. The scorn in his voice was as soft, as fragile, as the brush of a moth's wing. Everyone at the table felt it, felt the threat of his disdain, and knew that it would never amount to more than the gentlest brush. "I'm thinking of you, too, Louise dear, as we make this decision."

"Don't think about me."

"You have a right to a life of your own, after all this time," Big Tom said.

"What am I going to do," she asked, "with a life of my own?"

"Why, take a trip—go abroad, the way you've always wanted to do, go to Florida for the winter."

Mugsie put in, "You know you'll be able to see her anytime you want."

Young Tom's steak knife clattered on his plate, and the three adults glanced at him. He had been lost, vanished, the conversation washing over him. It was the same conversation, in all but the details, that he heard every time he had a bad idea. These were the same explanations—unanswerable, definitive—that, so it seemed now, had prevented him from doing most of the things he had wanted to do.

Then his mother—his beautiful mother—touched her face lightly with her fingertips, as though, Tom thought, there were mirrors in the tips of her fingers that could reflect any part of her face. Her blue eye shadow, a little bluer than her eyes, was smudged, and as if she had felt that with her fingertips, she snapped a tiny gold mirror out of her purse and peeped at herself. With the corner of a tissue she dabbed at the corner of her eye. After that, on cue, they all rose from the table, and the waiter stepped back just in time: he had been handing in the check. Big Tom paid and then, with a scooping gesture, he gathered both women under his arms. "Shall we go out on the terrace and get a breath of air?" he asked, sweeping them across the enormous lobby. Young Tom followed.

They stood in a row on the terrace, breathing deeply. Below them, other terraces led into the deep green valley; on the other side, the lone skyscraper in town stood out above a dim huddle of buildings.

"A beautiful view, still," Big Tom said with satisfaction, and then they all squinted, looking across the valley to where the sisters' house, nearly hidden by kudzu vines, stood among the wavering lines of the school. The house, solid green, without a window showing, resembled an enormous growth; the vines had not yet climbed over the chimney, however, and it emerged, cockily, at an angle, from the vegetable mass. "You ought to do something about that vine, Louise," Big Tom said. "Get somebody to come and cut it down."

With a scream of laughter, Louise said, "Oh, you know that vine! That old vine! Why, even in Papa's day, it got at the summer kitchen and pulled the roof off." She turned and looked at Young Tom, her face brittle and charming, and he understood for the first time why his father sometimes treated her as though she had been—but when?—"a remarkably"—yes—"a remarkably pretty woman."

No longer. Louise scuttled sideways as rapidly as a crab, moving out of the way so that Big Tom could speak to a friend, an acquaintance from the old days, perhaps someone he had known as a boy, during his year at the school. "Yes, yes." He was nodding, his feet planted wide apart, his hands clasped tightly behind his back, as he listened with all his might to the man's wheedling tale. "If I can, Hugh, if I can," he replied, warningly, and Tom knew that the man had transgressed. Had he asked for only a modest favor, Big Tom would have responded with gusto, a sideways wink, almost, at his waiting family. His heartiness would have indicated, to them, that everything was well under control;

that, also, it was no insult to them that he did not choose to introduce them, but rather an indication of the low place the supplicant occupied in his esteem. "You wouldn't want to know that man," he had told Tom once, after Tom waited on a street corner while his father talked and laughed with a stranger. Tom stamped his foot with impatience—he had a temper then—but his father looked at him with such disappointment that he walked the rest of the way in tears, refusing, at the store, to pick out a mask for Halloween, which was the whole purpose of the walk.

They wheeled now, with Tom following, and went into the lobby to the elevator, which was housed behind the huge fieldstone fireplace. Quotations from various sources were chiseled into the massive stones: "Lacrimae rerum," Mugsie read out, brightly, with a sigh. Then there was a long piece from some poet. Tom stopped listening halfway through. The elevator had descended by that time, and an elegant colored girl in an embroidered vest was holding open the door, but Mugsie would not go in until she had finished her quotation. They all waited, a little embarrassed—or were they really proud? Tom was not sure—while she stood with one foot in its expensive sandal planted in front of the other, like a girl at a recital, and in her clear, high, almost accentless voice (who would think Southern now?), read out the paragraph. A few people turned to watch her, surprised at first, then smiling, for she was as pink and pretty, still, as a girl.

At last the performance was over; someone—a stranger—clapped, and his mother stepped gracefully into the elevator. Louise had been encouraged to come up with them, to see their rooms and rest awhile. They got out at the third floor and skirted the palm court, with its white wicker chairs and writing desks where no one sat anymore, and its spindly palms reaching for the skylight. Big Tom had both keys, and he unlocked his son's room first, standing aside to usher him in. "Freshen up. We'll be leaving for the hill in an hour," he told Tom. Then he went along the corridor with Louise and Mugsie behind him. Tom shut the door and shot the bolt and lay down on the high white bed.

He closed his eyes for a minute and pressed his fingers against the lids until the blackness turned red and he felt a little pain at the back of his head. Then he let go of his eyelids and looked around the room. It was plain brown, left over from a previous generation. A television set was the only modern addition. Everything else in the room was made of highly shellacked taffy-colored pine, and everything, even the lamps, matched. Over his head a single bulb burned in a frilled glass shade, and he stared at it, concentrating, then closed his eyes again to see the bulb like a featureless face inside the glass bonnet of the shade. He sighed, got up, and switched on the television, turning the sound down low. Then he took out a cigarette and lighted it and stretched out again on the bed.

But the bed confined him; it was a narrow-feeling bed, although so broad. Years of bodies had worn a groove in the center of the mattress; he could not even spread his legs. The mattress and its deep quilt billowed up on both sides. He drew his elbows in and frowned at the television screen.

A woman with gross, loaflike arms was singing into a microphone; Tom thought she might be a comedian, but the sound was turned so low he could not hear the laughter. Her vast bare arms and unformed wrists reminded him of Shelby's; she had seemed gigantic to him when he was a child. Her flesh had been white and hard then, and when he held her huge hand, he had been surprised to find that it was warm and damp. He had also been surprised when he heard his father advising Louise to put Shelby on a diet; he had always assumed that she was built that way, hard white flesh that stood out over her collar and around the stained edges of her sleeveless dresses. She had had a booming laugh, too, and he had enjoyed her, rather timidly, as after some encouragement he had enjoyed the clown at the circus. It had not occurred to him to take her seriously, or even to be frightened of her, though he noticed that his father treated her like an embarrassing appendage of Louise's, an extra leg, enormous and space-consuming.

Then one day, when he was sitting idly in the garden of the old school, she had come down the wooden steps from the kitchen, teetering on a pair of tiny high-heeled shoes and laughing (he thought) at her own clumsiness. She came running down the gravel path, her feet twinkling, and he saw that she was as graceful and light as a giant balloon. She seemed to be holding her arms out to him, and he stood up, ill at ease, to be ready for her embrace. He was eight or nine then. When she got within a foot of him, she suddenly stopped, still laughing and balancing herself lightly, like a balloon on cardboard feet. She plucked up her wide skirt with both hands, still laughing, still balancing, and thrust at him a part of herself that he had never imagined, a hard white hump, belly or groin—he was never sure which— faintly speckled with dark hair. He turned his eyes away, shyly, a pale boy who did not want to appear rude or even uninterested, for it was obvious from her laughter and her excitement that she was offering him something important. "Here, here, here," she repeated, chortling and gesturing at herself with one hand. "Here, here, here." He did not want to look again and stared instead at the window of the old Colonel's study, flashing clear of the kudzu vine. After a while she turned, dropping her skirts, and ran off up the path to the grape arbor.

Afterward he had not thought about it at all.

Now, remembering, he wondered whether that had been a regular part of her behavior, and he thought of the late-night telephone calls, and his father looking tired over the morning paper. That was years before, when the two sisters had occasionally traveled, going to stay at a modest motel or spending a week in a housekeeping cabin farther up in the mountains. How had Louise managed Shelby on those outings? He had always thought Shelby strange, but he had accepted her as part of the picture, as everything within his father's ken was part of the picture. Nothing was explained because nothing needed to be explained: Shelby was one of the family, not a cause for sadness or surprise. Louise, he understood, was not able to be objective about it.

Well, no wonder, he thought, lying on the hotel bed. No wonder Father wanted to put her away; his father's action seemed perfectly comprehensible, only long delayed out of kindness. After all, it was always this way . . . the squalor of female life—no, he would not think of that. Even his mother, his beautiful mother, had never been able to convince him that women were clean. He had tried to believe in her, or at least in the part of her that she had carefully presented to him, sitting up in her cool, fresh bed every morning, wearing a white lace bedjacket with blue ribbons in the summer and a knitted shawl, also white, in the winter. She had always kissed him goodbye before he left for school. She had never smelled of anything, she had been as neutral as water. He still tried to believe in that, in her cleanness and sweetness, for he knew it was the most important lesson she had ever attempted to teach him, dwarfing even the love of the English language that she had also tried to impart. But he had to contend, always, with other evidence, some of it even hers. He had come upon unspeakable things in the toilet, bloodstained refuse, which he had made an effort not to see, looking away politely, palely, as he had looked away when Shelby held up her skirt. And of course at school he had seen girls who seemed bent on disproving what his mother represented, who wore stained cotton underpants and laughed in a knowing way and stuck their fingers up their noses.

He had tried to believe, instead, what his mother said; he had read the books she gave him when he was twelve or thirteen about love and making babies. "It is so beautiful," she had told him, sitting up in her cool, fresh bed, in the white jacket with the blue ribbons. "When you are older, you will understand the beauty of it." But he had also seen two boys in his class with their penises out in the bathroom; he had seen the evil crowns of soft black fur. His father always wore a dressing gown, an orange-and-yellow-striped one in the summer and a soft blue velour one in the winter, and the only time Tom ever saw him in bed with his mother, he was wearing white silk pajamas with his monogram on the pocket. "I will try to believe," Tom had said to himself when he was twelve or thirteen; he had said it to his mother, even, fervently, after she warned him to avoid certain people, vulgar little females especially, who had only one thing in mind. But in spite of his efforts, something had happened to him, something he could never have predicted, would not have believed: he had begun to grow hair himself, unsightly curly black hair, all over those portions of his body. The hair had been a betrayal; it had seemed to underline his loss of control over those parts. "'An unweeded garden that goes to seed,'" he said dreamily, his hands in his pockets, lying in the narrow groove of the hotel bed. Because that had been the worst part of it: he had felt some kind of delight, some kind of satisfaction, at the sight of his child's body, his perfect white child's body, despoiled by the invasion of those black hairs, by the invasion of feelings that no one in his world had ever had. "'Things gross in nature,'" he murmured to himself, trying to keep the dream and the shame perfectly balanced as he nursed his slow erection.

When he could keep the balance, he would feel, at the end of a long, strained period, something like relief.

A little later his father knocked on the door, and Tom was frightened. He shouted to his father to wait, and hurried into the bathroom to wash his hands.

He was alarmed to find his father gone when he opened the door, and he ran down the hall between the matched rows of dark doors. They were sitting in the palm court waiting for him, three middle-aged people sitting quite erect, propped up in the old unused-looking wicker armchairs. Louise was fingering her armrest with care, even concern, as though, Tom thought, the heavily repainted wicker was a set of veins. His mother was simply waiting, her hands folded on her lizard purse, and Tom thought again, with despair, that she was beautiful, a beautiful woman, who had remained somehow unlined, pink and perfect, in spite of the death of her younger son and the miseries of the world. His father—but he did not look at his father, frightened again by the shame he had felt when his father knocked on the door. Big Tom jumped up briskly when he saw his son and led the way to the elevator, and Tom wondered if he had actually felt, in passing, the flick, like the end of a switch, of his father's pale blue eyes.

The trim colored girl in the embroidered vest ushered them into the elevator, and they descended together in silence. At the desk Big Tom turned in their keys and spoke kindly to the gray-haired woman who received them. Flushing, with a darting gesture, she brought out from beneath the counter a little box, wrapped in bright paper, and tried to put it in Big Tom's hand. With kindly firmness, he refused to take it; he gave some sort of explanation that Tom did not hear. The woman slowly replaced the box beneath the counter, and Big Tom turned away, shaking his head. He never accepted favors.

Tom remembered a Christmas years before when he had gone with his father to return a basket of fruit. The people who had sent it were plain people, as far as Tom could see, the woman tense, gray, and frightened, the man plump, spilling out of his clothes, the house another of those brick houses with fake plaster pillars that his father always deplored. But after they returned the fruit—and Tom thought that the couple was, in the usual way, hurt, or at least confused—his father explained that the brick house was right in the path of a proposed state highway. Tom did not make the connection then. Instead he thought, quite inappropriately, about a time when he had cut out and pasted valentines for his friends at school, covering them with misspelled phrases of love, and his mother, afraid that he would be teased, had insisted that he replace them with regular cards, bought at the ten-cent store. He had always made the wrong connections as a child, unable somehow to find his way to the right conclusions about the things that went on around him. Later, when he was driven along the new highway, he recognized the lilac bushes that had stood in front of the brick house, and then he understood. The fruit basket had been a bribe.

His father led the way to the enormous front door, which a colored man in uniform was holding open. They passed through it into the thin high air. Big Tom stopped for a moment on the porch and opened his mouth wide, peeling back his lips so that he seemed ready to bite the air; his teeth were white and tightly packed, like the seeds in a milkweed pod, and Tom heard his jaws click. Tom stood behind his mother and Louise, watching a car unload a new portion of guests.

A driver brought up Louise's car, and his father allowed Tom and Louise to settle in the back.

"We'll have tea when we get to the hill," Louise said. "A pound cake the way you like it," she told Young Tom, "and Shelby helped me slice the cucumbers for the sandwiches. You know she always could slice them so thin. . . ." Her smile drooped. "What do you think the food will be like in that place?"

"I asked specifically about that, and they promised to send me a week's menu for an example," Big Tom told her. "Apparently they have some kind of a house organ, a newspaper— the patients run it themselves—and one of the main features is the weekly menu. I remember they said a big favorite was the lemon meringue pie."

"Shelby will never eat that."

"That was a week ago. They'll be having something else today."

"I doubt if Shelby will be up to eating much today." Mugsie, exhausted by her own kindness, allowed an edge of sharpness into her voice. "They're bound to put her on a diet. Her general health can't possibly be improved by the amount of weight she's carrying around."

Louise said, "We used to keep the cookie jar on the top shelf in the kitchen, but Shelby always got the stool and climbed up." She laughed, shaking her head. "She always did manage to get what she wanted."

"That was her main trouble, if you ask me," Mugsie said tartly.

"If they had diagnosed her early enough," Big Tom reminded his wife, "when something could have been done . . ."

"She simply wrapped your father around her finger. I remember it well enough. She used to come down to dinner in her dressing gown—that was the first winter I visited your people—with her hair every which way and smelling like she hadn't bathed in weeks."

"Darling," Big Tom said gently, "she wasn't well."

Louise was clasping and unclasping her hands. "She had her good times, too," she said with a smothered fierceness that startled Tom. "There were weeks when she was just as normal . . . she always was high-spirited," she continued incautiously, "and sometimes that bothered people. Just the fact that she would enjoy herself like a child and maybe laugh too loud."

"That never bothered me," Mugsie said.

"I remember at the football game . . . she jumped up and down and laughed, just like a child would, enjoying herself. But there was someone sitting behind us who tapped me on the shoulder and told me to quiet her down. Not that she was doing anything much, just jumping up and down and shouting and waving her pennant. They would have put up with it in a child."

"But she isn't a child," Mugsie said.

"She's forty-three years old, the baby of the family," Louise said.

"I am convinced, I am absolutely convinced, that this is the right thing to do," Big Tom said, looking at his cousin in the rearview mirror. "She'll be getting help, therapy, they'll do everything they can for her. I expect we're going to see a lot of improvement. There was just no way you could do as much for her at home."

"But I let her enjoy herself," Louise said. "They'll never let her enjoy herself in that place."

"They have doings there, too, dances—"

"They'll hold her down, put one of those jackets on her. I remember what it was like the last time."

Big Tom turned the car smoothly onto the bridge, and they began to climb into the hills. "The other place was different, Louise."

"Yes, and she came out of there with her head full of lice. I had to cut off all her hair to get rid of them. All that long beautiful blond hair. Mama would have died."

"That place was a mistake," Big Tom said wearily.

"That time, we were taking her to the movies, do you remember?" She leaned over the front seat, speaking directly to Big Tom. "We took her to see one of those cowboy shows. I didn't know she'd poured her medicine cocktail down the drain beforehand. But nobody saw her having the fit. It was dark out, and I don't think anybody even knew what was happening."

"That's neither here nor there," Big Tom drawled.

Louise sat back. After a moment she asked, very softly, "When can I go to see her?"

"Why, on Sunday. That's the visiting day."

"Just like the other place," Louise said. "One day a week."

"Well, you can see how they couldn't have people out there every hour of the day and night," Mugsie put in.

"A week from tomorrow," Louise said.

"You can go tomorrow, if you want. After we get on the train." Big Tom drove through the torn-off gates. "Here we are."

Young Tom turned to look out the window. He had not

seen the school for a year; away at college, he had missed the autumn visit. He had not expected there to be much change, since the place had seemed the same during all of his childhood. But the old brick buildings, always derelict, had suffered a further decline. The winter wind had blown down a section of one of the porches; it lay folded on its side in the yard, and the green wooden posts that had supported it stood tipped at odd angles. There was more broken glass in the long grass than he remembered; it glinted in the sun. The school buildings had not been used for a generation, but the kudzu vine had been kept back, and it was still possible to believe that if all the doors were closed and the window lights replaced, the place would look functional, if seedy, as though cadets in their stiff gray and white uniforms might still be standing or sitting along the porches or marching around the oval cinder track. But in fact—in fact—the buildings were passing beyond that hopeful fantasy, into a chronic state of decay that threatened to obscure their function. The narrow planks in the long porch in front of the west barracks were splitting, and the chimney on the east section had tumbled down and now lay sprawled in the box bushes. Through an open door Tom could see that the ceiling of one of the senior rooms had fallen in, and that the thin cheap lathing behind the plaster was bent into loops. Owls and other birds had built their nests there.

He remembered how he had frightened Paul when they visited the place as children: one autumn evening he had thrust him into the east barracks and bolted the door. It was still light out, and Paul, assembling his courage, had sat on the wreck of an old horsehair sofa, his feet planted neatly on a pile of military journals, his hands on his knees, taking up as little space as possible in the alien jumble. When it began to grow dark, he had called Tom over and over, and Tom, grinning, had danced with glee, peeping through the window at Paul on the sofa. Finally Louise, on her way to the mailbox, heard his screams and freed him. But Louise did not sympathize with Paul, who by then was sobbing hysterically; she said that he was old enough to take care of himself. Besides, by then Paul had wet his pants.

Tom had run off scot-free from that episode. Not being scolded frightened him, however, and he imagined that the punishment, when it finally came, would have gathered force; he was afraid that they would lock him up in one of the old buildings. To defend himself, he determined to learn all of the barracks by heart. He set himself to discover a new room every day, scrambling over piles of coal to find the teachers' sitting room, an old calendar still hanging on the wall, or a classroom full of spindly wooden chairs. He even penetrated into the cellar to explore the latrines. He forgot after a while about defending himself and began to feel at home in the school. The presence of all those boys—generations of younger sons or ill-explained misfits, set aside by stubbornness, slowness, or a slight physical defect—those boys, who might even have been Paul's friends, made the old buildings seem safe. He had grown to love the place, as though it represented the shadowy recesses of his own personality, and now he looked with dismay on its final collapse into the weeds.

"Shelby's garden," Louise commented as they bumped along the gravel drive, and Tom saw an enormous sunflower peering over the top of a chicken-wire fence. "We had to fence it in, the rabbits were so bad, but she had wonderful luck with her peas and tomatoes." Louise sighed and pressed her hand to the thin folds in her throat. "She had pumpkins in there, too, but they've never ripened."

She kept her eyes fixed on the sunflower, turning her

head to keep it in view as Big Tom drove the car up in front of the main house. Then Louise turned her face back, and Tom saw the bitter lines that bracketed her mouth. "She'll never see those pumpkins now," she said, her voice dry and harsh. Then, feeling Tom's eyes on her, she gave him a ghastly smile, the sweetness of her perceived personality barely covering the rage he thought he detected. Dear Louise, sweet as sweet . . .

"Maybe they'll let her out before too long," Tom said.

"No, they won't let her out, not for a long, long time," she said, still smiling and fixing him with her pale eyes. "Not as long as your daddy has any say in the matter."

Big Tom had already climbed out of the car. He came around to open Louise's door, and as she looked up at him her face submerged; the ill-humored, dry lines faded away, and she smiled her real smile, her true smile, which she saved only for him. "Why, Tom," she said as he helped her out, and she folded herself into the crook of his arm. "It's so marvelous to have you up here on the hill again!" He supported her into the house, and Tom and his mother followed.

The garden room, glassed in on two sides, was filled as it had always been with swinging baskets of ivy and fern; there were discolored places on the floor where the baskets had dripped. A canary cage, left over from a long-dead occupant, stood in one corner near several bookcases and a table loaded with magazines and newspapers, some of them years old. The armchairs and the sofa were ratty and comfortable. It was the only room in the house that Tom knew well, though he had spent a few nights as a child in the bedroom above. He knew that his father as a boy had spent a year in a room at the top of the house, but Big Tom never talked about that, in fact never referred to his boyhood at all. The bits and pieces Tom had picked up had been mainly gathered from Bessie, who did not know or was not willing to tell the whole story.

Louise settled them in the garden room, choosing the old cretonne-covered chaise longue for Mugsie and indicating chairs for the men. Then she knelt on the hearth to light the careful arrangement of logs and paper. As she crouched there, fanning the flame, Tom thought with dismay that she was scarcely larger than a child. Her hips and thighs were without weight or bulk, simply lines beneath the longer line of her skirt. He wondered, painfully, whether she had ever known sex, ever recognized, even, the sex of her own body, or whether she had lived since childhood inside a husk of self-denial so brittle and tough that even her own femininity had never been able to pierce it. She seemed so dim and chilly, kneeling there, that he could no longer believe in her furious smile. Surely her prime factor was her love for his father, and she would never, by so much as a breath, cross his favor. Yet she had said, "Not as long as your daddy has any say in the matter," and he had seen her eyeteeth, pointed, not quite white, in the corners of her smile.

He began to wonder if he might somehow help her out, but the thought sank under the weight of his revulsion.

"There," Louise said with satisfaction as the flame flared up, casting a clear light across the darkening room. She rubbed the palms of her hands together and then bustled off into the kitchen.

"Don't you think it's pretty hot for a fire?" Mugsie asked Big Tom.

"We always have a fire." He leaned back in his chair and closed his eyes. "I was worried for a minute when we drove up here. After all, that was the worst part, the real threat: Louise coming back here alone."

"Well, at least we're here with her."

"Yes. But she must be imagining coming back here alone tomorrow, after we leave. She has to imagine her whole life here, the whole thing, alone."

"I think she's over the worst part," Mugsie said reassuringly.

The conversation closed, gently. There was nothing more to be said. Tom's voice, coming a minute later, sounded like a child's, irrelevant, querulous. He had not planned to say anything.

"Why did Shelby have to go to the hospital?"

His parents stared at him. "You weren't listening," his father said patiently. "I explained it all on the train coming down."

His mother reminded him, "Your father explained that this is bad for everyone—bad for Shelby, who is deteriorating, and embarrassing for the rest of us. I mean, it might look as though we didn't *care*. Not that we expected the opportunity to come so soon," she added.

"I explained all that on the train coming down," his father repeated.

Confused, for he did not remember—but then his ability to concentrate on his father had been flawed by the same stream of erroneous impressions that during the spring had destroyed his concentration at college—Tom tried to cling to his original assumption. "I just wanted to know," he said tediously. "All I remember you talking about on the train was the school redistricting."

"Those poor people," Big Tom said. "Can you imagine putting a little child of six or seven on a bus at dawn, to ride two hours to school?"

"I certainly cannot. It's an outrage," Mugsie said.

"And yet it must be done," Big Tom said. "There is no other way to solve our problems with the schools. We must break up those old districts, and much as I hate to cause family disruption—hardship, even, for children—desegregation is after all of paramount importance." He paused before the full sail of his own speech, regarding it as though from a distance, critically.

"I mean, it seems to me Louise was doing pretty well with Shelby," Tom said.

"Well, of course, in a way, yes. But you only saw them on special occasions, when Louise had her all fixed up. It was a different affair the rest of the time. Louise told me so herself. She wrote me many pathetic letters over the last few years. About how Shelby would run outside stark naked, and it almost freezing. How she jumped out of the car once at the light on Walnut and ran down the old streetcar tracks for three blocks before Louise could catch her. All those shames, those humiliations, as well as the simple fact that it was dangerous—I mean dangerous for Louise—to live alone in the house with her. You never knew when she might get a hold of some matches and light the whole place on fire."

"Yes, or invite somebody up from town . . . I mean, she was reckless," Mugsie said.

Big Tom stood up and moved the fire screen closer to the blaze. "Well, I don't believe Louise would have allowed her to do anything like that. She watches her like a hawk. But it wasn't fair to Louise, either. She's carried this burden for more than forty years. She deserves a normal life."

"And don't think it's your father who's putting this off on Louise," Mugsie told Tom. "This is exactly what Louise wants—to get out from under. Only she'd never have the nerve to do it herself."

"I thought she seemed lonely coming up here," Tom said. His conviction was wavering.

"Well, of course she's going to have some trouble adjusting to life alone," his father said briskly. "But I'm going to book tickets for her to go to Florida for Christmas. She can spend a whole month down there, going to the beach."

"It's definitely for the best," Mugsie assured her son. "I respect your feeling for Louise, I always have. She's a dear sweet thing who ought to be protected from anything painful. But sometimes, you know, we have to suffer for the things we want. That's what has worried me about your dissatisfaction with college. I remember you told us the reason was you couldn't stand your room, the shade of blue it was painted. I mean, that's trivial, Tom."

"Well, that's all going to change this fall," Big Tom said.

"I can't explain it," Tom said hastily. He stood up, holding out his hands as though to fend off questions.

"Now, I'm not going to pry," his mother said, putting out her hand, too, so that their fingers almost touched. "God knows this isn't the time to go into all of that. But maybe when we get back home, it might be worth your while to sit down and write a list of the things you felt were wrong at college, so we can talk them over, calmly, before you go back."

"I don't know if I could do that," Tom said.

"Well, I mean, just try it, as a way of clarifying your own thoughts. If you don't want to show it to us, we'll understand." His mother's hand, having missed contact, hung as though forgotten in the air before she gathered it tenderly back into her lap.

Her tenderness startled Tom into a memory. Helplessly,

he thought of her breasts, and of the way she lowered them into the cups of her brassiere. She cared so much about the parts of her body, tending and cleaning each one, and yet it sometimes seemed to Tom that she had no sense of the whole, the combination, how these precious separate parts hung together. She had said to him once, "You have beautiful hands, Tom," and he had wondered if that meant that he, too, appeared to her in fragments, acceptable or not, with no thread or clue to bind them together. She spoke to him so seldom that her pronouncements tolled solemnly in the silences between them. Drifting, gazing at her, he tried to turn his attention from her by beginning to repeat the multiplication table. "See if you can help Louise get the tea together," his father interrupted, with his usual prescience.

Tom started towards the door that led into the hall. It was easy, when his father told him to, to break away from Mugsie.

He hurried down the stairs, noticing that the pale yellow walls were stained along the ceiling with long, jagged marks like stalactites.

In the kitchen, Louise was prying up one of the covers on the wood stove.

"Is there anything I can do to help you?" Tom asked.

"Why, I don't believe so, thank you, Tom," she said, brushing her palms down the towel she had tucked into her waistband.

They stood staring at each other uncomfortably. It had been a long time since they were last alone together, a long time since they took walks up to the parade ground or sat on the garden wall. Occasionally, then, Tom had held her hand. The comfort and ease were gone now; she looked frightful to him, a skinny old woman, witchlike in spite of her perpetual smile. He could not imagine how he appeared to her, though he remembered her telling him once that he reminded her of the portrait of her father.

"I wish I could help you," he said simply, looking towards the teacups on the tray.

"Help me get Shelby back," she said, and then she snatched up a knife and began to hack at the bread.

"How can I do that?"

She sawed, unevenly, then threw a lopsided slice into the garbage. "You can help me by talking to your daddy when the time comes. I don't mean now. It's hopeless now, I know that. That's why I don't try to say anything. But inside of ninety days they'll have to sign to have her committed. That's when I want you to come out and say something, Tom! Say something!"

"I'll be at college," he said, staring at the linoleum to avoid her eyes. It was entirely worn away in front of the stove; the wooden floor underneath was so highly waxed that the spits of linoleum looked like peninsulas in a black sea.

"Then write them a letter when the time comes. I'll let you know when."

"All right, you let me know," he said, in a droning voice that seemed to him to express rather than hide his uncertainty. And he smiled at her.

"Take the tray," she said, picking it up so abruptly that the teacups slid to one side. He took it from her and turned back to the stairs, knowing, in one part of his mind, that he had disappointed her.

But what had she expected? The carpet on the stairs was pierced and stained; he imagined the cadets tramping there in their boots, and then remembered that they had never been allowed inside the headmaster's house, except for tea on ceremonial occasions. Still, the host of boys gathered around him, comforting him, blotting out his pangs of guilt. They would have understood that there was nothing he could do.

He went into the garden room. His father leapt up in the middle of a word to clear the magazines from a corner of the big table so Tom could set down the tray. His rapidity puzzled the boy and then chilled him; he wondered if his father had finally assigned him to the category of those who must be helped.

"I can set it down over here," he said, putting the tray on the desk.

His father stood and watched with the magazines in his hand, aware, Tom thought, of the significance of this tiny act of defiance. Then Big Tom sighed and laid the magazines down. "That's a little inconvenient for Louise," he said.

"Well, it's right under the portrait of her father," Tom said, dazed by his daring. They all looked up at the dark oil portrait of the somber old man.

"Dear Papadaddy," Mugsie said in her reminiscing voice. "How he would have loved to be with us today. Sitting in the wing chair by the window with his spectacles down on the end of his nose." She sighed. "Let's leave time to go out to the cemetery tomorrow; I'll get some chrysanthemums in town."

"There are some in the garden," Louise said, coming in with the teapot clenched between two potholders. "Some of the dark-red ones that Mama loved."

"Yes, those small ones," Mugsie said, and then she went on quickly, "I can see her now, in that linen duster she saved for gardening and a pair of big workman's gloves flapping on her hands." She laughed gently. "I thought she was the most beautiful person. . . ."

"She was," Big Tom said gravely. "The most beautiful and

the most sweet-tempered woman in the world. Why, even when she was dying and in the most horrible pain, she never thought of herself."

"That's just the kind of person she was," Mugsie said.

Louise was still standing there, holding the big blue and white teapot with the potholders. "I'm going to serve the tea now," she said.

As she began to fill the cups, Mugsie continued to reminisce in the frail high voice that Tom associated with the past, with stories out of old times. His mother had assimilated her husband's family to such a degree that Tom had never thought or asked about her own. She went on describing that different world of almost one hundred years before, palely gray and blue, tinted with the melancholy of a long-lost war and the dear hard times that had followed it, times that had allowed for no pleasures or excesses but that had welded family relationships, strengthened family spirit, as no easier period could have done. "And then your parents' marriage," she was exclaiming to Louise, "their relationship! I remember thinking Tom and I would never be able to achieve such balance, such harmony. And then of course Tom's parents"—she turned to her husband—"why, those brothers had some special gift for love. I know it sounds corny," she apologized to her son. "I know children your age don't believe in that kind of thing. But if you could have seen him"—she gestured towards the portrait—"sitting out there on the porch with his wife, at this time of year, to catch the last of the sun, not even needing to talk, you know . . ."

"Watching the boys," Louise said.

"Yes, that's it—watching the boys, and enjoying each other's company."

"Do you have any lemon, Louise?" Big Tom asked.

"Here." She dropped a slice, with a splash, into his cup, and Young Tom realized that her movements were still uncharacteristically abrupt, as they had been when she spoke to him in the kitchen. She poured her own cup too full, and the tea slopped into the saucer and over her hand as she carried it to the chair in the corner.

"It was the school that kept them both going, in different ways," Louise said. "Papa would never have lasted to eighty-three without the school. He was determined, every year, to make it through till commencement time, so he could give the speech from the balcony upstairs. He knew how disappointed the boys would be if he failed them on that speech, the last day of June, before they went home for the summer. Why, they counted on that, the same way they counted on Mama going out to cut the lilacs. She always had two or three trailing after her. Her health was fine until almost the end, whereas for him the last five years were a struggle. All through the bad weather he would say, 'Only four more months,' or whatever, and people who didn't know him would think he just meant the weather. He kept his dress uniform in the wardrobe upstairs, and he would get it out at the end of May and have Mama go over it, in case the moths had got into it. Go over it and press it and shine the brass herself. He would do the sword, of course; no one was ever allowed to lay a hand on that." She looked at Big Tom. "Don't you remember that?"

"Of course I do," he said, stirring his tea.

"Why, the way he felt about that sword, and the times when it should be worn . . . Mama's pearl necklace he gave her on their wedding day didn't mean half as much as that sword did—I mean, to him. When one of the boys had done something wrong and been warned—he always gave them one warning, no one could claim that he didn't—and then went and did it again (like breaking windows, you know how he felt about that; throwing green apples at the classroom windows and breaking them, just for spite), he would take that sword down to the basement—the old latrines, I mean, before they built the new ones on the south barracks—and just simply let him look at it."

"And that did it?" Mugsie asked.

"Boys were different then," Big Tom explained. "They had an enormous amount of respect for the old ways, and the old men who had been there when it all happened."

"Sometimes looking was enough," Louise went on, as though no one had interrupted her. "I'll guarantee you that. Sometimes one look at that sword would put them into tears. He had a way of staring at you that could make you feel like dirt. Why, one time when Tom was here and we were playing—" Her eyes met Big Tom's, and her voice failed. "Why, he could make you feel like the lowest of the low, and that's something you don't soon forget. He never needed to do anything but look; there was never any need for him to do any more, except with the most hardened cases. That's why I just laugh when people say he used to beat them with that sword. As though he would have used it for anything so low."

"Did somebody actually say that?" Mugsie asked.

"People say all kinds of foolish things," Big Tom amended. "Out of jealousy, mainly. He was such a figure of a man. Absolutely erect, even when he was over eighty years old. My father had that same carriage. And neither of them was ever known to complain. Why, Father was the one who used to take the tea up to Mother, when she was having one of her spells, and he was just as patient and kind with her as he could be, although you could tell he simply couldn't understand—it just wasn't in him to understand—how anyone could have a sick headache."

"So when they tell me that—and you know, people still do sometimes, even after all these years; they come up to me and tell me that, just to rile me—I just laugh in their faces. That's what I do. Just laugh in their faces," Louise said. Her hand was trembling as she raised her cup of tea, and the liquid ran down her chin. She could not really be drinking, Tom thought, or tasting, and her eyes slid hastily around the room, as though she were looking for cover. The others drank quietly and waited for the moment to pass.

"Yes, I remember when I first came here." Mugsie once again took up the silk ribbon of her reminiscences, and Louise leaned back in her chair. "The first day I was here, there was something about my dress he didn't like; I believe it was too short. Dresses were awfully short then. And of course he wanted to tell me that in the kindest, most tactful way; he found words to do it that were so tactful—I wish I could remember exactly what he said—that they couldn't possibly hurt my feelings. Something about all the boys around, and how they were excitable, shut up without women for most of the year. Something, even, about my knees. No, I don't remember," she added hastily, "but I can see him as clear as day, sitting in this room, holding his stick across his lap, with his dear old face, and that fine white beard that was always as soft and white as snow."

"He washed it every day," Louise said.

"Yes, he had a way of expressing his opinion, but always in the kindest way. . . . I remember when we first brought Tom here, he was six months old that winter, and he hadn't been well, his nose was running . . ." She stared at her husband, seeming to search for the memory in the depths of his still face. "He was worried about Tom, that was it, it was his only grandchild, his only grandson, and naturally he was worried about the way we were treating his cold."

"He always hoped that someday Big Tom would take over the school, and then, of course, pass it on to his son." Louise said it neutrally, as though she were reading the words out of a book. "That was his great hope in life, since he had no sons of his own."

"Anyway, he brought me a handkerchief to wipe little Tom's nose, and he said . . . oh, I don't know what's wrong with me! I should have written all those things down. He had the most beautiful way with the English language; it came from his training in Latin and Greek, of course. And now I can't seem to remember a word he said." Mugsie struck her forehead lightly with the flat of her hand.

Tom, lost once more, was reciting to himself in the corner, pressing his quotations into the conversation as if, like wax, it would take the grand imprint. "'Old men forget, yet all shall be forgot'—"

"What's that?" his father asked sharply.

"Why, you know it," Tom said. "'Old men forget, yet all shall be forgot and he'll remember, with advantages, the feats he did that day. Then shall our names, familiar in his mouth as household words' . . ."

"*Henry V*," his father said. "Remember how we took you to the Memorial Auditorium when Gielgud came to town? You were only a boy, but you sat through the whole three hours."

"That was his main disappointment in life," Louise went on, fixing her eyes on Young Tom as if to seal his attention. "That there was nobody to carry on the school."

"And then later, when Olivier came to New York, we took you up on the train so you could see another rendition," Big Tom said.

"Yes," Mugsie said, "we had a fine time. Tom and I at the theater and you at the stores."

"I was looking for those English shoes," Big Tom replied stiffly.

"I didn't know you still remembered those lines," Mugsie said to her son. "I thought by now you'd have forgotten."

"I know the whole play—I mean the important speeches—and of course I know parts of all the tragedies. I memorized them last spring when I couldn't work," Tom explained, inspired by his father's embarrassment.

"Well, say something for us, then," Mugsie said.

Tom raked his chair a foot closer to the center of the room. He placed his feet on two swirls in the paisley carpet and laid his hands on his knees. His voice, as he began to recite, was unusually sweet and frail, almost piping, and he spoke rapidly, without tripping or failing: "'I come to bury Caesar, not to praise him.'"

Louise stood up suddenly, and her teacup fell onto the rug. It rolled over harmlessly.

"I'll start the cleaning up," she said, and she went out, leaving her teacup on the floor.

Big Tom's attention was immediately distracted. He sank hastily to his knees and gathered up the cup. Rising effortlessly, he held up his hand to stop his son, who had continued to recite, then turned to his wife and said, "I believe we really should get started back to the hotel if we're going to change before dinner."

Mugsie stood up and handed her cup to Tom. "Here, darling. Why don't you clear everything onto the tray and carry it out to the kitchen for Louise."

As Tom piled the cups haphazardly onto the tray, his father took his mother by the elbow and guided her to the window. "I believe she really is going to need something to help her sleep," Big Tom murmured. "Just for the first night."

"I have my prescription with me," Mugsie said, snapping open her purse.

Tom headed towards the kitchen and banged his elbow on the door frame. The pain made him wince, and he hesitated, shifting the tray. He felt blurred and lost, cast into outer darkness after the brief radiance of his father's attention.

"I don't mean she should use them indefinitely," he heard his father say. "That's why I don't want to say anything to Harris. He's likely to give her a jarful. I just want something to get her through the first night. Here, put it here; I'll write her a note."

Tom went down to the kitchen and crashed the tray on the counter. Louise was leaning against the wood-encased icebox, with her back to him.

Tom waited a moment, uncertainly, and then turned towards the other room. Louise snatched his arm; she had crossed the space between them with amazing speed. "Help me get Shelby back when the time comes," she whispered, her breath sour in his face.

"I don't know what I can do. . . ."

"I'll pay you back," she promised. "I'll make you glad you did it. I have a lot of things that should interest you."

He stared at her.

"You always used to ask me questions. Have you lost all your curiosity since you learned that Shakespeare?" Her horrible smile, pierced by her yellow eyeteeth, made him back away.

"Louise, I don't know what you mean. I haven't seen you for such a long time," he mumbled.

"I always thought you were interested . . . I always thought you cared about the family."

"That was Paul," Tom said.

"Paul's gone. And now you're just like a monkey on a string."

"I'm only in Kentucky for another week," he reminded her, stung. "Then I'll be going back to college."

"Would you write that down for me? Would you sign it?"

"Don't tease me," he said. "I haven't done anything to provoke you."

"I just don't want to see you get stuck at home like Paul. I want to see you get away. I had such hopes for you when I heard you were going east to college. And then it sounded like it wasn't going to work out. You can't live at home, Paul, you ought to know that by now."

"I'm Tom," he said.

"They loved you both so much, no one could ever say there was any discrimination, any favoritism; your dear parents, of all people, would never stand for that. Why, they never even wanted anyone to mention the prizes you won; they were embarrassed about it, afraid Paul would get some complex or other. As though in our family . . ." Her imitation of the family voice was so faultless that Tom could not tell whether or not she was mocking it. "I have some letters—just a few, not much—and some old papers," she said. "They should be of historical interest to you."

"I'm not a history major, Louise. English is my field."

She laughed, then seemed to give up. Her face drooped; the animation that had sparked it faded away. Almost feebly she asked, "Don't you at least want to know about Mama?"

"Your mother?"

"Yes. Didn't you notice? Your father has some notion of how she died. I don't believe he knows the truth to this day."

"You mean—" He hesitated. "You mean what happened to her?"

She nodded, barely interested. "Well, yes. What really happened. That kind of thing. You used to like the old stories." She looked at him slyly. "Of course you know what happened to Paul."

His hands, his big white hands, which had never seemed his own, never seemed to fit the rest of his body, now rose into the air and settled on her shoulders.

"All right." She shrugged her shoulders under his grip. "I mean, you were away at college. I was right there when it happened, you know."

"I know that," he gasped.

"Well, when the time comes . . ." She reached up to remove his hands from her shoulders, and he felt how cool her fingers were. "Well, when the time comes," she repeated wearily, "I'll see what I can do. The stories, you know, the skeletons—" She peeped up at him coyly. "I'll see what I can do for you and your big curiosity."

By then she had pried off both his hands.

"Louise . . . when?"

"Why, when the time comes to decide about Shelby," she said briskly. "Quid for quid, isn't it? You ought to know." And she smiled, freely and nicely, like the sweet friend of his childhood, as though she were about to present him with a peppermint stick. "You ought to know all about these arrangements!" she chirped, turning away and going into the hall.

He stepped behind her so quickly that the toe of his shoe knocked her heel, and she spun around, startled, and waved him off as she would have waved off a housefly.

Afterward, when his mother was gathering up her purse and her gloves, when his father was describing the restaurant he had chosen for dinner, when Louise was telling them that she had decided to wear her maroon wool dress for the occasion, and even later, when he was in the backseat of the car and the brick barracks were behind them and they were winding slowly down into town, and later still, when he was alone in his room, shaving, with his clean shirt laid out on the bed and his parents' voices through the wall, like the pleasant hum of bees on a sunny afternoon—even then he tried to believe that he understood what Louise had said: that she had promised him something, something unbelievable, even unthinkable, something that terrified him and yet must be actively sought.

At dinner, when they were eating their seafood cocktails and Louise was laughing gaily on the other side of the table, he looked at her, covertly, again and again, watching for a sign, a signal that she remembered what he thought she had said, that something definite had indeed been promised to him when they were alone together in her kitchen. But there was no sign. He had only his memory, ambiguous, dissolving. By the next day the memory had entirely melted. But her smile, and the way her eyeteeth pierced it—that, at least, stayed with him. He waited for a full week to hear from her; after that he left for college, believing that it had all been an invention, a figment of his hungry imagination. Lying alone in his bed at night, he remembered her teeth.

Chapter Three

Sunday: her first Sunday alone. Louise woke up at six, although she had not set the alarm. As soon as her feet touched the floor, she knew she would have to clean the whole house before she went out to see Shelby.

She stood at the kitchen sink and drank her coffee. The plastic mat with the cardinal on it was still on the table; she knew better than to look at it. She thought as she washed out her cup and tilted it into the drainer that she knew how to manage alone, or at least she knew how to try. It was a question of constantly working, planning each day, minute by minute. That system had carried her through the last time they took Shelby away.

Not that she could blame Big Tom; not that she could blame anybody, now, for being so shocked and mortified and even frightened by the sight of Shelby flailing on the ground as to assume that a hospital was the only possible place for her. She herself could not remember being shocked or mortified, or even frightened. Yet it made perfect sense to her now, in the morning, in the clear morning light, that someone like Big Tom, or Mugsie, would be mortified and would feel that it was a question of conscience—yes, a question of conscience—to have Shelby put away. Though why they hadn't thought of it before, or only once before in all those years, was still not clear to her.

She knew it was a beautiful day; a warm breeze rustled the blue-checked curtains over the sink, and she could hear the mourning doves in the bushes below the bluff. She did not dare to stop and look at the weather. Quickly she went to the closet below the steps and took out her pail and mop. Filling the pail at the kitchen sink, she began to sing, her high shrill voice almost as strong as the sound of the water. She sang, "Go Tell Aunt Rhody, the old gray goose is dead." By the time she got to the end of the second verse, the pail was full. She plunged in the withered mop, wrung it out with both hands, and then slung it at the kitchen floor.

Bella had had the nerve to try to do that for her the week before.

Smiling at the thought of Bella, down on her knees, her rear end hardly hidden by her short skirt, Louise finished washing the dark linoleum and went to sweep the back porch.

The morning caught her there, and she stopped for a minute, shading her eyes, and stared across the valley at the Pine Grove, where they had eaten lunch. How many birthdays, how many celebrations she remembered there; each one beautiful and the same. Her mother had never liked the place; she called it vulgar ostentation. Louise knew what she meant by that. The Pine Grove was where people went when they didn't want to know what was happening: where they married off their pregnant daughters with plenty of smilax and not one single sneer; where they took old relatives who were dying of mysterious diseases, and had a lot of steak; where young men fell down drunk on the floor and were helped to their rooms without a word. But she had always loved it; she had been too beggared to be a chooser, like her mother. Her mother had always put on her oldest black dress, shiny as a grackle's feathers, when one of the cadet's parents invited them to the Pine Grove for lunch; and yet as a young girl she had danced there in white petticoats.

Louise bent double to touch the linoleum floor. It was dry. She took out the can of wax and got down on her knees to apply it in dabs. Elbow grease was the only way to do anything. She rubbed each dab with a cloth until it spread, making an island of shininess on the drab floor. Finally she stretched out on her stomach to get at the area under the stove.

Pressing against the floor, she felt the hard warmth in her stomach and breasts. Still rubbing the dab of wax, at arm's length under the stove, she began to rotate her hips, pressing her belly into the floor and clenching her thighs together. After a while she sighed and put her face down on her arm. It was little enough. It was something. She would have a warm pain, like a match flame, in the pit of her stomach for the rest of the morning.

No one would ever understand the satisfaction in that, the way it warded off great pain, like a bonfire lit to contain a conflagration.

She went up and took a hot shower and put on fresh clothes from the skin out, singing again, but this time without words—a high, tuneless hum that seemed to come from the furniture in her father's room.

By then she was able to hurry. She got into the car and drove briskly down the drive, hardly seeing the wavering lines of the barracks, hardly noticing the newly broken window, its fragments flashing in the long grass.

She turned left on the county road to pass through the village, and stopped at Herman's store. Old Man Herman was behind the counter, and when he saw her coming he leaned over to call, "Hello, Miss Louise, how you?" in the overly familiar way she had hated since she was a child.

"Hello, Herman. Nice weather," she said, laying her purse on the counter. "I'm looking for a box of candy. What have you got?"

He bent himself quickly—he was lean and sectioned, like a measuring stick—and slid open the display case. He handed out two boxes of candy, one decorated with cross-stitch flowers and the other with a printed gold bow. They were both dusty and smelled dead.

"Don't you have anything fresh?"

"These just come in last week." He brushed at the dust with his sleeve. "Miss Shelby always has liked flowers. This one has cherries in it, too." He smiled at Louise, inclining his tall head and rubbing his hands smartly together.

"How much do I owe you?"

"Just three-fifty." He took the money and then, glancing at her brightly, said, "I'd appreciate it if you'd tell Bella to walk over here before dark. I need her to go over the inventory."

"Herman, she was down here yesterday. I can't do without her again tonight."

"Now, Miss Louise. You know I always try to oblige you when I can, but I have got to have Bella here tonight. I have to go over my inventory so when the supplier comes tomorrow I can get my order in. He's a hot-tempered man, and he won't wait for decisions. With you going to the hospital now, you can surely do without Bella tonight. That's an hour drive each way, and by the time you get back—"

"I'm not going to any hospital," Louise said.

"Well, as you say. But I would certainly be obliged if you would tell Bella to come over. Just for an hour or so."

"I'm not going to have her down here drinking with you," Louise said fiercely. "Drink alone, if you have to." She was not used to her anger, and she stepped back, aghast.

"Why, Miss Louise!" He was as surprised as she.

"I've known all along that's what you do, that and God knows what else," she went on recklessly. The slow burn of anger lighted her face. Drawing herself up, she remembered how her mother had complained, time after time, "It's these terrible mountainy white people! How in the world can we ever accomplish anything when we have to depend on these terrible mountainy white people? The niggers at home are lazy, but you can count on them to know their place. They may not get anything done, but at least they don't answer you back."

"Herman," she said, looking him in the eye, which veiled itself at once, like a sleepy owl's. "We've been through this time after time, and I'm not going to go through it again. Bella is here with you four nights a week, and that's all you're going to have her. That's plenty as it is. I'm not going to put up with it if she comes home drunk one more time, either. Carrying on at three o'clock in the morning, waking us up and giving us the fright of our lives." With the last words she turned and marched out, stopping at the door to call back, "You know darn well Mr. Tom said she was supposed to be with me night and day."

But that was going too far. She knew it as soon as Herman did. "All right, Miss Louise," he called after her, grinning.

The flush of her anger kept her warm all the way down the hill. She hardly noticed the heavy overhanging trees that walled in the road and the coal-truck shed and the cabin where some of Herman's relations had been squatting for the last year. She did notice the blond child sitting in the dirt in front of the cabin, and she wondered with blind patience how they—these terrible people, hardly better than animals!—managed to produce such beautiful children, full of hookworms and impetigo but with the most beautiful faces and pale gold hair. She had never yet heard of a child's dying in the shacks on the hill—there was a town, hidden behind the trees—or of anyone's having to be put away.

"The tallest trees are the ones that are struck by lightning," she said to console herself, remembering that Mugsie had said that, through her tears, when they were riding in the limousine on the way to Paul's funeral. Amazed, Louise had stared at her, then forced herself to feel some admiration. For after all, that was a pretty good way of looking at it. She herself had not been able to speak of Paul's death because of the rage it put her into: the sheer dumbness of it, the stupidity—that "accident."

Rather than be a tall tree of that kind, she would prefer to crawl over the kitchen floor on her belly for the rest of time.

She turned on the radio. One of the Sunday church sessions was in full swing, and she enjoyed the preacher's voice as he thundered against the sins of the flesh. "You can follow the first Adam or you can follow the last Adam," he shouted. "You can serve the spirit or you can serve the flesh, but you cannot serve both, my friends. It is your decision!" Louise smiled, wishing she had such a decision facing her. There was too little flesh in her life. The preacher's voice reminded her of her father's, though of course her father had been an educated man.

The memory of his voice scarcely left her on good days, underlining or redefining her experiences. He had spoken in a beautiful loud voice, too, when he addressed the boys in church, and Louise, sitting on a side bench with her arm around Shelby, had rejoiced in the knowledge that his thunder was never for her. She had always been one of his chosen, one of his blessed: "The only child in the world who has never disappointed me," he called her. That was mainly because he had given her a task from the beginning, and knowing the reward, she had never shirked her duty: she had always been Shelby's keeper. Besides, there had been no attraction for her—as far as she could tell—in the mysterious things her father proscribed; she had turned against them before she really even knew what they were, except that they had to do with noise, dirt, and bad manners. She had never wanted to run out with her hair in snarls or her hands dirty. Later she had realized that these transgressions, minor in themselves, led inexorably to the kinds of evil that compelled Shelby to sit in the grape arbor with that boy.

Well, she had never had much time to think about that. Taking care of Shelby, holding her on her lap even when the girl was really too large to be held, Louise had served her father in his own way, satisfied by the occasional glance he gave her or, very rarely, the full blue brooding shaft of recognition: "My sparrow, my wren." She knew how mulish the cadets were, how they broke his heart with their stubbornness and profligacy; she had seen him sitting at his desk with his head on his arms, exhausted, broken by the struggle. She had sworn that she would never disappoint him, and she had managed to keep Shelby from disappointing him too much, as well.

That had been her best gift. She had learned to braid Shelby's hair and tie the ends with blue ribbons, and she had learned to keep her quiet by stroking her arm. Later, of course, in adolescence, Shelby had begun to have certain feelings, which seemed to intensify her fits. Once she had run out on the parade ground in her nightie. (Louise knew about that, she knew all about that, she could not condemn Shelby for those feelings.) She learned to give Shelby facials with baby oil; she learned to keep her a long time in a hot bath. Perhaps it had helped. In any event, she had never disappointed her father, and she had prevented Shelby from disappointing him too much.

On his deathbed he had held Louise's hand, examining her face with wary avidity. "How old are you now?" he had asked. "Thirty, Papa," she said, and burst into tears. He nodded with satisfaction. "Out of the woods," he said, or at least she thought he said that, under his breath. And because of her, he had blessed Shelby, too, in the hours before he died.

Louise drove the car across the bridge and turned right, into the traffic. She kept in the slow lane and drove easily, barely touching the steering wheel, oblivious to the irritations she was causing by moving along at thirty miles an hour. A traffic policeman had stopped her once to reprimand her for driving so slowly, but she told him blandly that her brother had been killed in a car accident, and he let her pass. She knew the way to the hospital from Big Tom's instructions. It was a long way away, past the airport, past the old farms, but fortunately not quite as remote as the first place, which had been on the other side of the mountains.

She hoped Shelby had a view of the mountains from her room. A private place meant a private room, and she could already imagine that: a small room, clean and neat, with a bed and a chair and a closet for Shelby's things. Louise put her hand out along the seat and touched the box of candy. Yes, she hoped that Shelby had a view. Louise herself had long since gone blind to the low circle of mountains that surrounded the town; she knew everyone admired their hazy blueness, but she had never been one to pause in the day's occupations to stare into space.

On good days Shelby had sat on the back porch for literally hours, eating peanuts from a bowl in her lap and looking out at the view. Louise, in the kitchen, would hear her munching and smile, knowing that Shelby was happy out there—warm, clean, pretty, with perhaps a pink bow in her hair. That was the way Louise had planned to keep her, and she did not feel it was too much to expect others to put up with an occasional lapse—a bad moment or two—when all the rest of the time Shelby was sitting in a clean dress and a pink hair bow, admiring the view. Their father had understood that. Their mother had gone to her room and quietly closed the door whenever Shelby was having one of her spells. Louise had understood for a while why Big Tom could not put up with it, but her anger in Herman's store had burned up her patience. Big Tom should put up with Shelby. He should. He always had. But now he did not seem prepared to face even such a small trouble.

It was his house that had done it, she thought confusedly, all the things in it, the gold and silver and the enamel, the things that had to be constantly polished and dusted. It was all the people he had living with him now, the new cook, the Chinese one, the butler she'd hardly even met, the chauffeur who drove him to the capitol. It was Mugsie who had done it, or if not Mugsie then all her dresses, hanging perfectly pressed and perfumed in rows above matching shoes. It was the house and the hill it was built on and the servants and the cars and the friends and the people who voted for him and who would not be able to put up with such a small trouble. It was the long way he had come from being a sickly boy who couldn't sleep at night and needed a lot of sympathy. Oh, he was perfect now.

Staring, tense, Louise began to let the car slow down; her foot slipped from the accelerator as she gripped the wheel more tightly. Big Tom had said it was for treatment, but who cared about treatment? Shelby did not care about treatment. Shelby was her baby, her doll, her love, the only thing she had.

A station wagon passed her, horn blaring, but still she slowed almost to a halt before, with a convulsive shudder, she remembered and pressed her foot down to the floor. The car leapt forward, rattling. She raised one hand carefully to her eyes, as though to wipe away some obstruction, and thought of the old letters in the shoe box in her desk, the old poisoned letters that she had never even bothered to read since she knew their threats and their secrets by heart. In her time things had happened right out where everyone could see them, whether it was a fit or a birth or a death, it had happened right there, and she never could understand—here she heard herself speaking, into the microphone, while Dr. Dinsley, the gospel preacher, stood proudly by her side—she never could understand why modern-day young people knew so little about their families and didn't even seem to care.

Yes, the shoe box. She saw the wide green sign with the hospital's pretty name on it and turned off the highway.

She would wrap the shoe box up when the time came. She would have to look for brown paper and string. It had been a long time since she had needed to mail a package, but she knew she had saved the paper and the string from the last box that had come from Mugsie with clothes for Shelby. It had been full of Mugsie's old maternity dresses, which were totally unsuitable; Louise had sent them on to the home for lost girls.

Yes, and then a label, and she would take it down to the post office when the time came, and if anyone asked her what she was doing or why, she would make no bones about telling them. A boy, growing up, had the right to know about his people. She would even go so far as to insist that if more of the young people today took an interest in their roots, we wouldn't have the troubles . . . the drinking . . . the apathy. Roots. That was what they all needed.

She pulled into a parking lot and stopped neatly beside an ambulance, resting as sleekly as a white whale, its siren and its light turned off. She got out of the car, arranged her skirt, and paced towards the door.

Inside it didn't work, it never did; prepared though she might be, dressed, smiling, smelling her own light lavender perfume, she never succeeded in cutting off the sights and smells of the place. A gruff nurse in a bear's uniform—for size—showed her where to go, and she began to climb up a long flight of metal outside stairs. Stopping to catch her breath on the landings, she turned her back to the grilled windows. Yes, the mountains were visible, to the east. Finding a locked door on the top landing, she knocked and rang until a grizzled man in a doctor's white coat opened it from the inside and let her through. She asked for her sister, calmly, never moving her eyes from the man's dried-out face; his eyes were very bright, and she realized after a while that he was only some kind of trusted patient.

He seemed to know his way around, and he took her by the hand and led her down the long green corridor. She heard them making noises all around her, but most were sitting on low benches or on the floor, so that by keeping her eyes straight ahead she was able to avoid seeing them. Someone plucked at her skirt, but she passed on, breathing shallowly through her mouth to avoid the stench. "Where are the private rooms?" she asked her guide, who laughed and chattered like a monkey; she wondered if he was dark with age or illness or merely another Negro. He twitched at her hand, and she looked down to see a large fat white woman with no clothes on, lying on her side facing the wall.

Why, it's just like the other place, Louise thought, with calm recognition. It's just exactly like the other place.

Shelby seemed to have fitted herself into the crack where the wall and the floor met. The monkey man squatted down behind her shoulder and began to tweak at her hair.

Why, they've cut her hair, Louise thought, with the same mild recognition.

The man stood up, shaking his head and gesturing with his palms out, and then he went away for a moment and came back with a towel that he spread carefully across Shelby's buttocks.

He drew up a chair for Louise and then retreated, still chattering and shaking his head.

She sat down and folded her hands in her lap. After a while she pulled the chair closer to Shelby and angled it so that her back was towards the rest of the ward. "This place is private, you know," she said to Shelby, admiring the rise of her solid white shoulder. "The other place, anybody could go to." Her voice was pleasant and conversational, and Shelby seemed to respond; she moved one foot, at least, and pointed her toes. "Big Tom promised me it was the best treatment available, and although it may look or smell like the other place, that really doesn't mean too much. They'll be coming to you with treatment, and then we are really going to start to see some improvement."

Someone touched her shoulder, lightly and quickly, and she looked up to see an old woman in a bathrobe that was open to the waist. As she bent towards Louise, her spoiled breasts drooped out of the opening. "They put her on the list for shock," she whispered.

"Now, why would they do that?"

"First thing tomorrow morning. They always wait awhile, to see. But she was acting up something awful last night, cursing, and she peed on the floor. That's when they put her on the shock list."

"Can you tell me where I could find her clothes?"

"She won't wear no clothes," the woman told her brusquely. She turned away, yawning widely, as though suddenly and violently bored.

Louise opened the box of candy and leaned over to place it on the floor near Shelby's face. "These are Herman's candies," she said. "I know you must be hungry, with the diet they've put you on, but I hope you can make these last till the next time I come." As she drew back, her arm brushed against Shelby's shoulder. Crouching, she hesitated, then lowered her arm again until her wrist and palm were touching Shelby's soft white neck. "Darling, darling," she said, dully and softly, resting her fingertips in the creases of her sister's neck. "Darling, darling."

Some time later an attendant came and helped her up out of her crouch. By then it was time to leave, and she walked back down the ward with her eyes fixed at shoulder level and the tissue the attendant had given her clasped in her hand.

She drove home slowly, one hand on the car window and the other gently, lightly, on the steering wheel. Now and then she sniffed and wrinkled her nose, as though the stench of the hospital had caught in her nostrils. She did not think of Shelby anymore; instead she thought about the things she would need to buy at the supermarket, and the dinner that Bella was supposed to fix.

Bella was downstairs in the kitchen when Louise walked into the front hall. Louise listened to her rattling pots and pans, and then she went downstairs and stood in the doorway, watching her. Bella's long, pale hair was knotted up quite tidily on the back of her head, but every now and then a strand would come down and she would have to poke it up again. She had on her Sunday dress, a short green cotton with a white and red print, and her Sunday shoes, red, with very high heels. She also had on her new plastic apron.

"I told you just hamburgers," Louise said, after she watched her for a while.

Startled, Bella dropped the skillet top and then turned around to say, "Why, Miss Louise, I didn't hear you." She smiled. "I thought I'd fix you my special spaghetti sauce. I even brought the onions."

Louise sighed. "That will be nice," she said.

"How's Miss Shelby?" Bella asked, turning back to the stove.

"Why, she's just coming right along," Louise said languidly.

"Supper'll be ready in about five minutes. Why don't you wash up?"

But Louise still hung in the doorway. After a while, she said, "I told Herman you could not come down to the store tonight. I told him if you came, it would be the last time."

Bella did not look around. "It's just his old inventory," she said.

"Whatever it is, it won't be tonight," Louise said, and at last she began to feel the rising warmth of anger. She closed her eyes and leaned against the doorjamb, feeling the smooth wood with her palm. "If you want to keep this job," she added.

"Why, Miss Louise," Bella exclaimed, turning to stare at her. Louise flushed, almost to her eyes.

*   *   *

Asheville, N.C.
September 21, 1958

My Dear Tom:

I spent quite awhile this week reading over those old letters, the ones I told you about. Would you believe I never have read them before. I thought there was nothing more I could learn about the past, but I did learn some things. Nothing to surprise or confuse, but some details that I hadn't known until now.

None of it is likely to make much sense to you. They didn't write each other all the time, of course—no one in the family had time for that. So the letters come with years or months in between, and so much unexplained that it wouldn't make sense to you. I remember the stories and the things that were said, and so these letters make some sort of sense to me.

Anyway I decided the best I could do was to sit down, myself, and write you what happened.

I was there, after all—no one else still on this earth can say that—and it is of no interest to me to tell lies.

You want to know and you have a right to know the kind of people you come from. Even if all of it is not good news. . . .

First of all, about Mama. I write about her first because nobody but me can even remember her now. She's only been dead twenty years, but all of her generation are gone now, and your daddy, who knew her well at one time, says he does remember her singing but not much more than that.

I don't know if you remember the portrait of her that hangs in the upstairs hall here. It was painted just before she married my father. She was a pretty thing, evidently, with a tiny waist, and always full of life. Papa met her here in town, at the hotel where we had lunch. She was vacationing here from Virginia. Her family were well-off people and they didn't want her to marry Papa. I don't know exactly what the objection was; Papa was a handsome man and he had the military school and enough money. Maybe her people wanted her to marry closer to home. She was only up here for a week, that summer, but by the time she went home again, they had everything settled between them. Then there was some heart-straining for months because her people wouldn't agree. Papa went down to see them, but he never said one word about that visit, and as far as I know he never saw her people again. Certainly they never came here to the school. In the end they came around. I don't know how or why.

Anyway they were married. Papa was not a young man at the time, and it is reasonable to suppose that he didn't want to wait. I was born three years later, and Shelby two years after me. Mama was never a strong woman, she was little and slight, and she had trouble with all her births. She had two that died, after Shelby. Then I used to hear her crying, at night and pleading with Papa. After a while, if she didn't stop, I'd go and take her a glass of cold water. She would be sobbing and carrying on, sitting up in her long white nightgown in that maple bed Shelby uses now. "He says I'll have another and it'll die, the last one wasn't even baptized it went so fast." She always had such pains in her stomach, such terrible pains. Even the hot water bottle didn't do much good.

I don't believe she ever had many friends around here although of course there were plenty of acquaintances, people they saw in church. And then it was dawn-to-dusk work, trying to run the school, and times were not easy.

Anyway she came to love the boys, and they liked her too. Every year she'd have a favorite, usually one that had gotten into some trouble, and he'd follow her around like a dog. She used to say it made up for only having daughters.

Then she had one more baby that died, and I guess that had something to do with what happened. I was fifteen at the time, and Shelby was thirteen. Old Herman told me one time that Mama had some kind of sickness, some kind of incurable disease, but I never believed that. I mean, if that had been the reason she would surely have told Papa, and he would have told us when the time came. Any truth is better than none, don't you agree with that?

I used to wake up at night after she was gone and see her standing in the doorway, in that white nightgown she used to wear. I knew she was looking for Shelby.

After the last baby died, Aunt Edith (Papa's sister) came to take care of us. She was a harridan—a harpy as your daddy used to say—always looking in our ears and examining our scalps for lice. She didn't like living in the school because she said the boys were unclean. She never would let us have anything to do with them. Of course, that was Papa's rule too. Shelby outwitted her from time to time but I didn't try. She taught me to knit and crochet and make watermelon-rind pickles and that's about all I got out of life until I was seventeen years old. Your daddy will doubtless have told you about those days. He used to come on visits now and then, even after his year here was over.

Now the truth about Mama that I wanted to tell you is that she didn't want to live anymore. I don't know if it was the dead baby or the hard work or something else that happens to women when they stop being altogether young. Anyway whatever it was I would have known nothing about it if it hadn't been for Herman's niece Bella who was there when they brought her back. Bella didn't want to tell me, of course, but I plagued her about it for years. The French Broad River is deep near here, as you know—you used to swim there when you were little—and we always kept a rowboat so the boys could fish on Sundays. She had never been near that place before—the boys used to swim without clothes—but she made her way down there somehow, carrying some bricks to tie to her waist. Yes, bricks and string. They found them on the shore because of course she hadn't been able to arrange things the way she wanted. Someone came, I don't know who, and she went into the river just the way she was, in her clothes. They shouted I guess or maybe they didn't but it didn't matter anyway because she just kept on walking, holding her arms up— Bella is sure about that—holding her arms up over her head as though she didn't want to wet her sleeves. Just kept on walking until she went under. I never understood how she did that, but the sorrow or whatever must have been so heavy she knew she couldn't go on.

They tried to make a scandal of it and say it was because of one of the boys she'd tried to help who had somehow misunderstood but after a while it all died down and everybody agreed it was an accident. Everybody was bro-kenhearted. She was so pretty and sweet.

I am telling you this not to make trouble or fan the flames of old gossip but because I am afraid someday somebody will tell you she had some kind of incurable disease—cancer, or something, something that could be passed on—and I don't want you misled and scared into the bargain. Because she had nothing that could be passed on to you or anybody else in the family. She was just unhappy.

With love,
Louise

Cambridge
1958

Chapter Four

Sitting near the window, on the edge of his desk, Tom read Louise's letter and then carefully folded it up and put it back into the envelope.

"What's that?" Dennis Stevens asked. He was sitting on the couch, taking off his shoes.

"Some letter from a cousin of mine. Nothing," Tom added. He and Dennis were not close; they hardly knew each other, in fact, although they had been sharing the same two rooms for two weeks.

"You get a lot of letters," Dennis said gloomily. He leaned back on the couch with a sigh. "You been to supper?"

"I wasn't hungry," Tom said. He was still thinking about the letter, and feeling disappointed. Louise had seemed to be promising so much more.

"What's it like down there, where you're from?" Dennis asked lazily.

"You'd have to see it." Tom considered for a while. "It's not really the South, you know."

Dennis yawned.

"I mean, there's no Confederate monument in front of

the courthouse. In fact, there's no courthouse. The square's gone except for two benches across from a gas station. The old courthouse was torn down a few years ago, and they put up a skyscraper. The windows keep falling out, though," he added, to himself. "It never seems to work the way they want it to down there. They want something brand-new down there, something up-to-date, sophisticated, but what they get is some kind of cardboard second-rate skyscraper with windows that keep falling out. They haven't killed anybody yet."

"Yeah, but it's still the South," Dennis said, propping himself up on his elbow. He was a good-looking, blond-haired boy who had done the same things as most other boys at college. He had gone to prep school when he was thirteen, had traveled abroad in the summers, and hardly lived anymore in the New York suburb where he had been trapped as a child. He did not, however, have very many friends, which was why, Tom knew, he had allowed himself to be placed with Tom, an outsider, a nobody.

"Well, in the Civil War I believe it was neutral," Tom said. "I don't know for sure, but I believe it was." His hands made one of their curved, apologetic gestures. "I mean, my father doesn't take much interest in all that. He says all that is old hat, sentimental. But I know one time when Mother was talking about it, she said Kentucky tried to be neutral. After the start, anyway. It's a border state," he added. "They're all border-state people. They came from Virginia in the beginning, so they had all those ways." He hesitated, doubting that he could explain to Dennis how the myths of Southern suffering and gentility were still more potent in that border state than they were in the real South. "It was a backwater, until the Second World War, at least; that's when they brought in some new business, a steel plant or two, and the town started to grow. But even then, when I was growing up, it was still a little backwater town with a Loew's theater with stars on the ceiling and a ten-cent store and a cafeteria. Everybody seemed to know everybody else, even if they really didn't. We all went to the public schools."

Tom loved it. He had always loved it, and it had been difficult for him to leave for boarding school and college; he had barely been able to resist going home again, like Paul. He did not try to tell Dennis that, of course. Instead he joked about what it had been like to go to the same Halloween party every fall (where they all knew he was afraid to touch the peeled grapes that were passed from hand to hand under a sheet); and the same Easter party, with eggs hidden in somebody's perennial border and even a few in the fountain with the statue of Pan; and the same Fourth of July party, with somebody's father lighting rockets and Roman candles on a terrace overlooking the river, answering some lesser display on the Indiana side, where there were, of course, no terraces, no Pan statues, and no perennial borders, just the flat, coarse cornfields of the Midwest. Tom had known everyone, he had known exactly what was expected, yet somehow he had always been on the edge of the crowd, and when, later, they had started drinking and flying around in cars (and killing themselves in cars, sometimes, with a random kind of violence, against the trees on somebody's drive or the narrow stone bridges over creeks with Indian names), he had been a little further towards the edge, clinging finally to the edge itself with a panic he couldn't identify. By then they all knew the kind of person he was, but they went on inviting him to their parties anyway, even though he seldom spoke and never danced, because the girls all, every one of them, wanted to be nice, and also because his father was rich and probably the most important man in town.

He did not tell Dennis that either; it had a kind of irrelevant significance that he knew Dennis would grasp.

"What about servants, didn't you have servants?" Dennis asked. "Colored people?"

"Well, we always had a cook, and a maid, to clean." He was hesitant, again, trying to head off Dennis's wrong conclusions. "They were there all the time I was growing up; they were even there when my parents were first married. They were not just servants," he said.

"Colored?"

"Our cook was part Indian."

"Did she bring you up?"

"Oh, no. They don't do that anymore. I mean we don't have colored nurses anymore. My father had a colored nurse, but by the time it was my turn, most of the people had either French nurses or German governesses or white nurses, but no more colored nurses."

"No mammies?"

"No. It isn't that way anymore." He did not know how to explain the difference, although he knew it was important, had sensed its importance the moment he saw an old snapshot of his father being held in the arms of a large old colored nurse.

"Her name is Bessie, and she comes from the country somewhere," he added. "She comes from a big poor family with a lot of children, and she was hardly grown up when she came to us. We were the first children she took care of, outside of her own brothers, and she never has taken care of anybody else," he said proudly.

"You mean she's still there?"

"Of course. We don't need her anymore, but she'll always be there. She does the sewing, now, and some of the cooking; she did a lot more before they got this new Chinese."

"You mean they keep her on, just for that?"

"She's not a servant," Tom said. "You don't understand. I

mean, they pay her, of course, but she's not a servant. She never was a servant."

"Sorry," Dennis said, with his easy irony. "I didn't mean to step on your toes."

Tom hardly heard him, lost already in memories of Bessie. He remembered hot summer mornings when he would wake at six, waiting to hear her pad into the bathroom. As soon as she had washed and dressed in her crackling white uniform, as soon as she had rolled up her stockings and laced up her thick white shoes, they would go out to take their early-morning walk, creeping through the silent house and leaving the front door open so that no one would hear it close. He would run ahead of her, barefoot, down the warm drive, skipping and shouting the minute they were out of earshot of the house. Walking behind him, more slowly, she would stop to break off a flower or a weed and then show him, carefully, the way the petals were put together. Or she would stand, her hands on her hips, and watch a bird, never knowing or caring what its name was but simply admiring the way it was put together, the way it flew.

"That takes a lot of money," Dennis was saying, after some thought. "I mean, to run a place like that and support all those extra people."

Embarrassed, Tom said he really didn't know.

"Well, there are ways of telling. How many bathrooms have you got?"

"I never counted." (That was a lie: he had counted every room, every bathroom, and every closet to brag once to some boys in school.)

"You must have, when you were little. Maybe you didn't count the rooms—it would have taken too long, maybe—but you must have counted the bathrooms, and they're a square root."

"Well, I remember one time . . . somebody asked me then, too. I believe there are nine bathrooms, counting the top floor." Tom looked away from Dennis as he said it. He had never been easy with the knowledge that if he had nothing else, he had an enormous house with nine bathrooms that would be his when his father died and that for reasons that seemed stronger than sentiment could never be sold, never even lived in by anyone except his father's son. It made him feel smaller and more silent to think of all those bathrooms, all those pale-pink or dark-blue bathtubs with the chrome baskets for sponges and soap, all those mirror-fronted closets (many full of his mother's out-of-season clothes), all those nine pale-pink rattan thrones covering the nine toilets.

"That means it's a thirty-room house," Dennis said, calculating rapidly. "And your parents live there alone? You're an only child, aren't you?"

There was something gross in the question, and Tom was painfully offended. After all, he had asked to room with a stranger to avoid this kind of thing. He stood up and went to the window, clasping his hands tightly behind his back. Outside, the lights were on in the dormitories across the quadrangle, and it was raining thinly. "You'll have to stop asking those kinds of questions if you want me to tell you about it," he said. Dennis sighed and flung himself back on the couch, which was made out of a door.

"You don't seem to have much natural curiosity," he told Tom. "I used to count the rooms at home once a month at least. But there were only fifteen. Don't take it as an insult," he added quickly. "My parents have a lot of money, too."

"Everybody here has a lot of money," Tom said gloomily. "That's what I'm trying to get away from, don't you see? Money has nothing to do with it. That's just your way of looking at everything. I'm trying to tell you about the way it was, and you start to talk about money."

Dennis folded his arms behind his head and stared patiently at the bare bulb in the ceiling. "It's already nine o'clock, and we haven't even gotten over the money question. I'm supposed to be working on my Dante paper."

"Work on it, then," Tom said bitterly.

"Come on!" Dennis sat up and stared at him. "I told you I wanted to hear. I told you that the first or second day, after I told you everything about Mount Kisco."

"Go write your paper," Tom said.

"I can work on it before class."

"Yes, and probably get an A."

"Hell, that's not my fault, Tom. I'm just naturally quick," Dennis said, standing up with a little leap. "Just naturally quick, the way you're just naturally slow. It's the climate, you know, the hot weather you come from. I wouldn't be surprised if you had a natural sense of rhythm," he added, lifting the side of his shoe and nudging Tom in the backside.

Tom put his hand back quickly and caught Dennis by the foot, and they fell together heavily to the floor.

Dennis was larger and heavier than Tom, and he rolled him up like a sausage inside the rug, rolled him up entirely from his heels to his chin, and then sat on his stomach. "Now tell me about your Upper South! Now tell me about your border state! Tell me about your money, too! We've lived here for two weeks at arm's length, and now I want to know." He was flushed, careless, pleased with this game or any other. "Because I already know one thing about you, and that's you're not an only child."

Tom struggled to free his hands from the rug. "Get off me!" he shouted. He could feel Dennis's solid weight through the folds of the rug, and he felt paralyzed—but pleasantly so, as he had felt when Bessie pinned him under the bedclothes. He began to claw at the rug. "Let me out of here, you weirdo."

"I'll let you out if you'll tell me about your brother," Dennis said, getting up off the sausage roll.

Tom undid himself slowly and sat up. He ran his eyes around the room before answering. His Miró print was on the wall above the defunct fireplace, his books were lined up on his side of the bookcase—Dennis's side was empty—and he had folded his newspapers and magazines into a sheath that he had jammed into the armrest of the old wicker chair. The room was neat and cheerless and rather chilly—a radiator began to tick against the wall behind the couch—and he thought, as he had often thought before, that it was really *his* room, even though they shared it, because he had decorated it with his own things and had brought the curtains and the couch cover from his room at home. The bedroom they shared was devastated by Dennis, who slept on the lower bunk and left his clothes heaped everywhere, his shoes scattered, his books poured over the whole, but the sitting room was really Tom's, and he kept it neatly picked up, knowing that if his parents ever came to visit, he would serve them sherry and dry biscuits there, and they would sit, quite pleased, beside the defunct fireplace.

"How did you know I had a brother?"

"Somebody told me," Dennis said casually. His interest had collapsed in the interval; he turned on his side on the couch and closed his eyes.

"Three years younger," Tom said. "That is, thirty months. I don't remember life without him. He was always littler than me, though. Lighter. Blonder. He was a whiner," he said.

Dennis made a sleepy questioning noise.

"I mean, he was always whining. Always crying and

whining, and going to my mother with complaints. 'Darling, what is the matter?'" He imitated her high precious voice. "'What has Tom been doing to you now?'"

Dennis said, "I have two younger ones, too, both girls, if you want to hear about trouble."

Tom did not want to hear. "He never could seem to do anything on his own. I mean, anything independent. He always had to have someone to copy. If he couldn't copy me—because it was hard for him to keep up, you know; I was three years older—then he'd just sit and stare. Like a little lost dog." He did not tell Dennis how often he had longed to kick Paul, how seldom he had been able to resist the urge. "He never could do anything," he went on. "Not at school, or sports, or anything." Then, hating his own voice, he explained quickly, "It wasn't his fault, really. Something happened to him when he was born—I mean, not something big, but something that put everything a little out of whack. He couldn't seem to learn to read—he saw the letters the wrong way—and he was always left-handed, though they tried to change that. I remember he never could hop on one foot."

"What happened to him?"

"Well, it was an accident, you see. He fell out of a tree."

Dennis turned onto his back and stared at the ceiling. After a while he asked, "What do you mean, he fell out of a tree?"

Tom was annoyed. "You asked me what happened. That's what happened. I wasn't there, so I didn't see it. It was last spring, if you want to know. He'd come home from boarding school because he'd been sick." Again, he screened the hatred from his voice. "He was up in this tree, at home. We'd made a treehouse. At least, I made it, a long time ago, and he always used to want to go up there. . . . He fell out."

Dennis stood up, stretched, and looked at Tom. He

studied him methodically, stroking his chin with one hand. Finally he shook his head. "I can't figure you out, Tom. You haven't spoken to me once in the last five days except to ask me to close the window. I thought you were mad or something. So I try to lay aside some time in my crowded schedule to get to know you, since, after all, we spend a lot of time together in this room. Not speaking and in the same room! So I lay aside some time, and I ask what I hope is a personal question, and all I get is some kind of hogwash. I mean, I can't believe it, Tom," he said, looking hurt. "If you don't want to talk about it, I can understand that. It's pretty upsetting, after all, and all you need to say to me is you don't want to talk about it. But instead you go and tell me something . . . I mean, I can't believe it, Tom. A sixteen-year-old boy falling out of a tree?"

Stiffly, Tom said, "That's what happened. You can believe it or not, it's up to you. That kind of thing happens down there all the time. People get killed running into bridges. For no reason—not because they're drunk or anything. Or they drown in the river when they know how to swim. I can't explain it. It's just the way it is down there. He fell out of a tree, that's all I know."

"Okay," Dennis said, looking at him. "There's no need to get yourself all worked up. We'll talk about it when the time comes, when you're ready for it. As the dear shrink used to say, 'When the tree is ripe, the fruit will fall.' I'm going to go across the hall and see if Latelle's done his Dante yet."

He was moving all the while he spoke, and at the last words he was out the door.

Tom walked to the closed door and then stopped and turned smartly and marched over to the couch and sat down. The scratchy green material, off the daybed in Bessie's room, was still warm where Dennis had been sitting, and he got up quickly and crossed to the window. It was raining; drops crawled down the glass. The trees, already losing their leaves, drooped in the courtyard, and the crisscrossing paths were slick and black with water. He began to speak to himself, orchestrating the words with his hands, which moved gracefully through the air on two levels. "You have every right to want to know about me, and the only reason I can't explain is that I don't understand. It isn't that I don't like you or trust you—quite the opposite, in fact. I am one of a lot of people you know, but you are the only one, so far, that I know. We get on well in this room. I have never gotten on so well with anyone else"—except my nurse, he added, to himself alone—"and I don't want to spoil it with the wrong words. Last year was pure hell because my roommate knew me from home and he supplied all the words, he knew everything. But he knew it all wrong. He only knew about the money. I couldn't stand to have him knowing it all wrong, and telling it for me. My father: his importance. My mother: how pretty. My brother's death: how tragic. I wanted to room with a stranger this year so I could begin brand-new, think the way it was, tell the way it was. Only now I don't know. I don't know anything. It's all confused and mixed up and I can't describe it. It is as simple as that. It is as simple as that. It is as simple as that."

Staring out at the courtyard, which was running and blurred with rain, he remembered his mother's face the day of Paul's funeral, the way her lips had stretched beyond the neat line of her lipstick, and how he had smelled her breath and seen her tongue quivering inside her open mouth.

"No, you would not like me if you knew that," he said out loud, and he imagined Dennis, in his place, taking the distraught woman in his arms, comforting her, letting her lean her terrible face on his shoulder. Dennis would never have stood in a corner by a door, grinding his hands together behind his back, biting his lips at the spectacle, the horrible spectacle she was making, arousing guilt and terror in all those who were watching when in fact she was the one . . . she was the one who had allowed it to happen.

Dennis would not even have had those thoughts.

Tom turned around abruptly and pulled his raincoat off a hook and shuffled it over his shoulders and went out of the room. On the stairs he heard Dennis's voice in the room across the landing, and then he heard Gordon Latelle laugh. He felt frozen with hatred and disdain at the thought of those two, those great animals, impenetrable, unthinking.

He ran down the stairs and out the door and felt the coolness and wetness of the rain on his face. He stopped, lifting his face up, trying to let the unsaid words wash out of his mouth. He was tied and bound by unsaid words, fettered by them, hardly able to raise his hand to his mouth, to feed himself, even, because of the sharp pull of the things he did not dare to say. Then why do I think them? he pleaded with himself, knowing that it was because he had been born weak and spare—"unmuscled," his father had said once, objectively—unmuscled to fight off the furies of his perceptions. He began walking quickly towards the street, started to run, the puddles on the path flashing up reflections, flaring like burning oil, he thought, beside and beneath his feet as he ran out of the courtyard.

He walked down the dark street, passed a window of evening clothes, black jackets on white dummies, past an ice cream shop that was full of strangers, past a movie letting out (now the sidewalk was jammed; he walked carefully, his elbows in, afraid of touching), past the big store where he bought his books (and where, sometimes, he stood for ten minutes, unable to get a clerk's attention, unable to try), and around the corner to the shabby coffee shop he loved. He had never been there at night before—his nights were consecrated to studying—and he was surprised to see that the place was empty. (Not that it was ever crowded; he would never have gone in if it had been crowded.) The chairs were upturned on the tables, and a man was mopping the floor.

Tom went up to the counter and perched on the edge of a stool, waiting to be noticed. The hard doughnuts under the plastic dome seemed to have been forgotten, too, and Tom imagined them lying there until they turned to dust.

Tom stared at the man and thought about asking him for a cup of coffee. He raised one hand, but he could not speak before the man, by looking at him, gave him permission. And the man was lost in mopping, a middle-aged colored man with a high, furrowed forehead and a tall head bristling with gray.

Squaring his shoulders, Tom stared fiercely, the fury of his silence, of his inability, boiling in his veins. "Calm down, Tom," Bessie had warned him when he was having one of his wordless scenes, screaming and thrashing on the floor. ("Like a wild animal," his mother had said once, remotely fascinated, as she would have been by a writhing snake.) "Calm down, Tom, I've brought you some nice hot cocoa." Bessie would crouch beside him with the steaming mug in her hands, and as soon as he stopped yelling, if only for an instant, she would begin to spoon the burning liquid into his mouth. The sour smell of her sweat would combine with the sweet steam of the cocoa, and after a while he would swallow and begin to grow calm. She had believed that cocoa, or anything hot, had a magical effect on his silent fury, but Tom had known it was not that: it was Bessie herself. Her care took the place of the explanations he could not find; she had never even asked him why he was screaming. So now, although the magic was out of it, he always drank a cup of cocoa at meals. Even when he could not eat, he could depend on being able to swallow the hot, sweet cocoa, remembering Bessie, remembering her wordlessness, her freckled, broad-palmed hands.

Invigorated, he slid off the stool and went towards the man with the mop. But at the last moment he could not do it, could not interrupt the dark concentration, sullen, impervious, that the man was bestowing on the tiled floor. Tom stood a few feet away, his hands held up from his sides, as though his long, thin fingers might at any moment break into signs.

A cup of cocoa please, sir . . . if you please . . . if I could interrupt you . . .

A gust of damp air from the opening door touched his attention, and he turned towards the girl who was hurrying in. She dragged a chair down from the nearest table and dropped into it, slamming down her books. "You're not closed, are you?" she called to the man with the mop.

Tom was amazed when the man looked up and said, quite calmly, "Yes."

"Oh, damn," she said, beginning to gather up her books again. Then she asked, "Can I sit here for five minutes? It's raining and I don't have an umbrella."

"Uh-uh," the man said uncertainly, putting his mop in the bucket. "I've got to lock up in a minute, miss."

"Well, just till you lock up, then," she said crisply, and she opened one of her books.

Tom, invisible between them, did not know whether or not he dared to stay. After a while he began to edge towards the door.

The girl glanced up at him as he passed. She had a thin, pretty face, like a young fox, with long, delicate jaws and points of brown hair covering her ears and temples. "Hey," she said, looking at Tom almost as though she recognized him. "What's the matter with you?" And then, embarrassed, she laughed and put her hand over her mouth. "You look like a drowned rat."

Tom had not realized that he was wet from the rain; he glanced at his clothes, ashamed. His hands, hanging from his sleeves, made an independent convulsive gesture. "It was raining," he said.

"It still is." She studied him with amusement. "Are you going out again like that?" Swiftly she ran her eye over him, seeming to sum him up; Tom took stock of his feet, his ragged sneakers, and the long damp legs of his corduroy pants. He looked up at her timidly, as though expecting to receive some kind of verdict, but she was smiling, a sly smile that showed she had indeed summed him up but was, oddly enough, not displeased with the result. "Sit down," she said. "You might as well sit down"—again she touched her mouth, retreating into amused embarrassment—"at least until he throws us out."

Tom brought a chair over from the next table and set it down opposite the girl. She watched him, smiling, as he arranged himself, sitting down cautiously and then backing the chair a few inches away from the table. Carefully he crossed his legs, and banged his knee on the edge of the table. Again his hands performed their unplanned ritual, hovering over the injured knee. Her eyes followed his hands, as if she had already learned where to look for interpretations. "Did you hurt yourself?" she asked.

"No," he said solemnly, lowering his leg and bending forward to glance first at the window behind her head, which was streaming with rain, and then, cautiously, quickly, at her face.

"I guess I ought to introduce myself. Catherine Street," she said, holding out her hand.

"Tom Macelvene. I'm from Kentucky," he said, taking hold of the ends of her fingers.

"Well, I'm from Vermont. Haven't I seen you before, in some class?" She drew her fingers back deftly, after a slight pressure. "Don't you take English 101, on Mondays and Wednesdays at nine?"

"Yes," he said. "It was to get me out of bed. I have a bad habit of just lying there . . . but anyway I'm usually late, so I sit in the back."

"Well, I sit in back, too, sometimes," she said.

After that it was difficult to go on. Catherine looked at her books, stacked on the table, with some longing; then she glanced at Tom, who had begun to shiver. "Why, you're freezing to death," she said, leaning across the table to peer at him more closely. "You're going to catch a terrible cold if you don't warm up. You're practically soaked through!" she added, touching his sleeve gingerly with her fingers. "I'm going to get you some coffee." She stood up and addressed the man with the mop, who had reached their corner of the floor.

"This boy is freezing to death," she said. "Show me where the coffee is so I can get him some."

The man tried to refuse, but Catherine was already on her way to the counter. "I can see a full pot from here," she called, letting herself in through a little gate and going back to the shelf where the cups were stacked.

Tom turned to look at the man, who was frowning. "That's just the way they do, every time," he told Tom, wiping his forehead with the back of his hand. "That's just the way they do." Shaking his head over this shared conclusion, he snatched up his bucket and strode towards the back of the room. "I'm switching off these lights in three minutes," he shouted back, then lapsed into mumbling as he emptied the bucket into the sink.

"That's against the health code, emptying that water in the sink," Catherine said, bringing over two cups of coffee and a sugar dispenser on a small tray.

She placed Tom's cup in front of him and then returned to her own chair. When she offered him the sugar, he found himself staring at her hand on the dispenser, staring at her fingers, which were stubby and dark over the knuckles. He could feel the exact degree of intensity of her grip on the sugar, and he usually was not able to imagine anything about strangers.

"Yes, I'll have some," he said. When he made no motion to take the sugar, Catherine tilted it up and poured a steady stream into his cup.

"Say when," she told him, but, charmed, he did not speak; his eyes were still on her hand. She stopped the sugar and looked at him with a wry smile. "Say, you really like it sweet!" But her humor did not match the peculiar intensity of his stare, and her face grew solemn as she watched him. "You're not well, are you?" she asked, frowning.

"I guess the only trouble is—" He shook his head sharply, and his dark hair scattered over his forehead. "I'm just not used to it here."

"Do you know people? Have you got any friends?"

"Well, yes. I have my roommate. He's a boy from outside New York. Of course we haven't gotten to know each other very well yet. You know how it is. There's so much going on. He spends a lot of time running; he wants to make the track team. And then he studies in the library and I study most of the time in the room."

"I guess you're just lonely."

"Well, no, I wouldn't say that." Talking quickly, hardly

aware of what he was saying, he glanced at her face now and then as though to gauge his meaning from her reaction. "I mean, I'm used to being alone, I was always alone most of the time. I never went around with the crowd, you know, I was always pretty much on my own. At home, I mean."

She was intent on his words, as though he were speaking in a code that she was learning to decipher. She leaned forward, trying to look directly into his eyes. "What about your family?"

He turned his face slightly and felt her glance lightly brush his cheek. "Oh, they're all down there, all at home," he said.

"Don't you have any brothers or sisters?"

"No," he said. "I'm the only one."

He had not said that to anyone before, although he had planned to say it ever since Paul's death, had in fact written the phrase several times on the back of an envelope so that it would come out smoothly, naturally, at the right occasion. But no one except Dennis had asked him about his family.

"You look like an only child," she said. "I grew up in a big family—I'm the third of six—but I guess I can imagine how it feels to be the only one. And people here don't seem to care very much."

"Well, I wouldn't say that," he disagreed hastily. "I mean, my professors were very nice; last year my English professor told me all kinds of things, things I would never have found out on my own, like extra reading. I mean, that wasn't something he had to tell me, it wasn't written down or anything. But he was concerned—you know—he thought I could get more out of the course."

Catherine laughed. "Well, that's something."

Straightening his shoulders and pulling his chin back with a sharp movement, he stared at her.

"It *is* something," she explained. "It's just that I expected so much more."

"Well, we didn't leave home—at least I didn't leave home—to be babied." He said it rather grandly, then took up the coffee cup.

"I'm sure you didn't," she agreed. "But you see, I've always lived at home, with a lot of people, and everybody sort of took care of everybody else. I mean, if a button dropped off my coat, I would never sew it on; Mom or Julie or somebody would before I even noticed, and then, of course, I would do the same thing for them. Not sewing— I'm not much good at sewing—but making a cup of tea for somebody when it's raining. You know what I mean?" She watched Tom for a moment, but he had lowered his head and was gazing into his cup of coffee. "Then, when I came here," she went on, "I had some trouble getting used to the fact . . . well, you know, this year there are thirteen hundred in my class. I guess it's a little hard for everyone to get used to being on their own."

Tom said sullenly, "I had a nurse once who used to do that kind of thing. But by the time you're seventeen years old—"

"Oh, I agree with you," she said. "It's like loving peanut butter. By now you should have outgrown it."

"I'm going to turn these lights out," the man behind the counter said, and as they stood up, he switched off the big tin chandelier and the fluorescent tubes. For a moment Tom was afraid to move in the darkness, but then he saw the window glimmering and went towards it. He walked quickly, forgetting that he was not alone. At the door, he turned back and jarred against Catherine. He felt her shoulder against his arm and was amazed by the solidity, the roundness of it under her sweater. He had never realized before that a girl's shoulder was not angled in the familiar way. She went ahead of him out onto the sidewalk.

"I've got my bike here," she said. "I was at the movies and then—" She shook her head. "It's awfully late, isn't it?" She bent over to unlock the chain on her bike, and he realized that she was a small girl; he wondered if he would be able to lift her. "Well, good night," she said, slinging the bike chain around her neck.

"I'll walk you home," he said.

"All right." She leaned forward to look at him. The square was deserted, nearly dark, and the space between them was solid with falling rain. Tom turned up his collar and hunched his shoulders, thrusting his hands into his pockets, which were torn at the edges. Catherine walked along beside him, wheeling her bike, her hands on the plastic grips. When he glanced down and saw the dark points of her hair, plastered against her cheeks, he was overcome with disbelief and stopped walking.

"What is it? Did you change your mind?" she asked. "I can make it home on my own, you know."

"No, that's not what I was thinking," he said, catching hold of the bike seat to prevent her from starting off. "I just can't . . . well, this will sound crazy, but I just can't believe it."

She began to wheel her bike along again. "What do you mean?"

"I mean, walking here . . ." He laughed, hunching his shoulders, grinding his hands down into his pockets. "You won't understand," he went on solemnly. "This kind of thing doesn't usually . . . this doesn't usually happen to me. Usually," he repeated.

She was silent. They crossed at the light, in front of a few stopped cars; Tom looked at each one apprehensively. He would have liked to stand between her and the cars, but he did not know how to switch sides without awkward explanations.

"I mean, of course, I do this kind of thing sometimes," he said, maneuvering to walk between her and a dark row of trees as they entered the park. "But I'm usually asleep by this time. I'm an early bird. I was up late because Dennis wanted to talk."

"Is he your roommate?"

"Why, yes, and you see, he wanted to talk about himself, tell me about his family and all. We haven't had much opportunity for that sort of thing yet, and he's the type of person who believes in talking." Vaguely aware that something in his description had changed, been warped slightly by wishfulness, he peered at Catherine's face. She looked pale and tired; imagining that the bike might be weighing on her, he longed to take the handlebars out of her hands.

"He sounds pretty self-centered," Catherine said, facing straight ahead. "Doesn't he want to hear about you?"

"Oh yes, of course, that was all part of it. I told him all the usual things . . . schools. I haven't been to many schools, though; my parents just sent me to one place."

They passed through a pool of light from a tall street lamp. The rain was tapering off. Catherine looked up at him. "Did you tell him about your nurse?" she asked.

"Why, of course not."

"Why not?"

"It's not really very interesting. There are many more interesting things about my life. I can tell you about the place I come from—it's kind of unique. I imagine you've never been in that part of the country."

"I'd rather hear about your nurse," she insisted mischievously.

"Well, there isn't that much to say." Embarrassed, he stared at her feet, which proceeded along beside him, skirting the puddles as agilely as a pair of cats. "She was a woman, a young woman, from around there," he said vaguely.

"Is she dead?"

"Oh, no, she's still at home."

"Did she give you your bottles, and all that?"

"Well, yes . . ." He began to hurry, and the spokes on Catherine's bike wheel glittered as she pressed to keep up with him. "She's a nice woman, she did all the usual things. I used to sit on her lap at breakfast and she would feed me my cereal. I don't remember that, of course, but there's a snapshot somewhere. She used to give me my bath in the sink because for some reason I was afraid of the bathtub." He stopped, fending off the dark suspicion of fear, the tail that quivered like the tail of a crushed snake whenever he talked about his childhood.

"You must have loved her," the girl said.

"Yes, of course I loved her, she was the one who took care of me." Irritated, shrugging, he longed to change the subject, which was dry for him, devoid of interest, a dead patch of his past. "We could talk about more interesting things—She is a nice person, but why do you care about that? We could talk about more interesting things than the woman who changed my diapers."

"You don't know much, do you?" she asked, hesitating before crossing the street.

"Well, if you mean those things in books . . . those child-raising books, that is. I don't have much to do with those."

"I never had a nurse," she said thoughtfully.

"Well, it was a different kind of life." The horrible specter of money, and the wall it represented, made him hurry forward. "It was a way of doing things that was different, that's all. It had to do with the South. Women weren't supposed to strain themselves."

"Yes," she said.

"So that was the one reason I wanted to get away from home and come up here. You can't imagine how different this is from down there. Even being out at this time of night and walking a girl on a bike." He shook his head again, amazed. "It just wouldn't be possible down there."

"You mean everybody would be scandalized?" she asked coyly.

"Well, that wasn't exactly what I meant. Obviously things do go on. But people mostly live in the country or in the suburbs, so they have to use cars to get around. It's as simple as that. But I never had anything to do with all that, anyway. I never had the time."

"You didn't have a girlfriend?"

"I went to parties, if that's what you mean. Of course I did all that. But I was spending most of my time studying, I didn't have the time . . ." His voice trailed off, and he stared at the streetlight they were approaching. "Most of the people at home don't come east to college," he told her. "Not that I mean to boast."

"Oh, I knew you were bright."

Without saying anything further—as though, he thought, his brightness was irrelevant, ordinary—she wheeled the bike in to the circle in front of a large brick dormitory. Most of the windows were dark; the light over the porch showed four or five clustered couples near the door. "I'll say goodbye to you here," she said, stopping. She leaned her bike against a parking sign. Turning back, she put her arms around his neck and kissed his cheek.

He jerked back. The slight pressure of her fingers on his neck burned through the fringes of his hair, struck through his skin, and jarred the top of his spine.

"What's wrong?" she asked.

He turned away from her, bitterly ashamed, putting his arm up to shield his face. Pain, he knew, was not the right reaction. "Goodbye," he muttered, then spun away and began to run. She called after him, but he did not hesitate, splashing through a puddle at the curb and then darting across the street. He ran for three blocks, gasping, his breath scorching his throat. Finally, on the common, under the wet trees, he stopped and began to feel his face. He touched his chin and the edge of his mouth and then, like a blind man, he ran his fingers quickly across his left cheek. The kiss he had never wanted or expected had left it slick and ridged, as though scarred from an old burn. "She had no business," he whispered, fingering the place. "She had no business." Now, he knew, she would want more; she would not be satisfied to let him look at her, to let him admire her hands on the handlebars.

He walked rapidly back to his dormitory and ran up the stairs. Dennis was already in bed with the light turned out. Tom stood in the doorway, poised to tell him something, anything, his hands circling slowly at his sides. But Dennis was asleep and snoring. After waiting for a few minutes, Tom went to close the window in the sitting room. The wind had blown his history paper off the desk, and he leaned down to gather the sheets off the floor. Bending, he began to flush and grow warm. Straightening up, putting the papers back on the desk, he was still warm, and he stared at the metal desk where he had already spent so many hours and touched it cautiously, as though it, too, might have heated. But the metal was chilly. Tom was warm, warmer than he had been in several weeks, and the heat of his body reminded him of himself, as if he had come upon a set of footprints and known immediately that they were his own.

* * *

Asheville, N.C.
October 7, 1958

My Dear Tom:

Not having heard from you since my last letter I am afraid that something in it has offended you. As you know, I do not write to cause trouble but simply to set the record straight. It seems to me that I am the only one who can do this. And as you doubtless remember here in my kitchen you did seem to have some interest. So I am going to continue my sad tale unless you tell me to stop.

Here we are having beautiful fall weather and Shelby's pumpkins are ripe. I am planning to take one to show her when I go to visit her tomorrow. By the way, you may be interested to know that she seems to like the place she's in. I do not care for it at all but as you know she has a different standard. Anyway we shall see what we shall see.

Now that I have told you the story of Mama, it seems time to tell you what I know about Papa. Unfortunately, there is not much. He was not a letter writer. There are only two letters from him to Mama in the box and both of them are mainly instructions about the school. He seldom went on trips. They were almost never separated. Like you, he was not a talker though I often thought he did have things to say. I mean he was not a talker at any length. He would tell you what he wanted and expected right off with few words and just the right ones. But that was that. He never tried to explain things or talk about the past. I guess he thought

Mama did enough of that. Anyway his people were not much to brag about I guess although I am not sure even of that. Certainly, they were plain people without money or standing, schoolteachers recently come over from Scotland without a way of getting started or much except brains to go on. I know it always used to gripe him when Mama would describe how her people had lived in Virginia for five generations, in the same house on the same place. He would scowl, but he would never say a thing. He was in his way I guess a democrat.

The school was all he had. He had started it when he was hardly older than a boy himself. Then it was closer to the coast; the buildings are long gone but I believe there is a marker. That was not so long after the Civil War, when people in the south believed a military training could do wonders for a boy. You know there were many who were scarcely more than boys in the War who distinguished themselves in all kinds of ways. So the school was a great success right from the start, not meaning by that that it made much money but that it gave Papa the respect he craved. He was a firm disciplinarian but a good teacher, I'm told. I never saw him hold a class so it's hard for me to say.

The climate in the coastal part of the state is hot and humid, so before the turn of the century he decided to move up here to the mountains. That was when this town was just getting started as a health resort and all the big hotels were going up. It looked like it was going to be a fine kind of place. People from all over the South were coming up here to spend their summers, either in the hotels or in their own houses. It made sense to have a school where parents could send their boys who needed to get out of the hot climate or had some weakness or other.

So the school went on doing fine all through my childhood. We had as many boys as we could handle all that time. People looked up to Papa because of his firm ideas and the way he had of training boys, even boys who were weak, to be strong and manly. I think he did it mainly by example. You couldn't have missed him striding through the school. He was not teaching classes anymore since he had his hands full running the place but he knew every detail of what was going on. The boys were sent to him for punishment and I've heard it said it never happened twice. Apparently he had some way of convincing them. As I told you before this gave rise to some ugly rumors and it didn't help that by then Papa was often angry although his anger didn't find words. He had a black rebellious mood that would spread over his face until his face actually seemed to darken, I mean the skin itself would darken, and then we would all be afraid to speak to him. Even Mama would be afraid to say a word and sometimes it would go on for days. However, I never knew him to raise a hand against anyone even when he was in one of those rages. He had such control of himself. So I have never given any credit to those vicious tales.

After Mama died he couldn't seem to get his heart back and he spent most of his time in his room. Of course, the school suffered and enrollment began to fall. Times anyway were changing. There wasn't the call for the old-fashioned military training, the swords and parades and all. So Papa decided to close the school. He never told anybody about it. One year he just announced at commencement in June that the school would not be opening the following fall. There was a great deal of surprise and some criticism, especially from the teachers since it was a hard time to find another place. He wouldn't lift a finger to help them, not because he didn't care but because by then he was not leaving his study. He was not seeing anyone except me and only me because I brought him his meals. I made a mark on the calendar each day that summer that he didn't speak, and by the middle of August it was forty-seven straight days and before that only a request for aspirin. He had always been quiet and I had Shelby on my hands so I didn't worry too terribly much. Besides, he had always had such good control of himself.

What was actually on his mind I will never know unless it was Mama's death. They never had spent much time together, although they lived in the same house. Of course, he always had his own room.

One morning, August thirteenth it was, I woke up hearing a shot and went to his room and he had used his pistol. He always kept it in the drawer by his bed. One shot. That was all he needed.

They made a scandal over it and said he had left debts and indeed he had left debts—creditors ate up almost everything—but that was not his fault. He had gone on helping several of the boys who needed money. There was nothing wrong in that. People as you know will try to make a scandal out of any scrap they can find. It's usually just ignorance, just plain lack of knowing. Somebody wrote in the paper after he died that he had been a cruel man, a monster who beat the boys with the flat of his sword and that the debts were somehow connected with that. But I knew he would never use his sword that way. He had too much respect for it. He was a sad man who never seemed to find what he wanted even when the school was a great success. He never seemed to learn any words except the words for ordering and I suppose that made him feel cut off. I was very fond of him. He used to seem pleased with me and he liked me to take care of Shelby. Once he called me his sparrow.

Killing yourself is not a scandal when life is not worth it

anymore. I have always believed that. People know when life is not worth living anymore and when it is not going to change. Killing yourself then is reasonable. So I never have understood why people want to cover it up and pretend it is something disgraceful. Your father didn't want to put it in the paper that Papa had killed himself. He wanted to make it a heart attack. I believe it is the only time I have disagreed with your Daddy but I did that time. I told him straight. We had to write it the way it was. That was not a shame. That was not a scandal. He had no more reason to live.

He was like you in some ways, at least you remind me of how he looked when he was a young man in the portrait over my desk. Of course, the beard hides his chin but your eyes and your forehead are his. A fine broad clear forehead when he was young and fine large dark eyes. I have always been glad you were not fair like your brother and your Daddy and mother but dark and tall-headed like Papa. He had a noble face and a noble way of walking which is out of date today but can still be admired. And he had the same control over himself that you seem to have. Neither one of you is great with words. That is in itself a kind of strength, I believe. Other people are always chattering but what do they really say? Anyway I am always grateful that though he had no son of his own, Papa has a kind of copy in you.

Of course, with your good life and your advantages you will never need to feel cut off. It's enough, God knows, to look like him and I hope you can take pride in that, as I do every time I see you, dear boy.

With love,
Louise

Chapter Five

I t's just her way," Tom said when Dennis had read the letter. "She wants to tell me how things were because she's afraid I'll believe the lies."

"She shouldn't tell you at all," Dennis said. He stood brooding beside the fireplace, holding the letter in his hand.

"Oh, she always goes on and on. She has this interest in telling me things that happened years ago in the family. It doesn't really matter to me," Tom added quickly, hoping to put out the spark of Dennis's interest. "It's just old tales, gossip."

"But she connects it," Dennis said.

"Not to me. That doesn't have anything to do with me. My Lord, that was my great-uncle she's talking about. I never even knew him. He died when I was three. It doesn't have anything to do with me." He raised his arm and looked at his watch. "I'm going to shower and shave before we go to pick up Catherine."

"She's not expecting us until noon," Dennis said. He stared for a while at the folded letter. "You must have asked her to tell you, though. She says something here—" He opened the letter and looked at the first page.

"She made a big thing out of that. She was upset, she wanted somebody to take an interest." Tom felt annoyed, distracted from thinking about his day with Catherine. "I said I was interested, that's all."

Dennis, obviously bewildered, folded the letter up again and laboriously transferred his interest. "You don't need to get ready to go yet. We don't want to be an hour early." Tom was not listening. "Don't you want to see the map?" Dennis asked. "You've never even been out to Concord."

"No," Tom said. "You're the one who's going to drive." He walked slowly towards the bathroom, enjoying the grittiness of the thin carpet under his bare feet. He had been living in warmth for the last two weeks, wrapped and confined in warmth, and he seldom noticed anything except for the quality of his comfort. Catherine had done that for him, wrapping him in her attention, warming him in her care. It clearly irritated Dennis, and he would sometimes say, "You're like a rabbit in clover, it's enough to make me sick the way you gorge yourself," but Tom would only smile. He managed for the first time to feel rather sorry for Dennis, which justified his taking him along now and then. Besides, Dennis had a car. He also made sardonic remarks which helped to fill the silences, silences that seemed luminous to Tom, portentous, filled with the green light that went before a summer thunderstorm.

Tom went into the bathroom and studied his face in the mirror. He was still pale and unfinished-looking, with the long jaw that had always seemed so ugly to him, so much like an animal's, but he did not mind now that Catherine had told him he looked like a starving aristocrat.

He began to lather his face. Dennis, in the sitting room, put a record on the phonograph and began to sing in one of his several voices: a great churchgoing bass. After a few minutes he came to the bathroom door to look at Tom. "'Almighty Father, strong to save,'" he roared against the feeble phonograph, "'whose arm hath bound the restless wave.'" He frowned at Tom. "I always thought I would be the first to make it. It never even crossed my mind you would beat me to it." He punched Tom's shoulder.

"Quit," Tom said, carefully lowering the razor.

"Well, it's too much, that's all. I wasn't prepared for such a surprise. I thought you told me you never had anything to do with girls, and here you bag yourself one before Thanksgiving."

"She bagged me," Tom said, beginning to shave.

"How did you do it? I never thought you were much to look at, and you still don't talk worth a damn."

"She likes me," Tom said. Recently he had found his way to simple answers, and they seemed to work as well as or better than anything else.

"I know that," Dennis said. "She's spending more time here than she spends asleep. You look innocent as hell when I come back from the library—and you have noticed, I hope, that I never come back before eleven—but it's not in me to believe you don't do anything besides studying."

This had been discussed before—or rather, Dennis had suggested possibilities that Tom found unacceptable and even incredible. "Let's not start all that again," he said sharply, hoping to cut off the stories of underpants found on lampshades and strange shapes half perceived in the backs of cars. He did not quite dare to try to explain to Dennis that this thing with Catherine was old as warm milk in a bowl with a blue lamb on it, old as a blanket with a satin rim.

"I don't want to offend your innocence," Dennis continued mildly. "Last time I made an uncouth remark, you nearly killed me."

"You exaggerate everything." Tom dried his face. "All I did was punch you."

"And nearly knocked my front teeth out. What's the matter with you, anyway? You used to be so damned quiet, and now you've decided to get mad about things nobody else takes seriously."

"Well, I don't know how to explain it. That's just the way I feel." Tom thought of saying more, but the words were not available; he made a gesture with his right hand, pinching thumb and forefinger together. Then he went to hang up the towel, which was dirty. "Why don't you get the towels and things downstairs on time so the co-op people can get them? That's supposed to be your job."

"Hell, I can't bother about that," Dennis said, turning away. "You don't even strip your sheets."

"They don't get that dirty," Tom said uneasily. He had been worried about his bed because Catherine sometimes sat there, waiting for him to put on a tie before he took her to dinner. He did not want her to know that underneath the bright orange cover, which he tucked in neatly every day, the sheets were turning gray; he knew that would offend and alarm her, and she would jump up, exclaiming. Yet somehow he had lost the ability to take care of the details that had always seemed so important to him. He had been using the same razor blade all week because he couldn't seem to get himself to the drugstore; the work for his courses was taking up less and less of his time, although it still consumed a good deal of blank staring and sitting. Everything was soft and vague, except for the hours he spent looking at Catherine and listening to her talk. She smelled of some kind of soap, with a hint, perhaps, of mothballs, since she had only just got around to unpacking her sweaters. He wondered if that meant that she, too, had given up on details. But he had seen her in her dormitory window, watering a tiny plant with a paper cup, every evening after she told him good night. Feeling a slight chill of dismay, he had watched her bend protectively over it. He sighed, loving her sweetness yet afraid that somehow, in spite of everything, he was her opposite—an animal, a swine, although he showered every day.

He had begun to be bothered, again, by dreams, like the dreams that had tormented him in the spring. Nothing he did had any effect on those dreams. He would not have minded them so much if they had had nothing to do with Catherine, but some piece of her was always caught in that mess: her ankle, or her thighs inside her corduroy pants, or her soft little belly, which he had seen pressing up against her belt. All of her never got into his dreams, only some piece or patch, grafted onto a monstrosity, a female animal that sauntered beside him on his way to class or suddenly devoured his attention in the middle of a lecture. She—the animal—wore a piece of Catherine, jeeringly, as an ape might wear a piece of female clothing. After one of those visitations, Tom would have to turn his eyes away from that part of Catherine, ashamed of the way it had been transposed.

"We have got to start," Tom said to Dennis suddenly, and in spite of his protests, he forced him down the stairs and out the door, where they began to walk briskly, nearly running, towards Catherine's dormitory. They were early, and Dennis complained and argued the whole way.

When they got to the dormitory, the girl at the front desk recognized them and even seemed to know that they were early. She put in a call for Catherine, and the two boys waited, staring at the bulletin board. Behind them girls in discreet robes were passing, carrying cups of coffee. Tom was eager to find Catherine and get out; he tapped his foot on the floor impatiently. He did not believe that she had any connection with these girls, who all seemed coarse to him. He had been shocked to see her once, walking and talking with the queen of them all, a hideous giantess with raw red cheeks who wore purple stockings and a skirt that was much too short.

Catherine came in. Tom felt her in the small room, perhaps a foot behind him, but he did not turn around. He heard her speak to Dennis and knew that his friend had put his arm around her; he heard the light smack of their kiss. He did not turn around until Catherine placed her hand on his arm. It was their sign. He slowly swiveled his head until he could see her and then moved his shoulders and the rest of his body, pivoting on his heels. She was there, filling his eyes. A small girl with dark hair, he had written to his parents, wanting to blare his pride but limited by his choice of words. Greedily, he checked each detail: the lobes of her ears, pearly white beneath the wings of her short hair; the pale parting in back of her bangs where he had laid his finger once, expecting to find a pulse; her wrist, indented, the bones so fragile; her feet, long and narrow, the toes shyly curling when she took off her shoes. At last he allowed himself to look at her eyes, her warm, pleasant, watchful dark-brown eyes, which made him stammer and wince.

"Hi, Tom," she said, and she leaned forward and kissed his cheek while he stood rigidly waiting. As soon as he felt her soft, dry lips, he broke into motion, like a creature freed from a spell. He lifted his hands and grasped her elbows and brought her so close he felt her skirt crush against his legs. "Catherine, Catherine, Catherine," he muttered, blind to the girl behind the desk, who was watching with a smile. "So you made it through the night."

"And the morning, and got up, and dressed, and had my breakfast," she said, gently prying herself from his hands.

"Let's get started, shall we? I can't wait to get out of this place."

Tom followed the other two out the big door, moving freely and smoothly since her kiss. The effect, he knew, would wear off in about ten minutes, and he would begin to feel cold and stiff again. But he knew he could depend 'on her to touch him or kiss him as soon as he indicated, by looking at her or moving a little closer, that he needed it.

Dennis opened the car door for Catherine, and she jumped into the front seat; Tom scrambled into the back. Dennis got behind the wheel and started the car and drove them rapidly out of the square of dormitories.

"Hold the map," Dennis said, shoving it at Catherine. Tom was always amazed by his brusqueness towards her. She took the map and unfolded it. "Are we going to take the main road?"

They drove out of town, Dennis accelerating and braking abruptly, throwing Tom forward against the back of the front seat. Tom reached over and grasped Catherine's shoulder, kneading the pointed bone through the coarse material of her dress. After a moment she became restive and offered him her right hand instead. She smiled at him as he took it and pressed it against his cheek. She let him hold it for the next three minutes, but the position was cramped, and she pulled it away again, nodding and smiling to show him that she would think of a better arrangement. All the while, she and Dennis were talking about the place where they were going, a big house in the country owned by Dennis's uncle and aunt.

After a little Catherine extended her left hand into the backseat; that was less awkward, and she could still talk to Dennis. Tom snatched her fingers and pressed them tightly between his palms.

Later they left the highway and began to wind along

narrow roads between low walls. There were trees here, large, old trees, bare except for a few fluttering leaves, and Tom, looking out the window, was reminded of home. Beyond the walls there were small rough pastures; he saw a cornfield, the stalks dry and chattering in the wind. It amazed him that here, in the cold North, there could be pieces of the soft landscape where he had grown up. He squeezed Catherine's hand, telling her with the few words he could find that this place, this country, reminded him of the place where he had grown up—"though we don't have much corn; we have more pasture than anything else. The people next to us raise horses, so they have miles of green grass." Catherine seemed to be listening with one ear, but Tom was used to that; they had an agreement, reached without words, that Dennis would do most of their talking, since he was better at it, and Tom would hold Catherine's hand.

Leaving the road, they drove through a pair of stone pillars and followed a short graveled drive to the house. It was large and sat on a hill, walled around with privet. Two people were waiting on the front porch, which was open to the elements and set with wrought-iron chairs. Dennis leapt out of the car and opened Catherine's door, and the two of them went up the steps to the porch, talking and smiling. Tom came behind.

It was always difficult for him to meet strangers, but he had learned from Catherine simply to smile and hold out his hand. The woman was tall and severe, with gray hair pulled back in a knot; her face was lined in a way that startled Tom, who was used to women's faces' being carefully overlaid with pink makeup. Her mouth was too wide, too, and when she smiled, he saw a row of large yellow teeth. The man was neat and small, less alarming, though Tom was astonished by the number of dark hairs he saw in the open neck of his shirt. Still, his hand was cool, and less rough than the woman's. Tom wondered if, since they knew nothing about him, they would let him rest in silence. He was glad that Dennis was talking.

Dennis was, in fact, providing information about Tom's background, with bold exaggerations that made everyone smile. He claimed that Tom had been brought up by a Negro mammy. "She was just a plain woman, a white woman," Tom said sheepishly. He never could understand this insistence on his past, which both Dennis and Catherine seemed to find more interesting than anything else about him.

"His father runs the state," Dennis finished, with a flourish. "Why, yes, he does, too; it was a mess before he got it, full of racism and prostitution. But he straightened all that out." He winked at Tom, who was transfixed.

"Oh, the South," the strange woman said, with a sigh. "I know all about that. We used to have a hunting place in Georgia; I know all about the South." With another sigh and a shrug, she turned to lead them inside.

"That's not the same thing, Elizabeth," her husband murmured, behind her. "Dennis said this young man comes from—"

"Well, it's all the same," his wife interrupted, and she stood aside to let her guests pass through the door. The mahogany floor, highly waxed, full of reflections, reminded Tom of the floor in the great hall at home, and he paused before stepping onto it as he would have paused before stepping into a pool of dark water.

"Come on," Catherine said, putting out her hand, and he took hold of her fingers and followed her into the living room.

It was stiff and bright, with hard-looking chairs that Tom did not want to sit on. Finally he sat down next to Catherine, who was talking about life in her dormitory, about the meek girls in their hair curlers and pajamas and the reckless ones who smoked and stayed up all night on pills. The man and the woman were listening intently; during a lull, the woman handed out glasses of sherry.

"Now tell me what you've been doing." The woman turned to Dennis. "Your mother called to tell me she's only had one letter from you."

"Oh, God," Dennis exclaimed, flinging himself back in his chair and covering his eyes with his hand. "She will kill me with guilt one of these days. I wrote her," he claimed, "at two A.M. last Thursday, but the letter was full of unwelcome truths and I was forced to destroy it. You have to be in exactly the right mood," he explained to Catherine, "to write my mother the kind of letter she wants, the kind of letter she can read, sitting up in bed, and stuff into the side compartment of that wicker contraption she calls her breakfast tray. A breakfast tray with a two-minute egg and a slice of protein toast. Oh, God!" he repeated, looking from face to face, as though they must share his conclusion. "A two-minute egg! What a life!"

Catherine took her hand from Tom in order to smooth her hair.

"Your mother has a right to miss you, you know," Dennis's aunt said sharply. "She worked hard raising you, when it would have been much easier to hire governesses or send you off to camp."

"Raised by hand," the uncle said wryly.

"Well, I never asked her to do it. I used to beg her to let me go to camp; I used to write to the places myself and leave the pamphlets lying around where she would see them. I never wanted to take up so much of her life," Dennis said, appealing to his uncle. "You remember when you tried to get her to send me to that place in Vermont, just for a month, good God! And she wouldn't hear of it. She was afraid they 'wouldn't give "her darling" enough love.'" He imitated a sickly, prancing voice. "'Enough love!' I was fourteen and a half years old when she finally let me go."

"Well, you could still write her a letter," the aunt insisted. Rising, she passed a bowl of nuts to Tom. "And I will telephone her after you leave and tell her you're going to do it." She smiled humorlessly at her nephew. "You're enough to make us glad we never had any children."

"Elizabeth," her husband said.

"Never mind." She was still holding the silver bowl of nuts under Tom's chin; when she saw that he was not going to take any, she slowly moved it away. "Catherine, try some of these." Catherine took a handful and surreptitiously pressed a few into Tom's palm. "Past noon," she whispered to him, owl-eyed. "If they get into family business, goodness knows when we'll eat." He chewed the nuts obediently.

Soon a maid in a dark uniform came in and mumbled something about lunch; the aunt flew out, apparently to see to some form of catastrophe. The uncle stood up at once and poured himself a glass of whiskey. Then he advised the young people to kill what was sure to be the long interval before the meal with a walk outside. Dennis could not be persuaded; he took up a magazine and stared sullenly at the table of contents, now and then laughing at some internal joke. The uncle sat down beside the fireplace and began to turn the whiskey glass in his hands. Catherine beckoned to Tom and went ahead into the hall.

She was throwing her blue coat over her shoulders when Tom found her; her reflection in the hall mirror was like the reflection of a nymph in a pool. She looked untidy, mischievous, and he stood considering her with some surprise. "I hate it here!" she whispered. "Let's get out!" Tom wound his scarf tightly around his neck, and they stepped out onto the porch.

"Let's walk down to the road," Catherine said urgently; she began to walk quickly, with Tom at her heels. Then she began to run. She ran in spurts, jerkily, like a leaf picked up and then dropped by the wind; Tom hurried after her, amazed as he always was by the rapid change in her mood. They stopped at the stone wall on the other side of the road, then scrambled over it, catching brambles, and hurried down the slope into a ragged field. The milkweed pods were full, but when Catherine broke one open, the seeds were dry and the little silken parachutes would not fly. Tom noticed how grim she seemed as she abruptly separated the seeds from their shell; he wondered what was going through her mind, and he felt chilled, as he often felt when she passed beyond him. "Catherine?" he asked. "Let's go back. I'm getting cold."

"When are you going to get yourself an overcoat?" she asked harshly, staring at him as though he had intruded on her peace of mind. Then, seeing that he did not know how to reply, she held out her arms to him, sighing, muttering something Tom couldn't hear. "Come here," she said. He went to her and she folded him inside her arms, folded him so tightly that he felt pressed, secure, limp, inside her protection. As he leaned his face on her shoulder, he caught her warmth, which was like quicksilver to him, running through his slow blood, lighting up his veins.

"Now don't be upset," she said. "You know I get into a bad temper sometimes. . . . Those people are all the same!" she added sharply. "Killers! Just killers!"

"Catherine," he pleaded, putting one hand inside her coat. "Let me get closer to you." He strained against her, overcome by memories of warmth and betrayal. "Honey," he moaned, burying his face in her neck, catching a wisp of her short hair in his mouth. "Let me get closer to you, honey." There was always a final barrier between them that he could not penetrate.

"All right," she gasped as he pressed her. "That's enough, Tom, let me go." She caught his hand and pulled it out of her coat, bursting off a button; Tom bent down to pick it up and turned to give it to her. His eyes were full of tears. Seeing that, she let him hold her for another minute and then slowly, firmly, she began to pull back. "Please, Tom, let me go," she said patiently, reaching behind her back to unknit his hands. "Let me go, Tom. I'll let you hold me again later, I promise. Let's just talk awhile first." Finally he dropped his arms and turned away, ashamed, swiping at his tears.

She sat down on a boulder, bringing her knees up and clasping her arms around them.

"It's not appropriate, all the time, to act the way you do," she said, choosing her words with care. "I know the way you feel, I appreciate that, I know you need me—but sometimes it's just not appropriate, Tom."

"I didn't hurt you, did I?"

"No, of course not. Why do you always ask me that?"

"Because I want to hold you so hard . . . I'm afraid I'll hurt you sometime, crack your ribs," he said with a miserable smile.

"You can hold me as much as you want," she said, "now I know that's all you want. It only scared me the first time."

"'All I want'?" he asked.

"I guess it wouldn't be, for most people," she said slowly. "But I grew up with sisters and brothers. I know. They always wanted to get in bed with me at night and hold on tight when they'd had bad dreams. That was one thing I used to do for my mother, so she wouldn't have to get up. I used to hold the ones who woke up with bad dreams. Jim, I remember, from the time he was three until he was nearly six, he was up almost every night. I used to tell him to squeeze me as hard as he could; it was the only thing that did any good. He saw monsters," she added.

"It's not the same," Tom insisted, resisting as he always did the long slide into her family past. "I'm not afraid, I'm not having a bad dream. I'm just cold; I can't seem to get warm."

"Yes, I know," she said.

"They used to put long underwear on me when I was little," he went on, hoping to make her smile. "It was woolen, and it itched. And they used to make me drink beef broth and barley, things like that, to warm me up. One time they thought it was because I was constipated and then they started to give me mineral oil flavored with garlic. It didn't do much good, I guess. I used to drive my mother crazy."

"Maybe you were too thin," Catherine said.

"No, I was a fat baby. It was only later, when I was two or so, I got thin. Mother put me on a diet when Bessie stopped feeding me; she said I was turning into a butterball."

"Why did she do that?"

"Well, apparently Bessie had let me get into all sorts of bad habits. Like eating butter with a spoon, or having cream on my oatmeal. That's not very healthy," he explained, seeing that she did not understand. "Anyway, the diet worked. I stopped eating and got thin. Though I think the main reason was I had never learned how to feed myself. Bessie always did that. Then when my mother took over, Bessie was afraid to tell her I didn't know how to feed myself." Embarrassed, he said, "I don't know how I got started on that."

"How do you know all that?" Catherine asked curiously. "You couldn't remember that far back."

"Bessie told me later, when she used to take care of me in the evenings, after they'd gone out. It's really neither here nor there," he said.

"Maybe not," she said, standing up. "But I like to hear about you, about what's happened to you before."

"You sound like you're making a study of me," he grumbled.

"No . . . but you are different, you know," she said kindly. "You know that, Tom, don't you?" And she leaned forward to look into his eyes.

"Everybody's different," he said, resisting her meaning.

"Yes, but you're more different than most." She smiled. "I'm not complaining. I like the way you are. You make me feel it matters whether or not I get up in the morning. I don't believe I'd make it to English more than once a month if I didn't know you were waiting for me, saving a seat; if I didn't know you wouldn't eat any breakfast unless we went together to get it. It's easy not to care about anybody here, but you won't let me. You're good for me," she said.

He stepped towards her with his questioning look.

"All right, one more time. Then we ought to go back and see if they've got anything for us to eat." With the gentleness Tom knew he could depend on, she spread her arms and took him in. He began to moan as soon as he felt her warmth against his chest. "Please don't make that noise, Tom," she said. "I know you don't have to make that noise. Try to be quiet," she pleaded. He was quiet, for a moment, stilling the racket that seemed almost to choke him; he had learned that lesson already, with great difficulty, when Bessie took him into her bed. "Now none of that carrying on," she had made him promise as she lifted up the sheet.

Suddenly he remembered Louise's letter, and the horrible description of her mother crying in the night. He hated Louise for forcing that on him. He had never wanted to know about that. Starving. He knew too much about that already. He did not want to know any more. Even his own mother had tried to make him know about that: "You never have loved me the way you love Bessie," she had told him once, long ago. He had turned his face away, not listening, really believing that he had not heard, but the words had gotten through anyhow. It did not matter. He wanted to believe that it would never matter. They could starve and cry and howl, and he would not hear; he would wrap himself in warmth, he would grow numb with satisfaction, as he had when he slept next to Bessie in her warm bed.

They had starved Paul that way. He had starved him, too, pushing him away when he came mewing for something. He had never been able to stand his brother's whining.

He pressed Catherine tighter, more fiercely, with a kind of spasm in his arms. She reached back once again and undid his hands. Turning briskly, she started back up the slope to the stone wall. Tom followed, watching her bird legs under the billowing edge of her skirt. How beautiful she was, how perfect, her child's body preserved inside the soft outline of her womanliness. He had never been able to describe that to her: how he could feel the tender bones of her childhood inside the firm sheath of flesh. Often the things he said to her when he lay in her arms on the couch seemed crude, heavy—coarse expressions of need that he knew she must reject. He could not seem to find the right way to say it, the child's way, the way that would have been acceptable to her. Instead she would laugh and shake her head—"Tom, you've got to stop saying those things"—and get up and tuck in her blouse.

She let him have her breasts now and then, and he had learned to lay his face quietly there, covering her nipples with his hands.

How different she was from Bessie, whose breasts were long, crisscrossed with shallow lines and small veins.

At the stone wall she stopped to take his hand, and they crossed together and ran up the drive to the house.

Inside, lunch had finally been laid out in silver dishes on the sideboard. Dennis and his uncle were waiting with plates in their hands while Aunt Elizabeth adjusted the flame under one of the dishes. "Damn," she said when the light went out, and she turned to her husband for another match. When she saw Tom and Catherine, her expression changed, and she forgot about the match. "Here you are!" she cried gleefully, and she handed them their plates with a flourish.

Tom was able to pass swiftly and smoothly through the meal, placing small forkfuls of food in his mouth and chewing carefully. He noticed the stringiness of the red meat, the puffed softness inside the rolls, but he was able to avoid tasting. The taste of food had for a long time seemed misleading to him, dangerous, bait in some kind of fearful trap; whereas textures led nowhere, they were an end. When Bessie had fed him his hot cereal, the graininess of the oatmeal had not been a threat, but the sweetness, the overpowering sweetness, had made him gasp and hold his breath.

All during lunch, Tom listened and bobbed his head as the aunt talked in her quick, shellacked voice, which seemed so angry to him, like his mother's. His mother constantly talked and smiled. "It is marvelous for us to have a chance to meet Dennis's new friends!" Aunt Elizabeth exclaimed at one point, and Tom, glancing shyly at her, saw her bright eyes flash. "But where is your girl, Dennis? Haven't you got a girl for us to meet?"

Dennis made a gurgling sound.

Afterward they sat again in the living room. The bright colors of the upholstery faded as the sun withdrew. "Only four o'clock and already there's less light," the uncle said. They sat in silence, holding coffee cups. After a minute the aunt got up and flicked on a lamp. They looked at each other, briefly, with a kind of amazement, and Tom noticed that the uncle's face was scarred around the mouth. He wondered if he had been burned. Then Dennis was standing up and saying goodbye with his graciousness reassembled, including all three of them in the ritual, so that Tom needed only to add a mumbled word or two and hold out his hand. He followed Catherine and Dennis down the porch steps and bundled himself into the back of the car, hugging his knees, nursing the accumulated warmth.

Catherine had warned him, the day before, that she would have to go back to her dormitory to study. They'd spent all Saturday together, ending with a late picnic supper in his room; it gave him a sense of certainty to share ten or twelve hours with her. He could not say, this time, that she had not warned him, but still, when he climbed out of the car to walk her to her door, he could not smile at her, and she seemed annoyed and told him that he'd have to learn to be less possessive.

*　　*　　*

Asheville, N.C.
November 14, 1958

My Dear Tom:

I suppose I must resign myself to never hearing from you in answer to my tiresome letters. I know your life must be very full up there with studying and social activities and so I am not going to allow myself to be hurt by your silence. I still believe that you are interested in hearing from me and I even believe that although what I'm telling you may seem strange or faraway now it will come in handy someday. Someday you will need to know all this and perhaps then you will refer to these letters and be glad for the light they shed.

Now I am going to plunge right in and tell you what I know about your Daddy's mother, your grandma. Of course, all the details are not clear to me since I never saw much of her. Apparently there were hard feelings between the two brothers—your grandfather and Papa—which prevented much visiting. In fact I never saw those two men together in my life. There had been some problem or dispute when they were growing up which was never resolved. It seems strange since from the old pictures I know they looked a good deal alike and were no more than two years apart. Papa was the oldest of the three brothers, and it may be that something to do with the inheritance (what little there was of it), caused the bitterness. More likely it was something to do with the school. They were both straight and tall and hard-driving, teachers, with a powerful moral bent. Neither of them was very long on humor.

Well, that's the best I can do to explain why there was never much visiting. I remember the one time Aunt Rose— your grandma—came here to visit, at Christmas, she was so full of fun, such a girl with her jokes and her pretty dresses, that we were all nearly amazed. She was from Boston, you know, the only northerner in the family, and she always was spoken of as a belle. I suppose that didn't sit too well with Papa, either; she was a young debutante from some rich family up there, and she never had to do much but enjoy herself before she married or afterwards. I mean they always had plenty of servants. So she was like a butterfly you might say to us plain folks. I remember she even had her initials on her underdrawers.

Your Daddy was wild about his mother. Just plain wild about her. There was no other way to describe it. I remember he would talk about her by the hour. How they would go on drives together and he would hold her hand. How she was always there to tell him stories and sit with him when he couldn't sleep. I tell you it was like a fairytale. When he came here to spend a year for the sake of his health, he used to write her a letter every other day. I used to plague him to let me read them but he never would.

The worst part of what happened was that he was with her. They had gone to France—it was the summer after he left here—and they were staying down in the south, at the beach. She was determined to take Tom on a drive to show him some of the views, and although they had a chauffeur, of course she insisted on doing the driving herself. Apparently the roads are very narrow there, with cliffs. They were driving along, laughing and joking, having a marvelous time, with a picnic hamper in the back. And then something happened. Your Daddy has never been willing to tell just what. The car went out of control, or the brakes failed. They went over the edge and the car dropped down the cliff. Your daddy broke both legs, and she was killed.

Now, this is something he has never been able or willing to discuss. Whenever I saw him, I would try to get him to talk about what had happened. I had a feeling that it would do him good. He was never close to his father, and after his mother died he was always alone. He would hold his hand up as soon as I got on the subject. Never say a word, just hold his hand up. I didn't have the heart to go on.

Of course, as you might expect, there was a lot of talk. People couldn't seem to let the story alone. It was simple enough, it seemed to me, but people are never willing to let things alone, they have to go ahead and ask questions. It seems that some people didn't understand how she could have been killed when your Daddy only broke his legs. Then there was some talk that the car had never been found although, of course, it might perfectly well have fallen into the water. There was some talk of an autopsy or something like that but your grandpa wouldn't hear of that. We never talked much about it here; it was one of those things you really don't want to discuss. Your grandpa of course was broken up over it and your Daddy didn't get his spirits back for several years. He was so quiet then.

After a while your grandpa remarried and he had yet another wife before he was through, but you know all about that, I expect. They were both nice women but the way I see it they did not measure up to the first. At least your Daddy never would have anything to do with them. They were both kind-hearted women and they did what they could but he would not have anything to do with them. By then he was old enough to go off to school and he arranged it so he was seldom at home. He took himself off into another world. By the time he was nineteen, he was himself again—at least that was the way it seemed to me. He was lighthearted and debonair, with a cutting edge that hadn't been there before. The handsomest boy and man it's ever been my luck to see. Of course, we didn't see him much between college and the military and his marrying your mother. He would come for visits whenever he could and every time I would think to myself how lucky I was to have him here again, even if only for an hour.

I still think that whenever I see him. I still think he is the best, the very best. Whatever those old stories may mean, they haven't done anything to him. So you can see that gossip and scandal and even real misfortune don't have to blight somebody like your father. Whatever he knew about what happened to his mother didn't matter in the end. He knew it didn't matter.

With love,
Louise

Chapter Six

Tom crushed the letter and threw it away. Then he jerked a page out of his notebook and sat down at the desk to write. His writing was stiff and slow, and he pressed the pen nib deeply into the paper. YOU ARE LYING TO ME. He sat for a long time before he realized that there was nothing more to say. Then he pushed the page into an envelope and sealed it and asked Dennis for a stamp.

Dennis eased one out of his wallet and passed it to Tom. "What's the matter with you now?" he asked, staring at him. "You look like you've seen a ghost."

"I'm just cold," Tom mumbled.

"Well, you can turn the radiator back on. I turned it off last night."

"Don't ever turn the radiator off!" Tom shouted.

"It's on full blast all day. It's not healthy to sleep in that kind of heat."

"Don't ever turn the damn radiator off, I tell you!"

Dennis sighed. "All right, you fool. Why did I have to draw you? Of all the people in this place, why did I have to draw you and your crazy problems?" He was grinning, half in earnest, his hatred as thin and slick as a layer of wax. Tom turned away from him and licked the stamp, smearing it onto the envelope. "I'm going out to mail this," he said, propelling himself towards the door.

Dennis went to the window and watched him hurrying, with his strange oaring hands, across the courtyard. He looked as if he were parting a heavy sea. "Oh, God," Dennis muttered, catching hold of his hair.

Then he went into the bedroom and pulled open the drawers of the dresser, examining Tom's neatly folded shirts and ties. He lifted up a dark-blue pullover and sniffed at it. Tom's smell, as mild and dense and stale as the smell of a closed-up attic, made him groan. He could not understand Tom, and he could not stop trying. He felt as though he had worn himself out in the pursuit of some doomed cause— given all his money to the legless beggar who sat outside the subway. Enraged by his own fascination, he went back to the window to watch for Tom.

In the fresh air, Tom paused and beat his hands on his chest, breathing deeply. It was a cold day. The envelope was clenched in his hand; he stared at it. The writing on the front looked clumsy, enormous, slanting downhill like a child's ugly scrawl. He could almost see his single sentence, blackly printed, through the envelope. He realized that he could not mail it without opening the door to further lies, presented in the guise of further explanations. He knew how her next letter would start: "I understood when I wrote you last that I was running a certain risk." He began to tear up his letter, slicing through the envelope. The page inside ripped easily, and he let the fragments rain onto the mud beside the path.

Then he felt a kind of relief.

Upstairs, Dennis had settled himself at the desk in front of an open book. "Listen, about tonight," he said in an abstracted way. "Is Catherine coming over here?"

Tom began to explain promptly. "She's meeting me for dinner at six. We're going to the dining hall; why don't you come with us? It's roast chicken, I checked the menu, and that's one of her favorites. She won't eat the potatoes, and probably not the green beans, either, but she will eat a good helping of the chicken, and salad with that thick dressing."

"Oh, God," Dennis moaned, rolling his eyes up.

"Then we're coming back here to study."

"Yeah, that's what I thought." Dennis sighed. "All right, it's your room, too, there's nothing I can do to keep you out. But try to be through with whatever it is you do by ten, will you? I've got to get some sleep. If I could get one early night this week, I wouldn't care if she stayed all night Saturday."

"She's always out by eleven," Tom said. "That's the rule. Saturdays it's twelve, but she's never stayed that late."

"I mean, you could keep her here all night Saturday if you wanted to. I wouldn't care. And the proctors never check on the weekends, you know that."

"She wouldn't want to stay all night," Tom said, gathering up his books for his next class.

"All right, if you say so. But why don't you ask her? Anyway, keep it in mind when I barge in at ten tonight, and don't start growling at me. Saturday night she can stay to breakfast."

Tom was already out the door.

He came back in the late afternoon. He had trouble opening the door; his arms were full of books, a grocery bag, and flowers, and he shouted for Dennis, then cursed and rammed his shoulder against the door. Finally he dropped the books on the floor and wrenched the doorknob around, propping the door open with his foot as he bent and dragged in the books. He was angry, glowering, full of a warmth that, if sustained, would become rage—an outburst of rage, like a spurt of blood. He jammed the bunch of daisies into a jar, then slammed the table with the palm of his hand when the jar, top-heavy, fell over. Nursing his hand, he laughed once, biting off the sound, and glared up at the ceiling. Then he loped across the room to turn on the radiator.

He stood for a while, listening to its ticking; it spoke to him querulously, acknowledging his demands. Its tone was familiar: "I know what it means to you to be warm, and I am willing to do what I can." The tartness and fatigue of the voice made it all the most reassuring; Bessie had always been tart when she was agreeing to help him. It meant that he could count on her, because there was no more anger in her than he could hear in the sharpness of her voice. He touched the radiator's iron hip; it was already warm. Cautiously, he patted it, pleased as always by its contentious response.

After that he ran water into a series of soda bottles and divided the daisies among them. They made a long row on the mantelpiece, and he was delighted by the effect. Then he unpacked the grocery bag and arranged a jar of peanuts and a jar of olives on the desk. He loosened the lids slightly, to make it easier for Catherine, but he did not remove them; he wanted her to know that everything he had laid out was fresh. It was important to them both to begin each evening new, so that any possible disappointments or misunderstandings would not carry over from the previous day. He brought out the bottle of sherry, which was sticky; folding a paper tissue, he placed the bottle on top of it. Then there were the two shining glasses that he had bought in a little antique store. The edge of one was chipped; he placed it carefully so he would be the one to take it.

And so he began to wait for Catherine. He prevented himself from looking at his watch, knowing that the space of time ahead might overwhelm him if he knew its real extent.

He sat on the end of the couch, a hand on each knee, and stared fixedly at the window. The pale November sunlight began to seep out of the room, and he heard the courtyard clock strike the quarter hours with mechanical sweetness. He did not stir from his place. When the hour sounded, he started to feel the first terrible intimation of cold, a slight prickling in his toes and then a numbness.

It seemed that she was going to be late. He bent his toes inside his sneakers, unbent them and bent them again, never moving his eyes from the darkening window. It worked a little, as it always worked; it never worked entirely. Sitting on the wall by the gate at home, waiting for Bessie to come back from her day off, he had bent and unbent his toes fifty or sixty times, and although it had helped, had prevented him from freezing, he had still been beyond getting up to run to her by the time the bus let her out at the corner. She had always complained that he was not glad to see her, since he stayed on the wall.

At last he heard Catherine's feet on the stairs; released, he lunged up from the couch and threw himself down in the desk chair and stared at the notes for his history paper.

Catherine came in quietly and draped her coat over a chair. Then she walked over to the desk and leaned her cheek on the top of his head. He sat motionless while she slid her hand into the neck of his sweater; then he turned and snatched her onto his lap. Her face startled him each time he saw it again. As he examined her, he was overwhelmed by amazement, as he had been that first evening. "It's not just something to say," he explained, running his finger along her cheek. "I just can't believe it, I never can believe it, Cathy." He took her firmly by the shoulders and laid his head on her breasts.

She took herself away from him after a little, and searching for her, he stood up. She was already a foot away, with her back to him. "Tom," she said, "we've got to talk."

He walked around her and looked at her face anxiously. "What have we got to talk for?"

"We have to understand what's happening to us," she said calmly, hooking a wisp of hair behind her ear. "We're spending so much time together; I hardly do anything else. You remember, I told you in the beginning I didn't want it to be this way. I told you I wanted to have time to do my own things."

"Yes," he said, reaching for her hand. She let him take it, neutrally, as if it no longer belonged to her.

"It's not as though we're in love, actually, is it?" she asked with embarrassment.

Tom pressed his mouth against the back of her hand.

"I mean, this isn't love, is it?" she asked him.

"Cathy," he groaned, pressing her hand to his mouth.

She held herself away from him. "I don't want to hurt you. I like you, Tom, you know that, but it's not the same thing, is it?" She seemed to be pleading with him. "You like me to be with you, and you like me to hold you, but that's not really it, is it? Other people want to go to bed with me," she said. Then, horrified by his stricken face, she came closer and kissed his cheek. "Never mind, it doesn't matter. I can't stand to see you look like that. Never mind, poor lamb. I don't know why I started." Quickly she went to the door, locked it, and turned towards him.

He took hold of her shoulders again and ran his mouth lightly over her face. He could feel her more acutely with the skin of his lips than he ever could with the skin of his fingertips. Her taste told him that she had not changed. He had to find areas of his own skin that were not numb in order to feel Cathy, and after weeks of cautious experimentation he had found, with her help, that the skin on his lips, his cheeks, and the insides of his forearms was still living, sensitive. Intently searching for her, he pulled her sweater open button by button and then patiently, clumsily, unfastened the white blouse underneath. Her bra was loose, and he shoved it up under her chin. When he saw her smooth, pale, lightly freckled breasts, the tipped nipples crinkling, he began to moan.

She let him nuzzle and then nurse, standing with her back to the desk and supporting herself with her hands, planted palm-down behind her, among the papers. After a few minutes he was finished, and she slowly pulled down her bra and fastened the buttons on her blouse.

"Better?" she asked.

He nodded and dropped down onto the couch. His face was vacant, serene; she watched him for a while.

Then she said briskly, "Don't you think we'd better go eat?"

He stood up at once, but when he came close to her, he stopped and began anxiously examining her face.

"It's all right," she told him quietly. "Don't worry. Everything's all right."

Letting out his breath between his teeth, he seized her hand, and they started towards the stairs.

At dinner she was lively, attracting the glances of the other students. Tom was dazed by her attention and a little embarrassed. She cut up his chicken for him, leaning across the table and sawing diligently. She was flushed and pretty, and Tom, looking around the room, guessed that they were all jealous of him. He marched back to the counter, carrying the tin tray piled high with their dishes.

On their way back across the courtyard, Catherine saw someone she knew. Tom watched her face and the face of the boy she was speaking to as though they were both subject to his will. He did not even ask her the boy's name.

In his room they divided the desk between them, making two stacks of books and pulling up, at the same moment, the two metal chairs. Catherine, reading, leaned on her elbows and frowned, and Tom adopted the same position, his chin on his clenched hands. The words streamed across the pages, the pages turned, and the clock in the courtyard chimed.

After a long time they got up without a word and began to eat some of the olives and peanuts. Catherine did not want the sherry; instead she asked, with odd imperiousness, for a glass of water. Tom took the antique glass to the bathroom, ran the water to let it get cold, and filled the glass to the brim. A few drops spilled on Catherine's blouse as he handed the glass to her, and he brushed the darkening spots with his hand. She turned away from him abruptly. "I've got another fifty pages to read," she said. Tom stood eyeing her uncertainly.

She was back in her chair by then, bent over her book. He sat down beside her. The words on the page no longer moved. Magnified, a syllable would fill his eyes, then crawl along to the right with infinite slowness. "You're not turning the pages," she snapped after a while, and when he looked at her, she would not meet his eyes.

As soon as the ten-o'clock bell rang, Dennis burst into the room. He had not been to the library. Instead, he explained, he had been taken to dinner by the parents of an old friend from Mount Kisco; they had gone into Boston and sat in the restaurant for hours. His face was bright and glassy; he seemed amused, or angry. "Hello, jailbirds," he said as he came in. "I know you were looking forward to seeing me." He went over and stretched himself out on the couch.

Tom and Catherine pretended to ignore him. By now they had built a low wall of obstinate inattention against his intrusions; the wall was one of their jokes. Dennis had begun to pick at it, to insist in his irritable, roguish way on being let inside. Now he stood up and passed rapidly behind them, pulling Catherine's hair and tweaking Tom's ear. "Wake up!" he teased.

They shouted back at him, but now he was laughing, leaning against the fireplace and gazing down at them, rubicund, like an insidious uncle. "That's enough, stop it," Tom said at last.

By then Catherine was heaving with laughter, too.

Tom was used to that. He stood up, turned his back on them, and rammed his hands into his pockets.

"Put the books away," Dennis said, waving at them feebly with his large pink hand. Tom turned around. Catherine began to gather up her things.

"I guess I'd better start back," she said, glancing curiously at Dennis.

"No," Dennis said. "We're all going to stay here together. Tom's going to treat us, we're all going to have some beer."

Tom stared at him. "I thought you wanted to get to bed early."

"I'll never sleep now," Dennis said, "not after lobster thermidor and brandy."

"You told me you wanted to get to bed early."

"Well, I don't. She can stay here till three in the morning for all I care." He tore off his jacket and threw it onto the floor. "Go out and get us some beer so we can celebrate."

"What are we celebrating?" Catherine asked, smiling.

"Our friendship. This wonderful thing that has happened to the three of us. This feeling that surmounts all. That blots out the essential truth. That prevents us from realizing that you are a fool"—he tapped Catherine's arm—"and you are a damn fool"—he touched Tom's—"and that maybe I am even a fool as well." He grinned. "Go get the beer, fool! And something in a bag."

Tom looked at Catherine.

"I guess it would be nice to have something," she said demurely. "I mean, I was thirsty before."

"But you only wanted water," Tom said.

"Yes. Well, I could use something more, I guess."

Dennis was scraping his wallet out of his hip pocket. "Here's some money."

Still uncertain, Tom could not find words to fend off their plan. He started towards the door, then came back when Catherine called, bending his head so that she could loop his scarf around his neck. "Take care, now, keep warm," she said.

He went down the stairs, into the courtyard, and out into the street. Across the way, dark trees tossed the window lights between their branches.

Tom walked to the package store. Without speaking, he got six cans of beer out of the case and put them on the counter. "Oh, and a bag of something," he added, almost in a whisper. He really had no idea what Dennis wanted. The owner waved him towards a metal rack, and Tom stood in front of it for a long while, moving his eyes slowly from word to word on the plastic bags. "What's the matter, don't you see what you want?" the owner called, and in a panic Tom snatched down a bag of potato chips and took them to the register.

Back in the courtyard, still frightened, he began to hurry, but at the foot of the stairs he stopped, cocking his head with a sly expression.

"If you look for the Easter bunny, you won't see him. If you watch for Santa Claus, he won't be there . . ." Bessie's jingle. He climbed slowly up the stairs.

With his shoulder, he edged the door open.

Dennis was standing in front of the fireplace, his back to the door. He had his arm over Catherine's shoulder, and his head was obscuring her face. As Tom watched, Dennis turned slightly. Catherine's lips were stuck to his. Over the space between their two bodies, Tom saw her body bending.

He put his hands up to his eyes.

*   *   *

Asheville, N.C.
December 7, 1958

My Dear Tom:

Not having heard from you I do not know whether or not to assume that my letters are a nuisance. However, since I am always persistent—ask your Daddy about that!—I have decided to continue to write you my little diary of family events. Perhaps you may wish to save these letters for another time, if at the moment you do not find them interesting. Sometimes in later life questions arise that can only be answered in terms of the past. This is difficult for young people to understand, I know. "The dead hand of the past" etc. Still it is the truth as far as I have been able to see it. I remember when your precious brother had his accident, the only thing your Daddy wanted to talk about was his Mother. It seemed to console him that there was no connection between the two things, nothing similar or catching at all. Do you know what I mean? Sometimes we are all afraid there is some connection. In the old days, they used to burn the bedclothes and even the toys when a child had been sick or died so that the disease would have no chance to spread. Now, of course, with penicillin and all there is no need for such drastic precautions. Yet there is a feeling that certain forms of illness or bad luck can be passed on. I am not, frankly, able or willing to judge this. I simply do not have the information. All I know is that your Daddy felt for a little while that there might have been some connection between Paul's tragedy and his Mother's; I mean, he had to fight against that thought. I told him, of course, that there could be no connection but he had to come to that conclusion himself.

I haven't spoken to him about it since and I do not think it would be wise to raise the subject. I believe he is all over that idea now. It was the first panic when Paul died. Your mother was most alarmed by the conclusions your Daddy seemed to be drawing. I remember her saying with some feeling that there had never been anything like that in her family, and since Paul was at least part hers, there was no reason to suppose that the other side of his genes had outweighed the good sense he had inherited from her people. She was always convinced that it was an accident, plain and simple.

Now I was there at the time, as you know. It was our spring visit to your parents which always falls between the first and the third weekend in April. May is their busiest time, what with the races and houseguests so we are always careful to get our visit over before then. Anyway, I have the habit when I am visiting your parents of not being in their way. There is nothing worse than having to entertain a houseguest. So I always take a walk, every afternoon between three and five. You know there is still that path through the woods that somebody cut—I can't remember who—in the old days, when the place was kept up. I have seen trout lilies there, it is so damp.

Paul was in the big sycamore where your treehouse is. I saw him when I came down the path. He was sitting on the platform which as you know must be a good thirty feet up in the air. Anyway I was going to call to him but I could tell from the way he was sitting that he didn't want to be interrupted. He had been a little bit under a cloud since he had to leave boarding school. We all knew it would pass. It was simply a question of time and adjusting himself to being at home.

So I went on down the path to the turn where the ferns are. You know the place I mean. I've always thought it is the prettiest part of the woods. I was just turning the corner and then I heard something, I don't know exactly what. I turned around. He was in midair by then.

Your mother told you how it happened, but she was not there. I was there, Tom. I did not see him go, of course, but I saw his face before he hit. He jumped, Tom.

I am not telling you this to cause trouble or wreak havoc. I know the story you have heard is quite different. However, it never seemed likely to me that you would believe that Paul fell out of that treehouse. He never fell when you were small, so why would he fall now? Also I have always believed that to know is the best defense. Even when the knowledge is most unpleasant and even painful. Anyway, I am depending on you not to brood over this. What is over is over. And in the last analysis, the only thing that matters is that he is gone. Don't you agree?

With love,
Louise

Chapter Seven

Tom put the couch cover in his trunk and then waited for the curtains. Dennis had climbed up on a chair to get them down. They were dusty, and the motes streamed in the winter sunlight. Dennis handed him a curtain and then watched him fold it into a small wad and jam it into the bottom corner of the trunk. The material felt crusty, and Tom wiped his palms on the knees of his pants.

"That wasn't it," Dennis was saying. It was the end of a longer sentence, a sentence that Tom had heard or half-heard a good many times. "Wait another week or so. Think it over."

Tom held out his hand, and Dennis gave him the first curtain from the other window. Again Tom folded it tightly and dropped it into the trunk. For some reason this curtain had a slightly smoother texture and he wondered if that was because less sun came through that window. He had never realized before how different the two windows were: one full of sun, the other full of shade.

"Drunk," Dennis said. Again it was the end of something Tom had missed. "You're not hearing me, are you?"

The room was quiet except for the tick of the radiator. It had been on all week.

"You don't want to hear anything, do you?" Dennis's anger was short. He turned and stared at the bare curtain rod. "She's just a girl, after all. You should realize that by now. You would know that yourself if you gave yourself time to think and didn't panic. They all take whatever they can get. There's nothing wrong with that; it's just the way they are. And you only wanted to give her one thing—"

Tom made a violent gesture, throwing his hands out.

"Never mind, don't do that, you know I'm not going to say anything. I only brought it up to try to show you what I mean. If somebody gives a girl something, let's say a little excitement, and then goes off and leaves her, as they say, unsatisfied—"

Tom's hand caught him across the mouth, flatly, with a dry smack.

Dennis grabbed his shoulders and twisted him around, pushing him down onto the couch. "You bastard," he whispered, licking his lips. "I told you the last time, you can't do that to me. You bastard. You can't hit me in the face."

Tom, on his stomach, opened his mouth and tasted the texture of the foam-rubber padding beneath him. Then he began to move sideways, twisting his shoulders out from under Dennis's hands. Dennis let go of him and stood up, brushing his palms together.

"I'll take you to the airport," he said.

Tom started for the door. Dennis called after him, and he stopped suddenly, not turning around. Dennis handed him his jacket and raincoat and his small canvas bag. "You don't have to run," Dennis said. "I won't take you to the airport if you don't want me to. You don't have to leave for another hour, anyway." But Tom was already opening the door, the jacket and raincoat sliding down his arm. "All right, then," Dennis said. "Goodbye."

Tom's back was turned; he was aiming towards the top of the stairs. "Goodbye," Dennis said again, following him. Tom began to shuffle down the stairs, watching his feet and sliding his free hand down the iron rail. Dennis followed, a step behind. At the bottom Tom pushed rapidly ahead and laid his hand on the outside door. Dennis caught hold of his shoulder. "Goodbye, Tom."

Tom stood rigidly, facing the door. Dennis let go of his shoulder. "You bastard," Dennis whispered. "Goodbye, you bastard. Get the hell out of here. I'll see you on Monday," he shouted, as Tom closed the door.

Tom went out into the courtyard, still watching his feet, and moved hurriedly along the sidewalk. He had planned his route the night before, lying in his bed while Dennis tossed. Now, without hesitation, he went out into the street and plunged into the traffic. At the island he paused and passed his free hand over his face, as though wiping away a film. Then he stepped briskly off into the street. He was aware of the gliding shadows of cars, aware of a distant grinding that he thought might be the subway under his feet but that was in fact the sound of brakes. He reached the sidewalk again and turned jerkily to the right, his free arm swinging fast and stiff. He began to march up the street, eyes ahead, chin up, his possessions dragging from his left arm.

He marched along under the walls of the girls' library, where crabapples arched bare branches and where he had sat once, waiting for Catherine, on a wooden bench under an ancient tree. Then he went into the common where he had walked with Catherine, and he remembered how he had wanted to stand between her and the row of bushes.

He passed a streetlight and a bench, and his mouth opened, as if he might be about to sing. The air rushing through his open mouth dried his lips and tongue, and after a while he clamped his jaws shut. He marched out of the common and crossed another street, lifting his feet carefully over the curbstone; then he walked down the last sidewalk, which was humped by tree roots. Down the last sidewalk to the gate of the dormitory quadrangle. He turned right abruptly and stopped and stood in the shadow of the first building. There were people all around and he was dismayed at the thought of being seen.

Cautiously, he ran his eyes over the facade of the brick dormitory facing him. He had decided the night before to go no closer than this. After studying the whole facade, he began to look for her window; it was the third from the left, on the second floor. He had never been inside her room, but he knew her blue and yellow curtains. He stood in the shadow and stared at them. The window was open a couple of inches; she liked the cold. He ran his tongue around his lips. His lips were chapped; he pulled in his tongue and shut his mouth tight. Then he turned and marched out of the quadrangle.

She was Frenching him I saw that. She had her mouth wide open I saw that. Five minutes alone and she was Frenching him. They think I don't know they think I don't know they think they fool me. I know what they do I've seen them she is always arching her back she is always opening her mouth.

After all you cannot blame her no you cannot blame her. You didn't do what she wanted you didn't even know what she wanted you didn't even know how to find out. You knew what you wanted and that was old old old. It was not what she wanted but what did you care about that. You never knew her you never bothered to know her you never bothered to find out what it was she wanted. He knew.

Marching back to the square, he tried to believe that he had punished himself enough and that now he would be able to be finished with her. She would not continue to exist for him. He began to think that it might be possible for him not to feel the pain, or at least for him to learn to control it, as he had learned long ago to control his blinking and his breathing whenever he was threatened by sharp feeling. He had learned how to make every movement, even the most automatic, conscious, how to think, breath, and then breathe deeply, gingerly. He had learned to blink on command and then to close his eyes blissfully, briefly. He allowed himself to function automatically only during the night, when he was asleep. During the day, in the face of pain, he concentrated on his breathing and his blinking, alternating them smoothly, efficiently.

He walked to a taxi and jammed himself inside, closing the edge of his raincoat in the door. They started off, and the raincoat belt began to bang against the outside of the door. He was angry when he had to open the door and pull it in.

At the airport he stood for a long time in the middle of an open space, breathing carefully, before he decided where to sit down. Then he placed himself in an empty chair and piled his possessions on his knees. He waited to hear them announce his flight, screening out the other sounds around him.

North Carolina

Kentucky

1958

Chapter Eight

Bella was already in the kitchen when Louise came downstairs. Louise called good morning and then turned, keeping the box of letters hidden under the flap of her bathrobe, and went through the closed-up parlor to the front door. Louise never used the front door, and it was thoroughly stuck. While she was tugging at it, Bella called to ask if she could help. "Fix me a cup of coffee!" Louise shouted back, to give her something to do. It annoyed her to have Bella underfoot, wanting to help when there was nothing in the world for her to do.

Finally the heavy door opened, doubling up the rug in the hall. Louise stepped out onto the front porch and nearly put her foot through a rotten board. She hurried down the steps and then quietly made her way around the back, to where they burned the trash next to a clump of sumac. There were some ashes smoldering in the bottom of the wire basket—so Bella, burning the trash before breakfast, had been of some use after all—and Louise opened the shoe box and began to take out the letters. She opened each one and smelled the dryness of the paper before letting it glide down into the basket. The letters, pale blue and pale gray, sailed and circled like moths, then fell into the rising flames with a crackling sound. The small fire grew hot. Louise stepped back. She saw her mother's faint, spidery writing on one of the pages and stopped to read. "Adored, adoring, always . . .": now who could that have been? She opened the next letter and sailed it into the fire.

During the night she had decided to burn the letters. They had done all they could for her already, and there was no sense in her keeping them around for other people to read someday. She knew perfectly well that she read them and told about them differently than other people would; every sentence, it seemed to her, was ripe with ambiguities. In the old days people hadn't called a spade a spade. Writing to Young Tom, she had made things pretty clear. If Big Tom had been assigned that task, he would have quoted the letters directly to prove what he said was correct. And he would have found the right words and phrases, too. Louise did not want the letters to fall into his hands, to fall into the hands of anyone who might use their ammunition for some other target. She had aimed only at the truth. Lacking love, the truth was the best she could give. The truth was her gift to Young Tom.

She sighed. Big Tom's last letter sailed into the flames. She looked at the empty shoe box. That was the past, she thought.

And so. It was the past. Of what use was the past to her? She had her hands full trying to do something about the present.

On her way inside, she dropped the shoe box into a waste basket.

"I fixed you scrambled eggs," Bella said, with pride. Louise sat down in front of the plastic mat with the cardinals. "All right," she said.

With a lot of rattling, Bella scooped the eggs onto one of the best blue-and-gold plates (there were only three left from Mama's wedding service) and slapped it down in front of Louise. Then, not willing to let well enough alone, she added two pieces of singed toast—cooked over the gas flame, as Bella had no faith in the toaster—and one thick finger of bacon. "This is more than I normally eat in the morning," Louise complained.

Bella set the guava jelly in front of her. "You want any butter?"

"No, thank you."

"We're out, anyway. I made you a list. Will you go to the big store, or should I go down to Herman's?"

Louise knew that trap. "I'll go to the big store later. I've got to go to town this morning anyhow."

Bella's silence was louder than a question. To block it, Louise said, "You can stay away from Herman's one day, I should hope. I heard you come in last night, or rather this morning. It was three o'clock. What is it you do down there?"

"Why, I help him with the place. Sweep. Dust. You know how men are."

"I should think you'd get your fill of sweeping and dusting here."

Bella laughed. She was wiping the kitchen counter with a sawed-off piece of sponge. As she leaned over, her blond hair fell into her face. She was rake-thin; the apron straps slid down her shoulders, and the long sleeves of her print dress were as loose as sails around her arms. There was always something sliding in Bella's appearance. "And I have to see to little Johnny," she added.

"I thought you had him boarded with your sister."

"Why, yes'm, he is. Only he misses me something awful. She says he cries all the time for his mama."

"Well, you should have thought of that before you had him," Louise said. "I thought you were beyond all that, anyway."

Bella laughed. "Miss Louise, I'm only thirty-five."

"Well." Louise took a decisive bite of the burned toast, washing it down with a sip of bitter coffee. "I meant, I thought you'd learned some self-control."

Bella dropped the sponge into the sink and turned on the water full blast.

"You've got five children already; I should think that would be enough," Louise went on.

Bella finally turned off the water. "I've got a soft spot," she admitted after a while, shyly. "I can't seem to get along without a baby."

"I wish you could bring him up here, but I know Mr. Tom wouldn't stand for it."

"No'm."

"He wants you to take care of me." Louise sighed. She ate one spoonful of the scrambled eggs. "Though it doesn't make a bit of sense. There's not much you can do for an old bat like me. Next thing I know, he'll be sticking me in an old-age home."

Bella smothered her laugh with her hand. "Why, Miss Louise. At your age! You've got plenty of time before you need to start thinking about that."

Louise stood up and pushed her plate back. "Bella, I'm sorry, I don't know what's happened to my appetite. I've got to get dressed to go to town." As Bella reached sadly for the plate, Louise said suddenly, "You know what I'd really like?"

Bella looked at her.

"I'd like to make them do what *I* want for once. All of

them," Louise said. "I'd like to make them hop and jump the way they've made me. Make them dance. . . . Tomorrow give me a bowl of cold cereal." She went out of the room and up the stairs.

Bella, in the kitchen, shook her head and giggled. Then she began rapidly cleaning up the breakfast dishes. She had put her coat on and was at the back door by the time Louise came down again.

"I'll be back around twelve," Louise called. "You can do the dusting this morning. Bella?"

"Yes'm. I'll do that. You want some canned soup for your lunch?"

"Anything you can fix will be all right." Louise opened the door to the glassed-in porch, then waited. She heard the back door close softly as Bella crept out. "I swear if she goes down there this morning, I swear . . . ," Louise said. She went across the porch, shaking her head, and stopped to feel the dirt in one of the potted ferns.

Dry as dust. It was the first time in years she had forgotten to water them. They were as big as baskets. Stepping back, looking at them, she wondered if she might simply let them dry up and die. She had been watering them already for more than fifteen years—since Papa died. They had been one of his pet projects. She remembered his rolling the ferns onto the porch in a wheelbarrow; that was before he stopped talking and took to his room. Not long before, though. She tried to recall whether he had ever asked her to water them, but she could not be sure one way or the other. As he had stopped doing things, she had taken them over.

She went out and got into her car. Turning the key in the ignition, she smiled. It was a cold day, gray and rainy, but that hardly mattered. She was off. She was on her own.

Halfway down the drive, Bella stepped into the wet shrubbery when she heard the car. Louise drove past without looking at her.

Dr. Harris's office was in the new building in the center of town. Louise remembered when he had practiced out of his house on Franklin Street, but that was years before, when they were both young. She had known Dick Harris for most of her life, and as she parked the car and climbed out, she felt fairly sure that he would not be able to tell her anything about Shelby that she did not already know.

The new nurse who had replaced poor old Miss Begley was not one of Louise's favorites. She had told Dick himself that she did not like her tone. However, Louise spoke to her, as usual, with special courtesy, and asked after her brother, who was an alcoholic. The nurse seemed pleased by the attention; she said her brother was about the same. Louise sat down and looked at a magazine.

She was the only person waiting, and she did not see why she should have to sit there for more than half an hour. She was about to say something to the nurse when Dick Harris hurried in the door.

He still had faint traces of last summer's golfing tan, and as soon as Louise saw him, she dropped her complaints.

"Louise, I'm so terribly sorry to keep you waiting." He reached for her hand. She felt his skin, dry and fine as writing paper, and caught his sweet smile. He had been a towheaded youngster, but now his hair was dark, with gray wings at the sides. He was even taller than Big Tom and carried himself well. Louise noticed the elegant lines of his dark-gray suit as he ushered her into his office. She could not help smiling as she sank into a chair; even the cold plastic upholstery could not faze her. She remembered picking blackberries with him when they were both about ten years old. She remembered swimming. He had had a mother who had lingered on for years.

"Now." He sat down behind his desk and drew a folder out of a pile. "I know just what you're here for." He put on his rimless glasses, then winked at her over them. "When are you going to come see me for some other reason?"

"I don't know, Dick," she said calmly. It took her a moment to marshal her questions; he was studying Shelby's folder, thick with a ten-year accumulation of papers. Big Tom had asked her once why she didn't transfer Shelby to a specialist, one of those brain people, but she had explained that what mattered about Dick Harris was that he was an old friend, a friend of the family. "Shoot," he said to her, after a while.

"Dick, she's been in there over three months now. I've gone out every Sunday. She's the same as she was the first time I saw her. They've got clothes on her now, and they've put her through the shock course, and they've got her on some new kind of medication. I've watched her and I've talked to her and I know nothing's happened. She's the same, Dick. If anything she's more confused. She has trouble listening. She wanders off. I can see it in her face. So what's the use, Dick? What's the use in keeping her out there?"

"What have you been doing with yourself?" he asked.

She sighed. "Dick, you know what my life is. I've been taking care of the house. Reading. Writing some letters. Tom's forced Bella on me, so I can't even cook for myself. I believe I've gained some weight."

"Well, it's very becoming," he said. "Tom told me you're going south for Christmas."

"I believe he has that arranged."

"That will be a nice change."

"Yes. You know he's always been generous to us. He's always sent us money and arranged things for us—or at least he has for quite a while. As soon as he knew how strapped we were, he started making things easier."

"He's a good man."

"Yes. You know I appreciate that. What he doesn't know and what you don't know is that I have trouble getting up in the morning. Trouble getting up in the morning and trouble sleeping at night. My life isn't any use to me, Dick. There isn't any point to it at all."

"Now Louise, listen to me. Has she had a seizure since she's been out there?"

"Not that I know of."

"Well, I know she hasn't. They've stabilized her. You know as well as I do that's all anybody can do for her at this late date. They can do that, though: they can see to it she doesn't have any more seizures."

"It was only one time I forgot the medicine, Dick." She was determined not to plead.

"It happened more than once. Now, I'm not blaming you." He leaned forward, his bland, handsome face alight with concern. "You've been wonderful to her; you've done everything you could. But we have to face facts, Louise."

"I need her, Dick. I can't go on like this."

"You need a life of your own. We all know that. I remember what you used to be like, before your parents passed away. How you used to enjoy the movies and a concert now and then. You haven't done any of that for years."

"I didn't like to leave Shelby alone with Bella. I never knew when she'd take it in her head to go down to Herman's."

"That's just it. You've been tied down long enough; Tom and I are in perfect agreement on that. Shelby has to stay out there for your sake, Louise," he said softly. "For the rest of her life."

With trembling lips, Louise said, "I don't want you to tell me that."

"You have to have a chance, Louise. To have a decent life of your own. This is the only way."

She stood up. "I don't want you to tell me what I need. You don't know any more than Tom does. You don't know what it's like for me to be alone."

"Why don't you get in touch with some of your old friends? Amelia Thompson—"

"So I can go and play bridge at the Pine Grove? So I can go on shopping trips? So I can sit down to Sunday lunch with women who never have had anything and never wanted anything?"

"Now Louise—"

"I've never had anything, either. I'm not putting myself above them. But at least I've kept on wanting. I'm not too proud to say that. And that's the difference between the quick and the dead, if you ask me: wanting."

"I certainly do give you credit for that."

"And I want Shelby. Whether it's what you think is good for me or not. Whether it's what Tom thinks is good for me or not. In the beginning you were all grateful enough to have me take over with her, but now that it's gotten to be an embarrassment for Tom, you want me to let her go. He's supposed to be thinking about me and Shelby. But I know how perfect he is—how perfect he's gotten to be. He can't put up with these little messes anymore."

Dr. Harris stood up abruptly. He closed Shelby's folder. "I think we had better put off discussing this until another time. When you're more in control of yourself, Louise."

In spite of herself, she flinched. She had not expected

him to dismiss her so abruptly. "Now wait a minute, I haven't had my say."

"You've said plenty," he said, coming out from behind his desk.

She began to plead. "You remember Tom as well as I do, Dick. You remember what he was like when he was little. He meant more to me than anybody. He was the only one in the whole family who understood. But now, since he got elected—" He was sweeping her towards the door. "Well, he's changed, that's all. You know that. How long has it been since he's bothered to call you on the telephone? I mean, when it wasn't business."

The handsome face twitched. "I know perfectly well how busy a man in his position . . ."

"We're just some more of the little messes," she said.

Dr. Harris opened the door. "I noticed they're having a sale across the street. Why don't you go over and see what you can find? I know you've always loved a good book."

The door closed behind her. She stood facing the nurse, who was talking on the telephone.

"Excuse me . . ."

The nurse glanced up.

Louise did not know what she had planned to say. She apologized and started for the door. Then she remembered and came back to get her coat.

"Goodbye, Miss Macelvene," the nurse said.

She stood on the sidewalk, gazing across the street at the bookstore. How many years had it been since she last went there with Papa? Before his illness it had been one of their favorite haunts. Not that they had ever bought many books, but they had both enjoyed keeping up with what was happening, even if it only meant looking at the jackets.

She crossed the street and went into the bookstore.

Chapter Nine

S itting in the airport lounge, Tom closed his eyes and allowed the long equivocal childhood memories to flow easily, sweetly, in time with his breathing. He had done without the memories for a long time; now they flowed back vividly. He was coming home from school to the silent house where Bessie was placing his glass of milk and his oatmeal cookie on a tray. He was standing in the front hall and feeling the silence and then running wildly back to the kitchen and throwing his arms around her neck. She was always waiting for him. She smelled sour and warm, like turning milk, and as he grew older she would laugh when he hugged her and quickly pry his arms from around her neck. "You great big monkey," she would scold, "when are you going to grow up?" He did not want to grow up, into silence, into separation, and he knew that coming from her, the words were not a threat. They were a conventional gesture, like a handshake. She would never force him away. He took the tray from her hands, with the glass of milk and the cookie.

Bessie had seemed to exist only to help him, whether he

was awakened by a dream in the middle of the night or shaken by one of his panics during the day. She might expect him, finally, to tie his own shoelaces, might grow fierce when he threw his clothes on the floor, but at night she would always come, sighing, in her long pink nightgown, to sit in the chair beside his bed. She would hold his hand firmly in her tough, warm hand and sing him the song he remembered from his babyhood: "Go tell Aunt Rhody, the old gray goose is dead." She had a soft, croaking voice, and she never sang when other people were around. Leaning back on the pillow, dozing, he let her words trickle through his ears. Her words, the words of the silly old song, were the only cure he knew for the fierce spurts of terror that tore apart his nights, for the guilt that Bessie caused and cured. He knew that he should not call her, should not need her, particularly after Paul was born. He knew that his mother hated that in him—the calling, the endless need. Still, Bessie's song took the sting from his guilt. She would sing until they were both asleep, Tom's hand growing limp and cool inside her hand. In the morning he would wake up and see her sitting in the chair, asleep, her face gray in the morning light. Then she would jump up, scolding, and hurry to her room.

His mother had never known that Bessie still got up with him at night. She thought that had all stopped years before.

Tom's flight was called, and he stood up and marched in the moving line to the gate. He found it easy to stand in the line, pressed forward by the crowd. He felt the other passengers' warmth and their haste, and he grew brisker and more assured, squaring his shoulders and raising his free hand as though to fend them off. That seemed to give him options; it seemed to mean that the crowd would turn on Sunday and bear him north again, an unwilling—

unconscious, even—member of the migration. He had not really decided, he told himself, whether or not he was going back to college. Perhaps eventually he would find his place there, too; after all, though he had packed the trunk, it had not yet been sent. Playing with the edges of his panic, he thought to himself that he was free to do either: stay at home or go back up. It was only essential to keep the warmth that sustained him as he was carried along by the crowd. Together they went down a long blue passage and across a windy strip of concrete and squeezed into the airplane.

Sitting alone by the window, he began rapidly to cool. The armrest separated him from a middle-aged man who already had his briefcase open on his knees. The detail was familiar, a brick from the wall that had always divided him from his father. Uneasy, Tom glanced at the stranger, searching for differences, running his eyes along the rim of the man's large, mottled ear. His father's ears were small by comparison, well shaped, neatly aligned with the sides of his head. Tom knew that his father had a tiny pair of scissors for clipping the hair in his ears and his nose.

The stranger, too, was unaware of Tom, and remained unaware as the plane lumbered down the runway and shouldered into the darkening sky. Tom could feel the beat of the air outside the metal skin. He drew the curtain over the window, and a smiling stewardess flicked on his overhead light. Her care was not continuous, it was a fraud, and when she passed again with her smile he was tempted to stick his tongue out at her, hating her painted face and her false smile that was like a doll's.

To fend off the cold, he began to sing to himself, tunelessly, silently, the words tumbling over and over inside his head. The words from the nursery song blended gradually with his own words, and the meanings were fused.

I will go home again and Bessie will wrap me up. She will wrap me up in the old smelly blue blanket which is on the end of my bed. The old smelly blue blanket with the satin binding where I used to stick my finger. She will sit me on her lap which slopes and is too narrow and I will put my head down and hear the heavy thump in her chest. I will put my arm around her back which is round and I will put my face into her neck which is soft and she will say, "You big monkey."

The stewardess slung a tray at him; it landed on his knees, and he stared in angry disbelief at the cold dabs of food. He did not touch any of it, and when she came to take the tray away, he gave her a look that was intended to convey his scorn for her miserable offering.

"Lost your appetite?" she snapped.

Then when I have sat there long enough, Bessie will say, "Come on down to the kitchen," and we will go and she will fix me French toast. The toast will be stiff on the outside but soft on the inside like a mouth. A clean mouth. Then I will sit down at the kitchen table and she will put out the mat with the sailing ship on it and she will sit down and fold her arms and watch me chew. "Now chew good, Tommy, where's the fire, you don't want to ruin your digestion." She will put out the bottle of maple syrup and the bottle of honey and if I want both she will just smile.

The intercom crackled with a human voice, and the man next to Tom closed his briefcase. The plane dipped and tumbled suddenly, and Tom's head seemed to swell; a bottle crashed in the scullery, and he heard the stewardesses squeaking like mice. The man next to him turned slowly and stared at Tom, his big face blooming and filling the space between them. "Goddamned airline," he muttered. "Last time I ride this goddamned . . ." The plane landed, thudding along the runway while the engines shrieked into reverse.

Tom stood up and hunched across his neighbor's knees, taking his place in the packed aisle. Supported behind and in front, he moved slowly along the narrow passage. As he approached the stewardess, he turned his head away, rejecting her word and smile. Then the crowd drifted away, and he found himself walking alone in the middle of the terminal.

Not a large terminal, Bessie, not a big building like the old train station by the river, the one they tore down. You used to hate to go there when we started on the trips, you used to say the place gave you the willies. What did people need with so much room? And the tall dark pillars and the red tiles on the floor—they shocked you in some way, they were too grand, they had nothing to do with what was needed (a clean restroom to change Paul's diapers and a place to sit down). You were happy, though, once we were settled in the train and the porter had heaved the suitcases up onto the racks and adjusted the window shade and looked to see if there was water in the silver bottle. You couldn't wait to close the door on his back. The room with the two berths was just right for you; there was even an upholstered seat over the toilet. You used to sit there and hum and I would sit by the window and tell you about the sights we were passing. You took no interest in that. "I'll get plenty of sights where we're going," you'd say, and I'd know you weren't looking forward to all-day rides in the car with Cousin Louise to Chimney Rock or that old Indian village. That was too close for comfort with Miss Louise, who somehow you never got to like although you always praised her to her face and behind her back. But the train ride going down there was just right. Later, when Mother would come and knock on our door, you would refuse to go to the dining car. "They put the chicken back on the bones," you'd claim, although no one was fooled; they knew you wanted to stay put with Paul. You never ate with us except on Christmas. The colored people served at meals but of course they never ate with us, although they heard what we were saying and sometimes I would see them trying not to laugh. You always had your place set alone in the little room off the kitchen: too good to wait on the table, and not good enough to eat with us. I used to eat there with you until I was old enough to go into the dining room. Then I never ate there with you anymore. Once in the train I didn't want to go to the diner without you and Mother got pale and pressed her mouth with her finger and you whispered to me to go along, bad boy, don't make your mother cry.

His suitcase was sitting by itself in a cleared space, and he noticed for the first time how shabby it looked. He picked it up and carried it to the door. The wind was chilly, and he stood for a while under the bright yellow lights, considering. Nobody had come to meet him because they hadn't known when he was coming, or even if he was coming at all. It seemed strange to him that it was so cold in November; he did not remember its having been that way in the past. Thanksgiving was always a clear blue day when you could go outside in your shirt sleeves. Thanksgiving and the grass still green! Now outside the terminal the wind was as cold as winter, and when a taxi driver asked if he was going to town, he climbed into the cab without answering and then, through dumb persistence, forced the man to drive him ten miles in the opposite direction.

To town, he scoffed to himself. As though anybody lived in town. At least anybody in the last forty years. His father had lived in town when he was a boy; Bessie had told him that, had shown him a clipping, thin at the folds, with a picture of a tall old house with a wrecking crane beside it. "Home of local senator to be torn down," the caption said. Now there was an insurance office on the site, and people didn't even go to town to shop anymore; they went to the shopping centers on the outskirts. The center of town was left to the colored people who still lived on West Street in shotgun houses, neat or not neat, with sunflowers or weeds in the backyards. The stores they used were full of cheap shoes and wigs and garish petticoats. The town was rotting from the inside out, Tom had read somewhere, but he knew his father didn't agree with that. The only life worth living still went on ten miles out, along the river bluffs where the big houses stood, blind as teeth, in groves of sycamore and tulip poplar.

"I'll have to charge you for the way back in," the taxi driver said, but Tom did not answer.

Because you can say what you like about fair and unfair, but most people never have time to think about anything except the best way to get warm, and the best way to get warm is either to be wrapped in the blue blanket or—opposite and less effective—to go in bathing trunks and lie on the hot concrete by the country-club pool. You have to worry about conversations there, and staring, and there is always the chance of a cloud's coming over the sun. Still it is the only known alternative to the blue blanket. There is even the possibility of sleeping, flat on a towel with your hands under your chest and the sun close and hot along your back and legs. People will respect you if you are sleeping and will pass by quietly; they will respect the thought that you have been out until three o'clock in the morning, parked with some girl by the side of the road and trying to get your hand up her pants. There will be conversations around you that hinge on familiar phrases—"well you know the way she is, you know there hasn't been a single darn day this summer"—and finally you will find yourself fitted into a corner of the crowd. Just Tom, "so bright you know, only he's very quiet." "Step over his back carefully, friend, he's probably sound asleep." "His father told my father the best thing to do . . ." And the nearly dependable sun along the backs of your legs.

*Whereas in some other place, some strange place, some cold place,
you might hear them saying, "Why, he isn't asleep at all, he's
listening, you can tell that. Why, there's something wrong with
him. . . ."*

"Is this the place?" the taxi driver asked, rolling down his
window and leaning out to look at the rust-colored brick
gates. The headlights caught the number on the sign and
the driver read it off incredulously. "Three seven five five
five Penhurst Drive?"

Tom said, "Go on through the gates." The taxi driver
rolled up his window and started up the hill.

*In fact this road has no name; this is no identifiable piece of
suburbia. This is the dream itself. This is the road where on Sunday
the cars drive, slowly, through the gates and up the hill and around
the circle in front of the house. If it is warm weather, the people will
be hanging out of the car windows, and if they see anybody, they will
shout "Just looking" or "Just admiring your lovely home," and then
they will turn quickly and hurry on back down the hill. Because this
is not a number or a street sign but the place that everyone is trying
to get to. The people who live in the wooden shacks by the river that
are raised on stilts so the floods won't get in, the people who have
signs in front saying Nite Crawlers for Sale—they are waiting to get
to this place, although they know they never will. The people who
live in the small houses closer to town and send their children to the
private school are waiting to get here, too; and when their children
come to birthday parties, the mothers stand in the front hall beside
the urns full of magnolias and wait until it is time to take the
children home. "Say goodbye and thank you, Mary Bee." This is the
place where the mayor hopes to come to dinner because here he will
be taught to eat off golden plates as though it came naturally. And
because the food is so good. And because the two who run this dream
have learned to make their visitors feel that the dream is really
theirs, that they can go upstairs and lie down on the brocade*

bedspreads or sit on the enthroned toilets or peek into the medicine cabinets at the rows of Mary Chess perfume bottles and forget about old age and illness and death and the fact that the baby is still waking up every hour all night. Because these two believe in goodness and fairness and generosity, just the way they believe in desegregation and local charities and tennis courts and swimming pools and fit lawns for croquet. It is all one and the same when you are on their hill. That is the magic they make.

The taxi driver whistled softly as he stopped in front of the ten granite pillars that supported the front porch. Tom got out of the taxi and stood gazing at the front door, a large sheet of glass ornamented by twisting metal vines. The driver shouted at his back, and Tom turned, already half gone in the memory of the place, and pressed some bills into his hand. He felt that he was being generous, but the driver continued to argue, getting out at last and coming to stand beside him on the marble porch. Tom was looking through the front door at the two big copper lanterns that hung in the hall, spreading circles of light on the mahogany floor. "My God," the taxi driver said, "I'll ring the bell myself," and he skipped nimbly across the porch and pushed his finger into the deep navel of the doorbell. Then he stood staring through the glass, with Tom waiting behind him.

Bessie came hurrying across the hall as though she had been hiding in the shadows by the stairs. She opened the door and took one look at Tom and then, without saying a word to him, turned to the driver and said, "All right, highway robber. What do you say he owes?"

"I told him he'd have to pay for the way back in."

Bessie ferreted a bill out of her apron pocket and poked it into the driver's hand. "Get away from here now," she said, and he retreated to his cab and drove away.

"Come on in and let me see you." Bessie moved to one

side, holding the door for Tom. He went in, then turned and waited for her to finish looking at him. Her blue eyes, as bright as he remembered, swept quickly, twice, up and down his face. She cleared her throat harshly, and he knew she was close to tears. "Let me get you something to eat," she said, pressing her fingers around Tom's arm. "They didn't know just when you were coming." Tom started towards the hall that led to the kitchen, then hesitated at the sight of an unfamiliar colored man in a white jacket, who was standing on a ladder to light the candles in the drawing-room chandeliers. "They're having company," Bessie explained.

She guided him quickly down the hall to the kitchen. The old table where they had sat so many times was covered with platters. Tom glanced distractedly at a plate full of tiny sandwiches.

"It's for the mayor," Bessie said, setting aside a curl of parsley and choosing one of the sandwiches. "Try this." She gave it to him, and he put it in his mouth.

"Good?"

He could not seem to find a reply. He stared at her, chewing mechanically, noticing the details of her clothes: the dark print dress that stopped just below her round knees; the thick elastic stockings that eased her varicose veins; the big black laced shoes. At last he looked at her face, feeling with his eyes for the familiar wide lines of her nose—her pig's snout, she called it—for the pursed mouth, pale lilac, and the lined, pale skin that was as soft as the insides of her arms. Her blue eyes snapped at him, and he saw her clamp shut her mouth, tightening it against the sobs that threatened her every time he came or went. Her thin eyebrows grew red, and she turned away to fuss with the platters. "Fifty people to dinner," she said, "and they're having squab. I always say it's more bones than meat, and sure to be dry." She looked at him briefly. "What's the matter with you? You look like a drowned rat."

"It was a rough flight at the end." He passed his hand over his face, feeling for whatever it was that she had seen.

"Well. You had no business waiting till the last minute to come. I don't know what possessed you to wait so late. They said you weren't coming at all. If you'd started home yesterday—"

"I had classes yesterday."

She considered him, propping her chin on her hand. "I expect you're starved. Come on and let's see what else I can find for you to eat."

Threading her way between two waiters, Bessie marched to the enormous cast-iron stove and threw open the oven.

The cook, a Chinese with a face like a walnut, shouted something at her from the warming table, but she paid him no mind. Snatching up a dish towel and a serving spoon, she drew out an enormous metal pot and began to fix a plate for Tom. "He's starved, can't you see that?" she asked the cook tartly, elbowing him out of the way. Then she placed the plate on a tray, plucked up a knife and fork, and gestured to Tom to get himself a glass. "Come on," she said, and she led the way to the little room that had served, once, for all their meals. There were prints on the wall of cats in pinafores, now sadly faded, and in one corner, with its tray in the air, stood the toothmarked highchair that Tom had used before Paul was born. "Sit," Bessie ordered. She sat down with a sigh and started talking as soon as he picked up his fork.

"They've been busy as bees all fall. I never saw anything like it. Your mother is just about worn out. First it was the trip to France, and she had to get all new clothes, and then the ambassador from somewhere, one of those little countries, came for the weekend and got sick with something and stayed, sick as a dog, in the canopy room, for ten days. I thought we would go crazy carrying up trays. Well. Then, after that—was it October?—they had all the bishops from the Southern sector, and they stayed for four days. Their wives as well, of course. And of course they all had their little ways. No sooner were they gone than it was time for the Red Cross drive, and you know they always have at least two hundred for that. Your mother asked me to make my chicken soup, and then they had all *his* little doodads." She jerked her head in the direction of the kitchen.

"They must be tired," Tom said. It occurred to him that he was not sorry for them.

"Just worn out. And then your father is back and forth to Frankfort every single day. He has that new driver, Buddy, Cora's nephew that was in the service. They say he can make it in under an hour." She sighed, shaking her head. "Tired! I never saw your mother like this. She says she can't sleep at night, she's so exhausted."

"I heard he was going south to shoot."

"Oh, he did that."

"Things must have quieted down some then, at least."

"Not by much. It turned out that was when your mother had to entertain those women who were sewing the new things for the cathedral. Apparently this was the only place big enough to hold them all. They were here every morning for a week. And that meant tea and coffee and Sanka and sandwiches, and I made cinnamon cookies. They ate like horses," she added reflectively. "The house tour was after that, and it seems to me it was mainly the same people. Only they got to go upstairs."

Tom pried off a tiny squab leg with his fork, picked it up in his fingers, and began to take the meat off with his teeth.

It tasted delicately of decay, like a fallen leaf. He finished the leg and fished for another. "Are they upstairs?"

"Yes. They're dressing." Bessie folded her thick arms on the table. She leaned across to look at him. "Well, how was it?"

"What, college?"

"Why yes." She continued to examine his face, and he turned away and wiped his mouth.

"It was okay, I guess. It was pretty cold."

"I told you you should take that overcoat."

"I couldn't wear that thing."

"Just because it was Paul's? It was practically brand-new. He went in and got it at Rhodes the day after he came back from school. You could have gotten a lot of wear out of it."

"Bessie, don't start that again. I'm not going to wear his things." It was the longest speech he had made in some time, and it left him breathless. His voice sounded shrill, like a mosquito's.

She shrugged. "You always have been stubborn. They all used to say you were the good one. But I knew well enough, and I've told them, too, that the devil was in you somewhere. Had to be. You know that as well as I do. It's only common sense. One can't be all bad and the other all good, not in this world. In you it finally came out in stubbornness. Block-headed as a mule!" she said with a brief laugh. "Remember that time you wouldn't eat for three days? You had your poor mother down on her knees."

"That was when you were gone."

"Yes. My last vacation."

"I guess that wasn't right," Tom said peevishly, stirring his wild rice with his fork.

"I never had any use for those vacations anyway. I used to sit at home with Ma and wait to come back."

"Mother wanted you to have the time off."

"Well, she always has tried to be fair. She didn't want me overworked. These days she makes me lie down for an hour after lunch, because of my legs. People ask me why I go on out here year after year."

"Bessie, you know you never would be happy anywhere else."

"Well now, young man, don't be so sure of that. I've given you people nineteen years of my life."

"That's just it," he said, smiling confidently.

"Well, it's the truth that I couldn't just go home and do nothing. There isn't another job in this town I'd want. What about some more of that squab?" She got up and reached for his plate. He let her take it, though he was not aware of being hungry.

While she was gone he sat with his hands on his knees and looked out the window. The floodlight had been turned on in the grove of pines outside, and it was weaving their shadows together. He knew that if he stood up he would see the little reflecting pool, tossed by spray from the frog fountain. That garden had been designed to be admired from inside the house.

Bessie came back with a heaped plate. "I can't eat all that," Tom said.

"Well, you can try. You don't look full to me." She sat down again on the other side of the table.

All the while, there was a ceaseless passing to and fro outside the door to their room. The waiters spoke to each other in hurried whispers, like ushers in a church. The doorbell had begun to ring, and each time it sounded, the largest arrow on the wall indicator would jump, and they would hear a subdued rush and scurry in the hall. "Where's the vermouth?" someone asked piteously, swinging open the kitchen door. The question was lost in a crash of pans. The Chinese cook was cursing.

"I don't pay any mind to them," Bessie said. "They'll all be gone tomorrow. Then I'll have some cleaning to do! *He'll* have the day off, and I'll have a chance to get my kitchen straightened up."

"Have you been cooking a lot?"

"Well, you know how it is. For dinner parties and things like that, of course, they want *him*. I couldn't cut up all those vegetables if I tried. And it's new and different, and people always like that. For just plain everyday lunch and supper I usually fix the main dish at least. I know their favorites. And I always fix their breakfast." She watched him pick through the remnants on his plate. "Did you make any friends up there?" she asked abruptly.

"Sure," he answered, used to her traps. "My roommate, and people."

"Well, did any of them get to be friends?"

"Yes."

"Who?"

"Oh, people I met in classes."

"I remember when you came back in June, that was your main complaint. You couldn't seem to find any people. . . . What did you do on Sundays?" she asked.

"I didn't go to church, if that's what you mean."

She laughed, puffing out her breath derisively. "Tom, you haven't been to church that I know of in two years. I long ago gave up on that. I mean, where did you eat your dinner?"

"I went out to the country once, to somebody's house."

"Once?"

"Stop cross-examining me," he snapped, dropping his fork with a clatter.

"You're too old for that," Bessie scolded. "Don't you try any of those tricks on me, just because you're home again. You're nineteen!" she exclaimed. "High time to grow up, Tom." Then, her voice softening, she said, "It doesn't sound like you had much fun."

"Well, it was better than last year. Besides, I didn't go there expecting fun."

"All work and no play. You always were too serious. Paul couldn't seem to buckle down to anything, but you never did anything *but* study. Better lighten up now, or you'll find when it's too late you've missed just about everything. Every dog must have his day."

"I'll manage," he said bitterly, standing up.

She touched his elbow. "You ought to go up and change. I had your dinner jacket cleaned, and I polished your good shoes just in case."

"You mean they're expecting me to go down there?"

"Why, of course," she said, prodding him towards the back stairs. "That's the first thing your mother's going to say when she sees you. She'll have a fit if you don't go down there. You can't sit upstairs when the mayor is in the house." Briskly she moved him along, treading close to his heels. They went up the dark oak stairs in single file, her hand behind his on the thick railing. "I'll start your bath," Bessie said when they reached the top; she hurried ahead of him down the long hall. He knew that with her infallible instinct for setting things right, she had gone off to tell his mother that he was home.

Bessie was not there when he came to his own door, and for the first time in his life he felt for the light switch on the wrong side.

His room had not been altered since he left for college; the alteration had come before that, when he was sixteen and away at boarding school for most of the year. That summer his mother had decided to have the room redone so it could be used by an occasional guest when the house was full. She had it painted blue; it had been white before, smudged, hung with crayon pictures of fighter planes emitting spurts of fire. She had had blue-patterned curtains made to replace the dusty old venetian blinds, whose clacking had always awakened him when there was a wind. His books had been moved onto shelves in the back hall, and the white nightstand, then as now, had been decorated with a single copy of *The New Yorker*. He had been, if anything, rather pleased by the change. To be treated as a guest instead of as a messy, smelly teenage boy (for Paul's room, that quagmire, had not been touched) had struck him as an improvement. Now, however, he was not so sure. The room seemed as bland as the sitting room in Cambridge. Tom wondered if his bed had proved wide enough for guests.

Crossing the carpet, he began to feel around under the pillow.

Bessie, coming in behind him, said, "Your mother must have already gone down. What are you looking for?"

"My blanket," he said, drawing his hand out quickly.

She stared at him. "My Lord, Tom, that blanket hasn't been there for years." She confronted him, folding her arms over her breasts. "You know that! What's the matter with you?"

His hands, at his sides, made a sullen flourish.

"Now don't begin that old sign talk," Bessie said, going to turn on the bath.

Ah, but there had been a time—he stood in the bathroom doorway, reminding her silently—a time when she had understood what each of his gestures meant. It had started as shorthand, a discreet signal, when he was trying to learn to use the toilet. She had not wanted him to shout out his need in front of other people, and so a certain motion with his forefinger had come to mean "I need to go." Two fingers had meant "And right away," and a sideswipe with his palm, despairingly, "It's too late." From that small root the other signs had sprouted, the configurations that told her when he was unhappy, when he was going to cry. They had often been in company, among grown-ups, and it had been most useful to be able to communicate without attracting attention. By the time he was eight, they had had a whole vocabulary.

He watched her stoop down to feel the water in the tub. "That way you had of talking always drove Paul wild," she said, straightening up. To his surprise, she was smiling at the memory. "You never would teach him what those signs meant. He had to be satisfied with plain words. Lord, it made him furious."

"You never would talk that way anymore after he got interested," Tom said.

"Well, it didn't seem fair. I mean, you had everything already. Good-looking, the image of your father and just as bright. Your mother told me once Paul looked like somebody in her family. And she wasn't pleased. On top of that, for you to have your own way of talking . . ."

Tom did not say anything. He wanted to repeat to Bessie that he had never meant to cut Paul out, but he knew she would not believe him.

Bessie poured a handful of lilac crystals into the water and turned off the tap. "Now take off all those clothes. They probably need to be boiled." With a briskness that he knew covered a vague alarm, she went out of the room and closed the door. "I'll wait here for those clothes," she said sharply, through the door.

Tom stood considering himself in the long mirror. It had always been his bathroom, though he had shared it with Paul. He had used the long green drawers that were built in on either side of the tub for his toys, and there were still labels on them: Soldiers. Guns. He had been extremely war-minded. He tried to remember where Paul had kept his toys, and at last thought of the old wooden chest in the corner bedroom.

The closets in the bathroom were covered by a wall of mirrors. His reflection now was overlaid with tissue-thin images, beginning with his scabbed, knotted knees the summer he was trying to learn to ride his bike, and going on to the narrow-shouldered, high-hipped adolescent body that had caused him such shame. He had first seen the hairs around his testicles in these mirrors.

"Hurry up and get in that tub," Bessie said through the door, and Tom began to undress, unbuckling his belt, unzipping his pants, all the while fixing his eyes on their own image in the mirror so as to avoid a confrontation with the rest of his reflection. Dropping his pants, he pulled his sweater off over his head and so was spared the sight of his long, hard, hairless thighs. Then, once again matching his eyes to the mirror eyes, he snatched off his shirt and with an abrupt gesture shoved down his shorts. Shivering, hunching his shoulders, he turned and jumped into the bath, slipping, falling heavily, and sending a spray of scented water over the side.

"I'm not going to mop that floor," Bessie warned him.

She had mopped the floor for Paul, over and over, and yet she had hardly seemed to mourn for him. When he came home for the funeral, Tom had found her cleaning out Paul's closet, carefully folding each shirt and sweater and piling it on the bed. "Bessie," he had said, trembling, close to tears, but she had spoken to him almost casually: "Your mother wants me to get this finished by lunchtime. She's got somebody coming that can use it all." Later, when she looked at him, he saw that her eyes were quite dead, lusterless, flat as chips of blue paint. But she never cried. She went around the house doing what she could to help the others; Tom felt that she was avoiding him, as though she, too, believed that somehow he had caused the accident. Or perhaps, he now thought, she had only been afraid that he would make her cry.

He glanced at himself in the mirror. Cut off from the rest of his body by the edge of the tub, his head looked like John the Baptist's on the platter. He smiled. Years before, he had begged his mother to take away the mirrors. It was not a spontaneous request. Realizing that there was something unusual in his fear of them, he had spent a long time thinking of a sound way to explain it. At last he decided to tell his mother that he was afraid of breaking the glass when he kicked off his shoes. But when he stood by the side of her bed—she was eating a soft-boiled egg, one hand cupped under her chin—he lost hold of his argument. "I don't want those mirrors in my bathroom. In my and Paul's bathroom," he blurted out. "Send George or somebody to take them away."

"George is on his day off." She had regarded him oddly, used to granting his reasonable requests. It was one of the things Paul had held against him—for Paul had always asked with tears.

"Well, then, let me paint them over," he had insisted.

"Why, what's the matter with them?"

"Boys don't have mirrors," he had said with great decisiveness.

She had agreed with that, smiling slightly; but she had

pointed out that when he went away to school, the bathroom would be used for guests.

He wondered, now, why she had not reminded him that his father's bathroom had more mirrors than any of the rest. He soaped his armpits hastily with the soft pink washrag and then backed out of the tub, leaning down to pull the plug.

"You didn't wash," Bessie complained from the other room.

"I wasn't dirty," he replied. It was part of the formula.

He reached for the clean clothes that Bessie had laid out, at some earlier moment of certainty, on the chintz-covered chair. As he put on the stiff shirt, he stared at the bluebirds on the chintz. The chair had never been re-covered, and he knew the smell of the dust in its seams. Long ago he had hidden an arm from one of Paul's lead soldiers between the seat and the back. He ran his finger deep into the seam, but the arm was not there. He wondered if Paul had finally found it, and hoped that if he had, he had remembered, at the same time, the way he had screamed the afternoon when it was lost. "He can't be a one-armed soldier!" he had screamed when Bessie tried to find a way out of the crisis. And then he had fallen down on the floor to roll and shriek. Tom had watched him, frightened and guilty but afraid to admit that he had hidden the arm. As the scene rolled on and on, Tom had heard in the back of his head the drumbeat: there is something wrong with Paul, there is something wrong with him. His brother's oddness had made his own isolation seem less vivid.

Pulling on his pants, he remembered the bleak bathroom at college, with its cold, staring tiles and the yellow toilet seat standing up like a declaration. He glanced at himself in the mirror as he began to fasten the suspenders to the buttons on his pants, seeing something blurred and distant, an amiable ghost in evening dress. "Was this my grandmother's bathroom?" he called to Bessie.

She came to the door and opened it a little. Her voice was reflective. "Well, I believe it was. Of course, that was long before my time. I remember somebody telling me she had a bathroom all to herself. Miss Rose." She savored the unused name. "Annie Brown told me that, I believe. She was one of the servants from the old days. She's been dead a long time now. She told me once, way back, your grandmother had this bathroom to herself, down at the end of the hall. I don't believe Annie told me why. She certainly had a lot of clothes to keep somewhere. That locked-up room in the attic is still full of them. Maybe she needed more closet space. Are you ready?"

He pulled his jacket on and turned to be inspected. Bessie checked him carefully, then handed him his tie and sat down on the bluebird chair, smoothing her dark skirt. While he tied the bow, she went on, "I believe it must have been because of the clothes. Of course, their bedroom was up at the other end of the hall. Your parents' bedroom, you know. That was their room." She looked at Tom. "Why do you always want to know that old stuff?"

"What was she like?" he asked.

"Your grandmother?" Bessie hesitated. "I don't know much about her, Tom. She died young, I do know that. I never heard anyone say anything much about her. Your grandfather, now, that was different. People always used to say what a fine person he was, so generous and considerate. Handsome, too. Your father used to say you looked like him." She stood up suddenly and went to one of the mirrored closets. "I bet you never knew what was in here." Tom stood behind her as she opened the door and then ran her finger along one of the short green shelves. "There's a way to it," she said, and then, as though she had touched a spring, the shelves began to fold themselves up, accordion-like. Behind them, a darkness appeared, a shallow pit that smelled strongly of dust. Tom stepped back. "What's in there?"

"Nothing, now." Bessie watched the shelves subside. Then she darted her head forward and peered into the opening. "There's nothing there anymore." She started the shelves up again with a pat of her hand. "I used to keep our food coupons there during the war."

The smell of dust hung in the bathroom even when the closet was closed. Tom turned away.

"What's the matter?" Bessie asked.

He stopped in the doorway, feeling the jamb with his hand. The hook was still hanging there, but his mother had wrenched the eye out with a pair of pliers years ago, after he closed himself up in the bathroom for two hours one afternoon. It was the only time he had ever seen her use a tool, and even in the midst of his hysterics, he had admired her dexterity.

"I waited all these years to show you that," Bessie grumbled, "and now you don't even appreciate it."

"Why should I appreciate it?"

"That was where your grandmother kept her jewels."

"Well, they're not there now. Nothing's there, except that awful smell."

"Just dust. You have to use your imagination," Bessie said. "You always used to have enough of that. Don't tell me it all dried up at college. You of all people ought to be able to see it as clear as I do: the diamond crown in the little soft bag and the necklace she had made out of rubies and pearls, that hung down to there"—she gestured to her stomach—"and the big gold ring with the green snakes on it and the diamond from your grandfather."

"I thought you said that was before your time," Tom complained, annoyed by her face, as afire with imagining as it had once been when she told him fairy-tales.

"Well, I don't mean I actually saw those things," Bessie explained, as though he were dull-witted. "When Ma was sick, during the war, and I was sending her ten dollars a week out of my salary just to cover the cost of her medicine, and she needed an electric heater because her room was so cold—why, I used to come here then and make that secret place open and think what I'd do with them if they were still there. The jewels, I mean," she said patiently.

"What happened to them?"

She shrugged, her interest drained. "For all I know, they buried them with her." She gathered up Tom's dirty clothes, shaking out the pockets of the pants.

"How did she die?"

She was turning his socks right-side out. "Now how would I know that?"

"You might have heard."

"All I ever heard was that she caught something when they were in France and went downhill fast and was dead within a week. Your father must have been about thirteen."

"Caught what?"

She turned away. "Don't ask me that, young man. Ask your father, if you're hell-bent on knowing. I'll tell you one thing, though: even if you do find out, it won't mean a thing."

He touched her arm. Her eyebrows began to redden, and then she threw her arm around his neck and kissed his cheek. "Why, Tom!" she exclaimed, brushing at her eyes. "Now look what you've done."

"I want to talk to you," he said.

"Well, we can't talk now. It must be almost eight, and you know they always sit down to dinner by eight-thirty."

"Is Father . . . ?"

"Oh, he was dressed and down in the basement an hour ago. You know how he is when company's coming. He had to check the wine. He came back up, though, to have a spot taken off his jacket. Amos did that, fast. I don't know what he'd spilled."

There was a pause.

"You have no business thinking just because they're busy . . . ," she began harshly. Then she stopped. "You go on downstairs now."

"I wish I'd known they were having people."

"What difference does it make? Now come here and let me brush you off."

She took the silver clothes brush off the bureau and whacked his shoulders with it a few times. "There." He turned to face the bedroom door, and she hurried ahead of him to open it. "Come tell me good night later. Now behave yourself. And smile!" She stretched her mouth, setting him an example, and hastened away down the hall.

Tom stopped at the top of the stairs and listened to the voices below. He kneaded the velvet pad on the banister, feeling for the metal rod that ran through it. Buried in down like a soul in flesh, he had once thought, pleased by the image: unspoken words had come easily to him then, and he had been known to grown-ups as a bright, well-behaved, silent child. Realizing that he was likely to stand and remember for a while, he went down one step, so that if someone came, he could at least claim to have started down. The voices in the hall soared as the front door opened, and he heard, for the first time, his father's laugh.

I have stood here before, a lot of times, he thought. When Bessie was busy with Paul, or later, when she was busy in the kitchen. I have stood here and listened to all that going on downstairs. His father's laugh shattered his concentration; he patted the velvet pad. Well, he likes to laugh, he likes to talk, he thought vaguely. Whenever he tried to remember, his impressions grew vague and contradictory. He could not seem to pin them down. There was only a detail or two, beautiful, charming: his mother's green satin evening slippers, his father's watch chain stretched across his vest. Well, what does it matter? Tom thought. The significance escaped him.

Other people had used the stairway, too, he remembered. He would have liked to believe that they, too, had hesitated before going down, as though there were something terrifying in the descent itself, down the narrow steps, the runner held back on each one by a brass bar, and touching the mahogany railing that ended in a lion's face. Yes, but they had not hesitated, not in his memory. He had seen his mother float down like a hawk on an air current, her long dress swaying, her mouth preparing its smile. He had seen his father march down the steps as though he were branding them with his footprints.

When Tom had last seen Paul, he was sitting astride the banister, pressing the wood between his thighs and listening to the noise of the Christmas party below. Tom had told him sharply to get down. He had been shocked to see his brother sitting there; no one had ever sat on that banister, and it was certainly not Paul's place to begin. Paul refused to budge. His face had always been more constricted than Tom's, with fine lines and dry patches. By then his face looked as if it had lived through a furnace; it was baked and parched. That had maddened Tom—Paul's appearance; there was no reason for it. Simply, he had begun to drink too much and some girl had stood him up. That was no excuse for him to grow silent and parched. Finally, that Christmas night, Tom had passed him and left him and gone on down alone, for he was the elder, after all.

Then, of course, later that evening, Paul had come down. The rest was family history, the edges off. He came down naked, with a long white flower box in his arms—"covering the worst," Bessie said afterward, hopefully. He placed the long white box on the dinner table, in front of his father.

His father had chosen to smile. Paul had sworn that he was not going to give Christmas presents to anyone, so this was a reprieve. His father chose to ignore Paul's nakedness, his harmless penis dangling. "Why, what is this, a present after all?" His diamond stickpin had dazzled like his sapphire eyes as he slipped the ribbon off and opened the box. Then he started up, coughing, grabbing his handkerchief.

"What did he have in that box?" Bessie had demanded later, snatching Tom's arm as he brushed past her in the hall.

"Oh, it was just a joke—poor taste, though," Tom had said. He had not wanted to think about it anymore. His mother, coming behind him, laughed. "Why, Bessie, he had horse doodoo in there," she explained, wiping her eyes on a tiny handkerchief.

"My Lord," Bessie had exclaimed, her hands flying to her mouth.

Less than four months later, Paul was dead.

To avoid all that, Tom began to walk down the stairs. He had gone as far as he ever went, remembering. A sharp line divided him from his brother's death.

The hall was empty except for the coats swinging on the mahogany rack. He could smell the log fire in the library.

Stopping by the marble table, he picked a rosebud out of the arrangement in the vase; it was hard and pink, like a tight mouth, and he felt it carefully with the tip of his finger. Then he stepped into the crowd in the library, still holding the rosebud in his hand.

For a while he was invisible. Then someone said, "Why, Tom," and the room opened up to receive him. Several people pumped his hand or slapped his shoulder; the women pressed their mouths to his cheek. He smiled and spoke, restlessly peering over their heads until he saw his father, standing with his back to the fireplace. Then Tom began to make his way towards him.

"Why, Tom," his father said, and he held out his hand.

Tom, without thought, handed him the rosebud.

"Well, yes," his father said, looking at it. He put it into his lapel and then introduced Tom to a man who was hovering nearby. "You remember my son. Back for Thanksgiving. Isn't that so, Tom?" Before Tom could reply, his father once again offered him his hand, tanned from the sunlamp, each nail as clear and shining as a fragment of the moon. "How have you been?" he asked. His blue eyes seemed to lighten as he stared at Tom.

"Fine," Tom said. He struggled to find the right words; one hand twirled at his side. "It is really interesting there. I've been taking some interesting courses."

"You have?" The bright eyes were fading. "You must tell me about them sometime."

Then his father turned to the other man and began to ask him about a scandal in the police department. The man took a step back; he seemed confused. Tom's father stepped forward. "For schoolchildren to hear about this"—he sighed heavily—"I take that seriously. This country can't afford to disillusion the young." Then he glanced at Tom. "How long are you here for?"

"For the weekend, I guess," Tom said, looking cautiously at his father's ears.

"That's what I assumed." He touched Tom's shoulder. "Classes again on Monday, of course. We're going to drive out to the country tomorrow, have our Thanksgiving feast at a charming old inn—oh, delightful," he assured the other man, as though he had protested, "—in Green County." He tapped Tom's arm. "I see you've taken off some weight. Excellent. In the spring you'll be in fine shape for crew. Go fix yourself a drink." He glanced at Tom once more, his pale, benign eyes focusing for an instant on the boy's face, as though on a distant star. Then he turned back to the other man, encouraging him, with sweeping gestures, to introduce a less painful topic of conversation.

Tom started briskly for the bar. Waylaid by kisses, he lost his momentum, and it took him ten minutes to remember and thread his way to the drink table. Amos, who had once been employed as a yardman, had risen to the position of bartender through good manners and good luck: the incumbent had been killed in a car crash driving home from the country club with a trunkful of half-empty bottles.

Amos began mixing a glass of bourbon and water as soon as he saw Tom. "Welcome home," he said, handing him the glass. "Now don't tell me you want beer."

"Hi, Amos," Tom said.

"Last time I saw you, it was nothing but beer. I figured another couple of months up there would grow you up some." Amos smiled, clasping his hands. "That Bessie is something. She told everybody you'd be home this evening. Nobody believed her."

"I didn't write. I didn't know when—"

"Never mind that. Miss Bessie knew." Turning to fill another glass, Amos studied Tom. "What happened to you up there? You look like a picked chicken."

"Nothing much. I didn't get out much. You can't get around up there if you don't have a car."

"Take your bike up, why don't you?"

"I haven't ridden that thing in years. Remember how long it took you to teach me?"

Amos laughed. "You had the worst time. You didn't want to do it, you cried. But I kept after you. Well, you learned before too long, I guess," he added quickly.

"I remember you running me down the hill on that bike. It seemed like we were going a hundred miles an hour."

"I never taught Paul," Amos said. "He wouldn't let me try."

"He was scared of everything," Tom said with his old scorn.

"I guess he just wanted to teach himself." Amos sighed. "Things haven't been the same around here, with both of you gone. House is as quiet as a tomb."

"Well, you've got plenty of people here now," Tom said brusquely.

"Oh, yes, guests—plenty of them."

Tom watched him bob and smile, fixing another drink. It still hurt to remember how much he had loved Amos, how he had waited in the kitchen in the early morning to see him when he came in for his coffee. Once he had thrown his arms around Amos's neck, and the man had flinched. "I want you to let Amos get his work done," his mother had warned him. "He can't get anything done with you trailing after him." So Tom had limited himself to watching while Amos weeded or pruned, not even offering to help because he knew Amos would not be able to refuse.

Tom moved off uneasily and hung, suspended, a little distance from his father.

Big Tom was talking to three younger men, and now and then he would rise on tiptoe, stretching his feet farther apart, and tighten his hands behind his back. He was shorter than the others, but each time he rose up on tiptoe, he seemed to tower over them, and they would all draw back slightly. Big Tom had always been expert at controlling the distance that separated him from other people. Now, when the correct space had been established, he did not rise up on tiptoe again. Instead, abruptly, he dismissed the group and made his way to a young man who had been standing for some time alone. "I didn't see you come in," Tom heard his father apologize.

"I was late. I had to speak to some people at the church, you know they're upset about that low-income development. I had to reassure them about that, and by the time I got home and changed . . . I don't know many people here," he added, touching the swept-back wings of his dark hair.

Tom recognized him with a pang. He had been in and out of the house for the last several years, at first self-effacing, awkward, a good-looking country boy with no special claims. He had been increasingly smoothed and polished by attention and good talk, so that now, though gaunt and inclined to wait his turn, he seemed taller than he had been, and certain that he was intended to shine. Tom felt sure that his country-boy apparatus might still come in handy when he was talking to people elsewhere in the state, but here, in town, it had been completely dismantled. He was running for the legislature, and Tom had always loathed him, in secret.

"I'll introduce you," Tom's father was saying. Turning, he

saw Tom and seemed surprised. "Why, Tom," he said, recovering, speaking with enthusiasm. "Of course you know Melvin Baird."

Tom accepted the soft hand.

"'Remember'!" Melvin commented with a smile. "Why, we practically grew up together. Remember the old Patrick School, at recess? They're going to pull that down. High time, too; it's a wreck," he added to Big Tom.

Tom hesitated, startled. "You must be thinking about Paul," he said.

"No, no, I mean you. Of course you were both a lot younger than I was. But I used to watch you both, to see what you were up to—to learn anything I could, I guess. Of course I mean you."

Tom could not think of anything to say. His memory began to diffuse. His father was gazing off indifferently.

"Remember the North Swamp at flood time?" Melvin went on blandly. "When you boys used to say you were going fishing for crocodiles? And that Pin Creek girl, what was her name? Dora—Flora—something like that. She went in up to her armpits in mud. Slipped." He laughed briefly. "I wasn't thinking about Paul."

"You weren't there when I was," Tom insisted.

"It's the strangest thing," Melvin said to Big Tom. "I'm sure you've had this experience, too. The things you remember most clearly—and then you find they haven't meant anything to somebody else. I can still almost smell that mud in springtime!"

Big Tom was smiling. "Why, Melvin, I don't know where you got all that. You were still up in Green County then. You were still going to Morgantown High."

Speechless, Melvin stared at him, and his face began to redden.

"You didn't get here till 'fifty-four," Big Tom went on kindly. "That was the summer you came to work for me."

"I don't know how I could have gotten it mixed up." Melvin struck his forehead lightly with his palm. "I guess I've just heard so many stories from your daddy . . . you don't have any idea how much he talks about you," he said to Tom.

Tom looked at him. He could not believe that that was what they talked about—his father and Melvin—when they walked arm in arm around the circle in front of the house.

"I've just been going too hard," Melvin said. "May Jane told me I ought to take a few days off."

"Don't do that," Big Tom put in. "You don't want to drop out of sight at a time like this." Rousing himself, he added, with cheerful malice, "You're just fitting in so well, Melvin, this place is so much home to you, that you can't believe you've ever lived anywhere else."

"That's not it," Melvin said stiffly. "Why, some of my best—"

Big Tom turned away to speak to someone else.

Melvin watched him go. With difficulty, he transferred his attention to Tom. "You and I have had some good talks, though. I remember last summer, when you came back from college . . ." He trailed off.

"Yes," Tom said. It seemed pointless to argue.

Melvin looked again at Big Tom. Slowly, he shook his head. "Your father . . . well, he hasn't been the same. You know that, of course. Ever since Paul died, he's had these vague spells. Nothing that interferes with his work; just these moments of distraction." He paused, pursing his lips. "It'll be a year next April, won't it?"

"April twelfth," Tom said.

"You were away at college." He shook his head. "Your

father hasn't gotten over it. I don't believe he ever will get over losing Paul. I do the best I can to fill the gap, but of course it isn't the same."

"No," Tom said.

Melvin looked at him sharply. "Why don't you talk to him? You always seem so . . . far away. He needs you, you know. Take the time and talk to him while you're here."

"He doesn't want to talk to me."

"Now that's just foolishness. He's always wanted to get closer to you. To you and to Paul. That's something he's always missed. He told me once he just couldn't seem to find a way to talk to you, you were so—" He had succeeded in catching Big Tom's eye. "Sir, can I get you another drink?" he asked.

"I don't believe so, Melvin. My wife just gave me a sign that we should go in to dinner. The squab will dry out." Big Tom started across the room.

"We were just talking about Paul," Melvin said.

Tom saw his father's face stiffen. The lines between his nose and mouth deepened, and as he looked down, his bright-blue eyes seemed to have been extinguished. His mouth drooped. Without a word, he hurried off.

"Oh, God," Melvin groaned.

"It doesn't matter," Tom said, impressed by his pain.

"I don't know why I had to bring that up. I mean, you have the right, if you want to, but I don't. I guess I just feel he ought to talk about it to someone, get it out in the open. But for me to do it!" He struck his shirtfront lightly. "Me, of all people. After all he's done for me. Why, he gave me my start, politically speaking."

"I know."

"What chance would I have had without him?" Melvin asked rhetorically. His eyes sailed over Tom's head, seeking a wider audience. "A boy from Green County. I hadn't even graduated from college when I met your father; I was working in the hardware store. He was coming through to make a speech. He told me to go back and finish college, and he told me how to do it. After that I went for my law degree." He narrowed his focus again to Tom. "I met him nearly ten years ago. I've stuck to him ever since, through thick and thin. You were away."

"Just last year."

"And then the tragedy. He wept on my shoulder, do you know that? I believe I'm the only man alive who's seen Big Tom cry."

Tom did not say anything. He was looking down the path his father had made through the crowd, which led to his mother.

"You act like you don't hear me," Melvin Baird said.

"I hear you. I've heard you before, though," Tom said.

"You used to drive Paul wild."

"Oh, Paul. He was temperamental. I used to almost get the feeling he was jealous of me. Not you. You never acted that way. I never saw two brothers more different—I mean, in personality."

"He was also shorter."

"Is that so? It's funny I never noticed that."

Tom tightened his hand on his glass. "Are you going to get elected, do you think?"

"Well, it's awhile off. If you pay attention to the straws—"

A pale girl in a pink dress passed between them and plucked at Melvin's arm. "Honey, I have to go and call home."

"May Jane, this is Young Tom."

She turned, startled, arranged her face, and held out a firm hand. "Who did you say?"

"Young Tom," her husband prompted.

"Please forgive me." She clasped his hand in both her own; her palms were dry and warm. "I had a baby a week ago, I'm so distracted—"

Amos passed behind them and said sonorously, "Dinner is served."

They separated to go in. Tom lingered behind. As the library emptied, the furniture reappeared, solid shapes rising from a mist. He looked at the fern-patterned armchair where he had once seen his mother sitting, a needle in one hand and a thread in the other and an expression of suspended despair on her face. He looked at the red velvet stool with curved runners, on which as a child he had rocked wildly around the room. He looked at the painted rocker where he had sat to listen to his father read aloud in his beautiful voice.

The glass doors into the dining room were closing; he saw a waiter he didn't recognize peering uncertainly at him. He turned his back and heard the doors click shut with sharp satisfaction. They had forgotten him.

He wandered over to the bookshelves behind his mother's desk. Taking out a poetry anthology, he ruffled through the pages, separated by tissue-paper inserts crowded with her tiny notes. "Unreal rapture," she had written next to the "Ode on a Grecian Urn." The book was twenty-five years old. Tom had often looked at it, finding in his mother's harsh notes proof of the face his father kept in a gold frame on his bureau: the delicate face with the high, smooth forehead and the widely opened, widely spaced blue eyes. "When I first saw your mother, she was sitting on a sheaf of corn," his father had told him once, unexpectedly, when they were driving to church. "She was Persephone."

"How could she sit on a sheaf of corn?"

"I don't know. She was the brightest girl I ever met, in addition to being so pretty."

That was a complication, or a contradiction, that Tom had not yet mastered. He pushed the book back into its slot and turned to his mother's desk, opening the lid and examining the pile of papers inside. He had never really understood what they were—invitations, bills, or demands of some more obscure nature. "I simply must attend to my mail," she would say every evening after dinner, getting up from the table with such haste that occasionally the heavy linen napkin or a fork would be brushed to the floor. Tom and his father, stranded in the cool air of her departure, would, with the same gesture—replete, resigned—fold their napkins square by square, so that the heavy monogram lay on top of the last fold, like a scarab.

He picked up her beautiful black pencils, each one sharpened to a perfect point. Laying them back in their enameled dish, he felt as though he had disarranged a set of occult signs. He had never touched her desk before, even as a child, when he had sometimes stood at her elbow while her hand and its pen hurried across the sheet of pale blue paper. "Where's Bessie?" she had asked once, noticing him.

"She's changing Paul."

"Well, then, you'll have to find some way to amuse yourself. Go outside . . ." She had looked at him vaguely. "You're a big boy now, Tom. You should learn to entertain yourself. You can't always have Bessie thinking up things for you to do."

Now, wandering to the bar, he began to fill a glass with ice cubes. Before he could finish, his mother came through the doors from the dining room. She waited, holding the door with her hand, until he noticed her. "Have you eaten?" she asked.

"I had something on the plane."

She sighed. "I would have told Amos to set you a place, but the table's already too crowded. I should have told them to set up the little round tables—so much better for conversation. I've got that dreadful old barbarian Max Chester on my right." She came closer to Tom, then hesitated. "I haven't even had a chance to say hello. You look well, though. We'll have a good talk tomorrow." She touched the back of his head experimentally.

"You look well, too," he said.

"Oh, do you like this?" She spread her sequined skirt, which glittered with a thousand eyes. "It's not new, I've had it for ages."

Tom did not say anything. Far away, on the edge of his vision, he saw her turning in a circle.

"Well, if you're all right, I'd better get back to Max," she said ruefully. "Your father's expecting a big donation . . . though I'd much rather spend the evening with you!" She pursed her lips and moved closer to kiss him. Tom winced away.

"What's the matter?" she asked in a changed voice, harshly. "What happened to you up there? You hardly wrote at all."

He turned his back to her and stared at the desk. It had been a long time since she last tried to kiss him, and the threat made the air around him hum.

"It was all right," he said.

"Well, I hope so," she said, mollified. She touched his arm with three fingers. As he slowly drew it away, she said, "Why, I believe you must have fallen in love!"

"They'll be waiting for you in there."

"You're right." Her relief matched his. "I ought to go back. Amos is likely to pour the white wine into the red-wine

glasses." She looked at him uncertainly. "You'd tell me if
there was something really wrong, wouldn't you, darling?"
"I don't know," he said.
"Paul always told me everything."
"He did?"
"We always got along so well. . . ." She put her hand to
her throat. "Well, just so long as we keep in touch—keep the
channels open." Smiling at him mischievously, she turned
and hurried back to the dining room.

Just as rapidly, Tom went to the hall and plunged out the
front door. His mother's touch had fired him, setting him in
motion.

Outside, it was dark and raining. Tom started down the
hill. He moved mechanically, slowly, but with great vigor, his
hands describing small circles by his sides. He hurried down
the hill to the path that led to the swimming pool, marching
like a tin soldier, his mind blank and bright, and then, at the
wet woods, he began to run, blundering, panting, towards
the patch of ferns and the tree. . . .

The branches were wet, and they shed their drops on his
head and shoulders as he pushed through. It was almost
entirely dark, but he knew the way. Coming out of the glade,
he continued running.

He stopped when he felt the ferns' wet beards around his
knees. Turning his face up, he stared into the darkness,
searching for the high branch that held the platform. But it
was too dark to see.

He threw his hand out, grazing the tree trunk with his
knuckles, then lunged forward. Stretching his arms around
the trunk, he pressed his face against the grainy ridges and
tore a wedge of bark off with his teeth. Spitting the bits out,
he whined, "'You're driving Paul crazy!'" Then he fell down
on his knees in the ferns, pushing them aside with his hands

and falling on his face in the wet mulch of leaves underneath. He rolled there, snatching up handfuls of leaves. "Paul," he moaned. "Paul, Paul, Paul." His voice shed its hysterical whimpering and became dull, monotonous, endless, as he thrashed, moving more and more slowly until he lay still at last, on his face in the wet leaves.

After a long time he got up and brushed at his clothes. It had begun to rain heavily. He started up the path, walking slowly, hunched, with his hands clasped tightly behind his back. He crossed the road and plowed up the bank, aiming for the lights of the house, sailing across the top of the hill. As he came around to the kitchen door, he heard the crash of dishes and the voices of the servants. He guessed that they had probably just finished serving dessert.

On the back porch he stopped to brush at his clothes again.

Going into the kitchen, he hesitated; it was hot and bright and full of strangers. A waiter carrying a tray loaded with coffee cups stopped and stared at him. The Chinese cook, collapsed in a chair, struck the table with the side of his hand, and the waiter turned and rushed off. "Get off my clean floor," the cook ordered Tom.

Trying to leave as few marks as possible, Tom crossed the kitchen and started up the back stairs. There was a great clamor of voices from the dining room, and he imagined that he saw his mother's voice, jeweled, sparkling, riding the crest.

Bessie's room was at the end of the back hall. The door was closed. Bending down, Tom saw that there was no light coming through the crack.

"Bessie?" he called softly. Then he turned the knob and pushed open the door.

He knocked into a chair on his way to the bed, and Bessie woke up. "Who's that?" she said, sitting up.

"Me," he answered. He knelt beside the bed, feeling for her, and caught hold of her soft arms.

"Get away from here, Tom," she said sharply. "You're too old for that stuff." But he held on to her arms and buried his face in her shoulder, smelling the faint scorched odor of her flannel nightgown. He began to sob, grinding his teeth.

After a while she raised her hand and stroked the back of his head. Later she sank back against the headboard, pressed by his weight. He stretched himself out beside her, still holding her arms, gradually moving his face into the pit between her arm and her breast.

"My Lord," she sighed.

Chapter Ten

L ouise had a basket of treats to take to Shelby on Thanksgiving. She had collected Sweetheart soap, a bag of sachet from their mother's closet, some chocolate kisses in silver wrappers, and a new pair of pink bunny slippers for Shelby's poor cold feet. She planned to take the basket to Shelby as soon as she was finished at the cemetery.

It took her a while to arrange everything there. First she put the chrysanthemums she had bought into the tin cup at the foot of her mother's grave. The flowers were for all the people there, but she thought it appropriate to put them at her mother's feet. They took the place of all the flowers her mother had not been given when she was alive; they represented the birthdays she had insisted on ignoring and the Christmases when she had had to be coaxed to open her presents. It gave Louise some satisfaction to think that now her mother could not reject the flowers.

She pulled up a handful of crabgrass and then stood with her finger pressed against her lips and reread the brief inscriptions on the flat granite stones. Those names and dates existed now only as tombstone definitions; she did not encourage her memories from those years. An uncle whom she had scarcely known was buried there, at her mother's right hand, near her father's parents, dead long before her time. Her father's gravestone, set a little apart, had a small urn carved into it—to signify his interest in the classics, she had always thought.

None of that mattered much. But the phrase on her mother's stone, crowded beneath her name and her dates, existed independently in Louise's imagination, flashing out at odd hours like a neon sign:

LOVELIEST AND MOST BELOVED

Now what had her father meant by that? She took her hand from her mouth and turned towards her car. He had not been a sentimental man; the statement must be precise, a summing-up no less valid than her mother's name and dates.

She wanted to believe that there had been something between them, something to contradict her mother's silence, her drabness, her never-ending round of duties. There must have been a gleam, an arrow of surmise, that had flown over Louise's head; there must have been some meeting of minds or bodies obscured by her parents' silence, by their dour habits of expression. Still, the epitaph shocked her a little. They had not been meant for display, those feelings—if in fact they had existed—and she felt that her father must have fallen prey to a stonecutter's sentimentality at the end. Their love—if it had existed—should have remained a secret, guilty in its intensity.

For after all, she thought, we are born to manage, not to love.

Except, of course, for Shelby.

That thought released her restraints, and she half ran to the car, slipping on the sloping lawn.

Then she pulled up short. One of the caretakers was lounging by her car, as though come on purpose to hear her complaints about the ivy. It hadn't been pruned for ages, but that was always the way with Eternal Care.

"If you don't do that ivy now, it'll be a mess in the spring," she warned him, across the hood of the car.

"I'll get to it," he drawled. He was a straggly blond young man from Elizaville, a worthless cousin—Louise thought—of Herman's down at the grocery store. "You going to see Miss Shelby?" he asked.

"I expect I'll see her when I get home, I usually do," Louise said, opening the car door.

"I saved her this." He thrust a magazine, well thumbed, across the hood. "It has a piece in it about the team."

Louise recognized the blue and white helmet on the cover, above a profile that Shelby, even now, would be able to name. "Why, thank you, Jed." Looking at him, she remembered years before when she had swung on an inner tube in the backyard of his mother's house. Jed had been a baby then, in sagging diapers.

"She'll appreciate this," Louise said, laying the magazine on the car seat.

"When they going to let her out?" Jed asked, coming around to her side as she climbed in.

Louise fed the key into the ignition. "Why, Jed, you know perfectly well—" She hesitated, looking at his checked shirt which was buttoned wrong. "I don't know when," she said.

"It gets to me," he complained. "Here they let every kind of crazy run loose. Moey Maclean, that beat that child to death—he's out already. Miss Shelby never did anything to anybody."

"Well, she could embarrass people."

"Hell." He spat on the ground and wiped his mouth. "She

didn't embarrass me none. Remember that time she run out in the road in her nightgown? Cousin Herman and I brought her back. It didn't amount to nothing."

"Well, the truth is, other people don't want to put up with her. I'm trying all I can to get her out, but right now it doesn't look like I'm making any headway."

He shrugged, disgusted. "You get her out of there. Get her home for Christmas." Stepping back, he watched her start the car.

She drove out of the graveyard, thankful that Jed did not know how little fight she had put up.

She knew what was holding her back. It was Big Tom's face. Every time she started to think of all the things she hadn't tried yet, she would see his face, sad, watchful, disappointed, like the face on her father's clock on the mantel upstairs. She was always letting him down, in thought or word or deed; but she had not yet let him down by getting Shelby out. "It's you I'm thinking about," he had told her, time after time. "It's your life." She had never been able to explain to him that her life had no substance, no meaning, unless she could take care of Shelby.

She had tried to punish him for not understanding. She had tried to get at him through Young Tom. That it hadn't worked, had had no effect at all, hurt her more than the shame. Those letters—but probably the boy had not even read them, and certainly he had not had time or taste to sort out the truth from the lies. She would have had a hard time doing that herself; truth built on lies, lies out of truth, guesses, half wishes—they had all come as weapons to her hand. Louise knew they had been feeble arrows, falling at her feet.

She had thought, too, that somehow her truth would help Young Tom. She had had that in the back of her mind. She had always liked him. He was supposed to be the bright one, the elder, the blessed, the one who would be like his father. As a child he had seemed wooden to her, lifeless, until she realized that he only lived to please. That had frightened her, especially when she watched him talking to his father. That had been too close to home. Paul, she remembered, who was not supposed to be anything but a little brother, had been such a pretty child, and full of the devil. Well, Paul was gone.

It hadn't mattered to her that he was supposed to be the dumb one—late-maturing, whatever the word had been. He had been so funny and alive, prancing around, making all kinds of mistakes but never being afraid. They drove that out of him by the time he was half grown. He didn't do well in school, that was the trouble, and Louise had heard him crying once over some page of arithmetic problems. It had been hard for her to realize how much that mattered. She thought that a place would be found for him, a shelter, a warm corner, as there had always been a place for Shelby. After all, there was nothing wrong with Paul.

She was on the thruway now, beginning to watch for the hospital turnoff.

Paul, and the ferns, and the treehouse: less than a year ago, but already as far gone in silence as her mother's death.

He had been nice, though. She had been fond of him. Once he had made her a necklace of dry oak leaves, strung on a thread.

If they had only been willing to let him alone.

She turned in through the hospital gates and drove up the hill to the main door. Although she had only been away for a few days, the building surprised her all over again. It was so enormous, with row after row of barred windows and rank after rank of metal outside stairs. She would not have thought the world had enough mad people to fill that place.

She parked the car and got out as quickly as she could before fear could overtake her. Climbing the outside stairs, she stopped as always to get her breath, and looked at the distant mountains.

She banged on the fifth-floor door, and it was opened immediately by a large nurse in a tight white uniform. The clanging noises and the zoo smell were overpowering, and Louise wiped her face with her handkerchief. Big Tom had told her over the telephone to cut down her visits; what was the use, he said, of her going to see Shelby when she didn't even know her own sister? Louise said something to Tom about the pleasant drive, about the view of the mountains. She was careful not to mention the stench, for fear that he would use that as another argument against her going. Now she held the handle of her treat basket firmly and went through the door, which the nurse closed and locked behind her.

"She's getting along real good," the nurse told her. "She's finished with all that fussing and carrying on. Just as gentle as a little lamb."

"What have you got her on now?"

"Why, just the same thing, the same stuff her doctor ordered." Briefly, the nurse looked offended; then her pride reemerged, and she took Louise's arm to guide her to her sister. They walked side by side through the milling crowd to an alcove where Shelby was sitting alone on a chair.

"And she's gained weight, too!" the nurse exclaimed. "She's just as pretty!" She darted at Shelby and smoothed her cropped hair. "You like the food here, don't you, honey?"

Shelby was staring at the palm of her hand.

"They had her on a diet before," Louise said, looking at her sister, trying to catch her attention.

"Well, they took her off that. She's not the type to be starved to death, if you ask me."

Shelby was wearing a short gray smock that Louise had never seen before. Her thighs, thick and ridged as loaves, were spread apart. The nurse swooped at her and pressed the skirt down firmly between her knees. "Look who's come to see you, honey!" Louise noticed that Shelby was wearing her own white socks and her blue canvas shoes they had bought together at Boltman's with some of Big Tom's money.

She leaned down and kissed Shelby's forehead. Her hair was clotted, smelling of grease. "Can't you wash her hair?" Louise asked angrily.

The nurse drew back. "We can't baby our patients, miss. We have too much work as it is."

"Show me where the bathroom is. I'll do it."

"The shower room is locked until five P.M."

"Then I'll wash it in the sink."

The nurse laughed. "I'd like to see you try that! She won't even wash her hands after she's been playing with her mudpies. Gerry and me had to hold her while Annie hosed her off." Shaking her head mirthfully, the nurse hurried away towards a disturbance at the other end of the ward.

Louise turned back to Shelby. "Sister?" She touched her broad flat hand. Shelby stared straight ahead, motionless, planted between the arms of the chair. Louise crouched down beside her and began to unpack the basket. "I brought you some Sweetheart soap. You've always liked that. Bunny slippers. And a sachet . . ."

The slippers slid off Shelby's knee, and the soap and the sachet followed. Quickly Louise began to gather them up.

She was afraid that the nurse would come back and upbraid her. Already an old woman in a stained cotton slip had wandered into the alcove. "Get away," Louise hissed, flapping her arms at the woman, who backed off. Then Shelby said something, made a soft chuckling sound in her throat. She was taking her hands from her knees to hold Jed's magazine, and slowly, by degrees, she was bending her neck. She brought her face down close to the cover, bending double, her large breasts mashed into her thighs.

"Jed sent you that. He knew you'd be interested." Straightening up, Louise watched her sister. "Shelby," she said at last. "Shelby, listen to me." Shelby was smiling and shaking her head at the magazine. Now and then she chuckled low in her throat and fluffed herself up like a big bird sitting on a nest.

"Shelby," Louise said again. "Tell me something. Don't you want to go home?"

Shelby did not look up. With one finger, she was tracing the football player's profile.

"Do you like it here? Because if not—"

The hefty nurse hurried between them. "Now what's the matter? You've got her crying again."

Louise saw two tears on Shelby's round cheeks. "Why, I'm going to take her home," she said.

"Not without the doctor's say-so, you know that. Nobody leaves this place without his name on the papers." She glared at Louise, her hands on her hips. "Some people are the damnedest. Here we're just starting to get someplace with her—it's only the last few weeks we've been able to keep the clothes on her back. Now that we've got her on this new stuff she's really starting to improve. She smiled at me yesterday. Yes, she did! And now you're talking about taking her home."

Shelby raised her head and looked at her sister. The tears, stirred into motion, ran the rest of the way down her cheeks.

"Shelby, I'm not going to take you if you want to stay here," Louise said. "I just don't see how you could prefer—" She glanced at the nurse. "Come on home with me, Sister," she said.

"Not without no papers, you know that," the nurse said.

"I'll get the papers."

Sighing, rubbing her hands together, the nurse turned to leave. "Well, I wish you good luck with her."

Louise concentrated on Shelby, who had dropped her head again and was studying the photograph on the magazine. There was no way to tell, really, what had caused her tears. "It'll start to get cold here soon," Louise told her. "Then it'll get to be Christmas, and what will they do about that? They probably won't do anything about it at all. And you know how you love to get ready for Christmas. We can make the fruitcakes pretty soon now. You know you always love to chop the candied fruit."

Shelby did not raise her head.

"Never mind," Louise said. "This doesn't mean a thing. We'll talk about it again the next time I see you." She bent down to kiss Shelby's hair and smelled again the heavy, gluey stench; her hair smelled like an animal's pelt.

Louise turned away and hurried off down the ward. She found the nurse pushing a cart covered with tiny plastic cups; she waved her hand at Louise and said something to an aide, and the two of them laughed. Louise stood still and let the procession pass.

"It doesn't mean a thing," she said out loud as she was driving home. "It doesn't mean a darned thing." And she wondered why she had even spoken to Shelby about going home. It was up to her, after all, to decide what was best for her sister.

She stopped off at Herman's to buy a loaf of bread. She had a suspicion that Bella was in the back room, but she did not have the energy to investigate.

Herman was grinning. When he asked her, as he always did, when Miss Shelby would be coming back, Louise told him, "Why, she's coming back for Christmas, just the way I said. And you can tell Jed for me she appreciated the magazine."

Chapter Eleven

It was bright morning when Tom woke up; the sunlight was pouring through Bessie's little window, filtered by the bare twigs of the Virginia creeper. He got up quickly and looked at the empty side of the bed, deeply indented, where Bessie had slept. Her broad bedroom slippers were parked by the nightstand. He knew that she was always up and dressed by six o'clock, ready to fix his parents' breakfast; he had often waited on the stool in the kitchen while she folded the napkins for the pair of trays.

Bessie always said, "If it's worth doing, it's worth doing right."

Staring at her nightgown hanging from its hook, sack-shaped, washed-out, he remembered, for the first time since he left Cambridge, Catherine with her mouth open; but the pain was far away, a half-forgotten throb from his childhood.

He went out of the room, pausing in the dim hall to be sure that no one was about. He did not need to imagine how his mother would look if she saw him coming out of Bessie's room.

He walked quickly down the hall to his own room, then realized with horror that the door had been left open all night. The lamp beside his bed was still burning, and the sheet was neatly turned down. He touched the neck of the lamp—it was hot—and wondered who had looked into the room and what they had thought. He was curious, as though from what they said or felt he might derive some conclusion about his own feelings. He went into the bathroom and stripped off his crumpled shirt, still damp and smelling of leaves. Then he began to shave.

Five minutes later there was a light tap on the door.

"Who is it?"

Instead of answering, his mother opened the door. She looked pale, with last night's mascara pooled beneath her eyes. She clasped her hands on her stomach, clasped them more and more tightly, rearranging the fingers as Tom had often seen her do.

"I missed you after dinner. Did you go somewhere?"

"I went for a walk."

"It was raining."

"Not too hard. I didn't really get wet. . . . What a beautiful day today."

"Yes. Did you walk far?"

He sighed and leaned over the sink, looking down into the soapy water.

"I don't mean to cross-question you," she said hastily.

"I went down to the trail."

She let her breath out quickly. "I noticed you weren't in bed when I came up."

"I came in later," he said, amazed at how easy it was, now, to lie to her.

"Well." She put her hand out cautiously and touched his arm. "I just wanted to be sure . . . I want you to enjoy yourself, have a rest while you're down here. After all, it's only for a few days."

"Yes." He let the water out of the sink.

She sighed again, turned away, then turned back and again lightly touched his arm. "I see you didn't put on your pajamas."

He had forgotten that they were still laid out on the chair in his room. "I guess I was too tired. I didn't even get under the covers. At college," he added briskly, "we don't bother with pajamas."

Again she seemed relieved; she smiled. "Well, if you need anything, be sure to tell me, Tom." She hesitated, her eyes fixed on his shoulder. "I know it hasn't always been the best." As she said it, her pale face seemed to shrink, and she licked her lips. "I haven't always been able to . . . well, it's hard for you to understand. After a cesarean . . ." She seemed to be wandering. "In those days you had to stay in bed for three weeks. By the time I was up, Bessie already had you settled in the bassinet in her room." She looked at him sharply. "I had planned to nurse you, you know . . . it didn't work out. Something went wrong, it wasn't clear to me just what; Dr. Lilly said I wasn't built for it. It wasn't done much in those days. But I wanted to. And then two years later, no, thirty months later, Paul . . . I'm sorry. You want to dress." Frightened, she turned and hurried out of the bathroom, closing the door neatly behind her.

Tom stood staring at the closed door. He had not understood what she was trying to say, but the swarm of words, light as butterflies, still hovered around his head. She had always used such small, light words, without much meaning, in large clusters—as though their colorlessness itself must communicate something. They were like her small dry touches, her meaningless pats, which seemed to graze his arm or his shoulder and then slide off into the void. They were meant to express love, but they were so light and ambiguous that she might only have been brushing off a speck of dust. He thought that was why she was so pretty, even now: she had kept a large part of herself in reserve, flirtatiously, perhaps, coyly, perhaps, but with rigid determination, like a young girl saving herself for a great romance.

He remembered Bessie's telling him "Go to your mother" when he was three or four. "I don't know why you always hang around me when I've got my hands full with Paul. Go upstairs and see your mother. Go tell her good morning. Kiss her goodbye. Kiss her good night, Tom."

"Why, Bessie?" he had asked, petulantly.

"Because she wants you to."

He had hoped that his mother would turn her attention to Paul. He had hoped that would free him to go to Bessie. But as it turned out, Bessie had Paul, too. She walked the floor with him night after night when he was colicky and couldn't sleep. Once Tom saw her sitting asleep in broad daylight with the baby on her lap. He kicked the rocker, waking them both. Bessie screeched at him, but later she tried to stop his hysterical crying. She offered him a lollipop. It was the only time he had ever succeeded in frightening her.

He left the bathroom and met his father on the stairs.

"Good morning. Have you had your breakfast?" his father asked. He was wearing a suede jacket, belted in the back, and a silk handkerchief tied like an ascot inside his collar. He looked to Tom as though he had just come from bathing in a clear mountain stream. There was not a seam or a line in his face; he was as clean and hard as a stone.

"I don't want any breakfast," Tom said.

His father was practical. "You'd better have something, it's a long time till lunch." His attention elsewhere, he walked down the stairs. "We'll be driving to the inn. It's a long way, almost two hours."

Tom followed him, noticing that his father's pale-green suede shoes matched his jacket. Of course he never would have admitted to working on that; he would have claimed they matched by pure chance. He was not the kind of man who paid attention to shoes.

"Your mother wants to go to Rose Hill first," his father said, aiming for the newspaper that was laid out on the marble table in the hall.

"All right," Tom said. He watched his father pick up the newspaper, rapidly scan the headlines, and then turn to an inside page. That was the signal; Tom left him and went to the kitchen.

As soon as she saw him, Bessie began to spoon hot oatmeal into his old brown bowl. "Eat up. You've got a long day ahead of you," she said crossly, slapping the bowl down on the table. Then she went to bang pots in the sink.

"What's the matter?" Tom asked, then added, glumly, "I'm sorry, Bessie."

"Don't 'sorry' me." She never had time for apologies. "Just don't act that way again." She looked at him over her shoulder. "Nineteen years old. You'd think you were nine at the most. How is it you can't give up your old ways?" It was said with amazement as well as anger. "You're a smart boy; you have everything you want, a good education, everything. How come you can't go ahead and grow up?"

"I'm growing up as fast as I can, Bessie."

She was not to be placated. "I thought you'd come back different this time. I thought you'd come back acting your age. I bet you left your clothes all over the place upstairs for me to pick up."

The tenderness behind her irritation made him smile. Freed, he said, "Bessie, I don't want to go back to college."

Without hesitation, she said, "You've got to go back."

"It doesn't make any sense up there. I can't remember anything I read. I sit for hours . . . It doesn't make any sense," he repeated, pleading.

"Let me tell you one thing, young man." She faced him, leaning back against the sink. The bright morning light deepened the lines around her mouth and eyes; she seemed witchlike in her apprehension, and Tom gaped at her. "If you think you're going to come back here and worry the life out of me, you are mistaken. I'll leave first. I mean that. I always said I'd stay to see you boys grown, but if you don't walk out of this house Sunday night, I'll walk out Monday." He saw her eyebrows begin to redden, and she swiped at her face with the back of her hand. "I've done all I can for you, Tom. I did it all a long time ago. Before Paul was born, even, before you were three years old. It just didn't seem to stick. It didn't seem to satisfy. I guess that's why I never could bear to leave. I don't know what it is about you, Tom; you never seem to have enough. Well, I can't help that now. I've done the best I can," she said, her voice rising. "I'm too old now. I can't go through all that anymore. I never have felt the same since Paul died. I just don't have the strength. So don't go thinking you can come back here and lie back and sop it up." She turned abruptly and leaned on the sink. He saw the high ridge of her knuckles as she gripped the edge.

"I wouldn't come back here for anything," he said sullenly, shoving the bowl of oatmeal away. It skidded across the table and stopped at the edge. "You always blame me for everything. I can't help the way I am. I can't do anything about what happened to Paul—"

"Now don't start that," she interrupted, turning around

again. "Eat that cereal." She pushed the bowl back towards him.

He was not to be stopped. "Everybody blames me for what happened to him."

"Who said any such thing?"

"You don't need to say it."

"Just because everybody decided you were the smart one. Paul had a lot of good, too. He had the sweetest nature." Again she swiped at her face. "Don't start me on that. Sometimes I think you're still jealous."

He stared at her.

"Yes, when he died, at the funeral, I saw your sour face. You didn't even bother to cover it up. It was the first time Paul ever got ahead of you, got the attention."

"Shut up, Bessie," he said, standing up and knocking over his chair.

"Don't use that tone with me," she hissed.

"I never was jealous of him in my life. It was the other way around. I used to feel sorry for him. I wanted to grow up and get out of here, that's the only thing I ever wanted." He banged out of the kitchen, dazed by his own anger.

"I'll go back on Monday," he said out loud. "I've got the ticket."

He went into the front hall, shooting out his right index finger to make his gesture of defiance.

His mother was waiting by the marble table. She was pulling on her gloves. Her pale face was carefully overlaid with a pink film; when she smiled at him, Tom forgave her her yellow teeth and her breath that was as tart as vinegar. "Are you ready to go to lunch?" she asked.

Tom nodded, not daring to speak, and his mother turned and led the way out of the house.

His father was on the porch, pacing rapidly up and down.

He gave an exclamation of relief when he saw them. "We'll go to Rose Hill first," he said, opening the car door for his wife.

Tom was about to slide into the backseat, next to the bunch of flowers, but his mother insisted that he sit beside her instead, in front. He could not remember when that had happened before, and he sat uncomfortably wedged beside her, feeling her thigh next to his through her coat.

"We thought it would be more entertaining to have Thanksgiving lunch at Halfway House this year," his mother began to explain as they drove down the hill. "They always have an amusing group of people there. It's not just an inn, you know, it's a beautiful old place, perfectly restored; Mary Ellen says even the fixtures in the bathrooms are authentic. I did want Bessie to have the day off," she added. "She's been getting so tired."

"She does look tired," Tom admitted gloomily.

"Yes, well, she still insists on getting up at some unreasonably early hour, even though it's absolutely unnecessary now. Your father and I only eat cold cereal in the morning—we're on Dr. Greene's diet—and there really isn't anything for Bessie to fix except coffee. But you know how she is, she always has to have somebody to fuss over, something to fix or arrange. She just can't seem to understand that times have changed since you were a baby. I mean, now, when we want a good meal, we go out to Renoir's. They have a French chef, and the pâté is flown in from Paris. There was nothing like that when you were little. Bessie still seems to feel that we depend on her, though. She made me a handkerchief case last winter—so pretty, blue and pink—and I had to hide the one I'd bought in New York."

"We should have let her go a long time ago," Big Tom said.

"Well, I couldn't do that. I don't know what she'd do. She'd never find another job. She doesn't have any skills. And she couldn't just go and sit in some little room in town."

"Hasn't she got relatives somewhere? A brother or something?" Big Tom asked.

Tom looked at his father, surprised by his sharpness.

"Well, she does have that brother in Cincinnati, but I believe he drinks," his mother said.

"We ought to let her go," Big Tom repeated.

Tom was absurdly frightened. He knew that anything he could say would only make matters worse. He tried to trust his mother's elaborate system of justice, which insisted on lifetime payment for a lifetime of service; he did not believe that she would give in. Not, he realized, that she liked Bessie, or even believed that she needed her; but all that was less important than the moral obligation.

He looked out the window and saw the river, brown and wide between low banks. Pleasure boats were riding downstream like a flotilla of fat white ducks. Tom remembered when there were only barges on the river, pushed by green and white sidewheelers. He noticed a new marina built out into the river; a cabin cruiser was backing out of its slip.

"It's beautiful now," his father said, looking proudly at the river. "We got that bill passed to stop the plants upstream from dumping their garbage, and the water's cleaner and the fish are coming back. They say some people even swim."

"Without typhoid shots," his mother added. She opened her purse, took out her gold-backed mirror, and glanced at her face briefly. "Oh, I look like a ghost!"

Tom and his father, their voices interweaving, hastily reassured her.

"We've been so busy," she said, sighing. "You know the new theater down by the river opened a week ago, and we had a party for that. The cast is all down from New York for the season, living with various people. Hope Gray has taken a pair of men . . . well, you know the kind I mean. I said to her, 'Hope, how could you?' You know she has a little boy. But she says they're the sweetest things, neat and clean; they even do their laundry in her machine."

"One of them is in the chorus in *The Student Prince*," his father continued. "I believe the other one does something about props."

"No, he helps with the costumes. Of course I just can't understand these things," his mother went on cheerfully. "I mean, who would want to act that way? It's like Bim and Mary Ellen's boy, he's tried to commit suicide twice, and he was the brightest boy in his high-school class. They've done everything for him, college, a trip to Europe; why, Bim even got him out of the draft. . . ."

"They had a psychiatrist say he was nuts," Big Tom explained.

"Well, I believe he was depressed. It doesn't matter what they said, they spared him a terrible experience in Korea. Now Bim's offered him a job at the distillery. Starting at the bottom, of course, just the way Bim did, but he'd end up at the top. If he was willing to work, which, of course, he isn't. I saw Mary Ellen at the airport last week, waiting for him to come home; I didn't dare to ask her where he was coming *from*. She took him straight to Our Lady of Peace, and he's right there this minute; they don't expect him home before Christmas."

"You mean Wright? Is that who you're talking about?" Tom asked.

"Why, yes, of course, who do you think? You remember Wright, you used to go to school with him until they sent him off to that place in Virginia. His father thought the military training might give him some backbone. I believe that's what did it to him," she added, inspired. "I never have had any faith in those places, no matter what your father thinks of them. You remember Wright," she repeated.

"He just can't seem to take any interest in girls," Big Tom said.

"Oh, that'll pass, that's not the real problem. It would kill Mary Ellen to hear you say that."

"Then what is the real problem? He's certainly always been bright enough."

"Well, he gets depressed, you know that. It's probably something physical. They had him on this new drug, and it worked fine for a while, but then it seemed to wear off." She looked at Tom. "Wright and Paul were very close, you remember. He was cut up about Paul. He was in bed for a week afterwards, his mother said. He just couldn't seem to get up." Her bright voice faded; she fell silent, studying her hands.

Big Tom said, "They never have been able to make that boy do a thing. That's his main problem."

"They gave him everything," Mugsie said sadly.

Tom asked, "Is he still in the hospital?"

"Yes, I told you that already. He's in Our Lady, and they don't expect him out before Christmas. I just don't know what poor Mary Ellen is going to do."

"Drink, as usual," Big Tom said.

"Why, honey, they're both just social drinkers."

"I guess I ought to go and see him," Tom said doubtfully.

"You won't have time today. It'll be too late by the time we get back." His father's voice closed the conversation.

"Maybe I'll go tomorrow."

"I don't know who could drive you in."

"He was Paul's friend, really," his mother said.

"I can drive myself."

"You wouldn't know the way. They've put up a new building, way out on Fourteenth and Main," his father said.

"I've got to go to the dentist tomorrow. I could drop you off," his mother said uncertainly. "If you really want to go."

"I don't know why you should go," Big Tom persisted. "He was never in your grade. He was in Paul's grade. Everybody says he looks awful, a wreck, some kind of skin infection—"

"No, he was in Tom's grade," his wife interrupted.

"You've got it wrong. He was in Paul's. Don't you remember when Bim telephoned us, the day he was born? It was the spring of the big flood. Paul was a baby."

"I don't know. I seem to be getting it all mixed up," she said.

"He was in my grade," Tom said, finally. "He was Paul's friend, but he was in my grade."

There was silence in the car.

"It seems to me we ought to be able to get these things straight," Tom said. "It seems to me we ought to be able to remember."

They stopped for a light. "That's where they're putting up the new office building," his father said, pointing to a desolated block. A house clung to the edge of the excavation, looking oddly tranquil, with a curtain flapping in an open window and a box of geraniums on the stoop. "They had to quit blasting till they can get those fools on the corner out."

"I just don't see why they can't get them out," Mugsie said with mild surprise.

"Oh, somebody's been paid off, you know how it is. I hear they'll be out of there next week." He nodded with satisfaction towards the crane that lay, its neck extended, next to the site. "They brought that thing all the way from Chicago. It's the biggest one in the business."

"The town is certainly changing," Tom said. He had recovered himself.

"Yes, this used to be the rattiest neighborhood. Nothing but a lot of boardinghouses full of hillbillies. Why, they'd pee right out on the street. Now we're going to have a new commercial center here, with a shopping center and trees."

"Why, honey, your own family used to live just down the street," Mugsie reminded him gently.

"Well, fifty years ago it was different. I'm not talking about that. The last people moved out of here around the First World War. That's when all the houses went to rented rooms. Once that happens, a place is doomed. There's nothing you can do but tear it down and start over." He drove slowly away from the construction site, looking back with a longing in his smooth face that Tom had never seen before. "It's going to be a beautiful place, a model for the Midwest."

"At college they think this is the South," Tom said.

"Well, of course, it does have a lot of that charm," his mother agreed.

His father shrugged. "Charm is not going to carry us very far. Your mother and I have done a lot about keeping the fine old places here: the library, and the warehouse down by the river they've turned into a theater. That's all well and good, but we have to let go of the past. The past wasn't all honeysuckle and magnolias, you know. I remember babies' dying every summer from dysentery and malaria, before the swamps were drained. I remember where the colored people had to live, out by the dump, with the fires burning like hell itself night and day. I remember when the only school for those children was a shack with no heat or running water down by the river. And it wasn't much better for the whites. We've made a lot of progress here in the last ten years; we've made things a good deal better for the poor people and the coloreds. If it meant letting go of some of the charm, I don't regret it."

His mother said, "Some of the people at the country club can be quite ugly about it. I mean, they want the old Franklin place to be turned into a shopping center, but they couldn't care less about what happens in the middle of town."

"Well, they're blind," his father said harshly. "Always have been and always will be."

"Now, darling, those are our friends," Mugsie chided him. After a pause she turned to Tom. "Tell us what you've been accomplishing this fall."

He had trouble answering. "Oh, nothing much, I guess. I've been trying to get settled." His parents' voices floated around him like paper streamers, coloring and filling the blank air. He had nothing to add to their decoration. "Working, of course," he added.

"I hope you've been making some friends. You never have needed to worry about the work."

"Give him time," his father said.

"I've gotten to know my roommate pretty well. We went out to the country one Sunday."

"Don't you have girls in your classes?"

"Yes, there're always a few." He looked across at his father and caught the flick of his interest, like a lizard's tail. "I've gotten to know one of them real well," he said recklessly.

His parents' exclamations were linked.

"Is she the one you mentioned in your letters?" his mother asked.

"Well, she's got dark hair." Tom tried to summon up a neutral memory. He chose words at random, surprised that they had no associations. "A good figure. A really good sense of humor."

"That's important," his mother agreed.

"Dark, you said?" his father asked.

"She must be a New England girl," his mother put in.

"Yes, she comes from Vermont. Her father's a schoolteacher." He could taste their pleasure, soft and dense as a spoonful of white sugar. Humbled by their delight, he went on talking, giving them details that did not pertain to myth or reality—stories from magazines, or a line he had read somewhere in a newspaper. "She comes up with the most original ideas. We were going to the beach one day—it was October—and she brought along a kite."

After he had finished, his father asked awkwardly, "Are you fond of her?"

"Oh, yes," Tom said.

"Now don't feel you have to rush things," his mother said.

"Just what do you mean by that?" Big Tom asked.

"Why, they don't even have rules in the dormitories anymore. The girls never have to go home."

"There are some rules," Tom said.

"It was no different in my day," Big Tom said. "There was always a way. There was always a car or a back road, if you wanted it badly enough. That used to make it hard for boys who felt shy or hesitant—the way a lot of boys feel at first. That used to make them hesitate awhile longer. Now there's nothing to hold you back but fear itself," he added with a laugh.

"I don't know what you're trying to say," Mugsie complained.

"I'm just trying to tell your son here that if he calls home one night to say he's in trouble"—again the laugh, which Tom did not remember—"well, I just want you to be forwarned and forearmed," he said, reaching across to squeeze his wife's knee.

"I certainly will not be, if I understand what you're driving at. Tom's always been a good boy. I've taken pride in that."

"Paul was a good boy, too. You brought up both of them to be that way," Big Tom said, and his son saw a flush spread across his cheeks, under the thick, smooth skin. "That's the only thing I've lived to regret—I mean, about Paul. I don't regret anything else. He had a good life, what he had of it; the best we could give him. He died a boy, that's all. It wasn't right. He was sixteen years old. By the time I was his age—"

"Tom, now don't," his wife said in a strangled voice.

"I'm not going to start all of that. That's over and done with, that's the past, it doesn't matter anymore." He turned the wheel sharply, and the car shot through the ivy-hung gates of Rose Hill. "It's the only thing I've lived to regret, that's all," he said, raising his hand to salute the guard. "Why, I believe that's old Saunders. I thought they'd pensioned him off."

"Paul did have a good life," his wife said. She was crying.

"Yes, he did." Reaching over to pat her shoulder, Big Tom met his son's eyes; they stared at each other briefly. "He had a good life, you have nothing to reproach yourself with on that score." His eyes, blue and sharp as bits of colored glass, flickered across Tom's face; then he winked, quickly and expertly, the wrinkled lid lowered for a fraction of a second across the startling eye.

Tom continued to stare after his father had turned away. DID YOU MEAN THAT? He wanted to ask him. DID YOU WINK AT ME? It was incredible, what he had seen, it had no place or explanation, and after a minute he knew he must have been mistaken. His father had not winked. It must have been some trick of the light.

They parked in a glade, shielded on both sides by hills that were thick with gravestones. Tom opened the door, got out and held it while his mother extricated herself. She wiped her eyes and composed herself; a half-smile appeared on her lips. Stepping neatly around the car, she took Big Tom's arm. Tom followed, his eyes on the heels of his mother's black leather shoes.

They stopped in front of him, at the foot of the grave. Raising his eyes slowly, Tom saw, beyond his father's bulk, the fringe of ivy, still quite new, that framed his brother's gravestone.

"I forgot the flowers, they're still in the car," his mother said.

Tom went back to the car. The flowers lay on the backseat, wrapped in newspaper. He leaned in and seized them, his fingers closing hard on the stems.

On his way back, he saw his mother kneeling by a little faucet to fill the tulip-shaped metal vase.

His father, his hands clasped tightly behind his back, stood at attention beside the gravestone. His eyes swept the rows of stones on the facing hill.

"It's such a pretty place," he said to Tom. "Why, in the spring, when the dogwoods are flowering . . ."

His mother came back, walking uncertainly in her high heels across the soft grass. She was carrying the vase of water. "Here, give me those," she said to Tom, taking the flowers and stripping off their paper cone. The yellow chrysanthemums stood up stiffly as she pushed them into the vase. "Stick it in the ground," she instructed Tom. He knelt and drove the point of the vase into the grass.

PAUL RANDAL MACELVENE

1942–1958

"I always thought we should have put something more," his mother said. "It seems so short, just the dates."

Big Tom lowered his eyes by degrees until his gaze merged with his wife's and son's. "Wouldn't have been any point in that," he said, in a choked voice.

Mugsie said, "I don't know why it is, but I can't cry here. I cry other places, but I can't cry here."

"It's so peaceful," Big Tom said. He took out a large linen handkerchief and blew his nose. "Somehow when you see the grass, and the trees . . . there's even a lake down further, with ducks."

Tom was choking with rage and despair.

"We'd better get started," his father said after a moment. He turned briskly towards the car, and his wife and son followed. Big Tom helped them into the front seat, closed the door, and, reaching in through the half-open window, stabbed the lock down.

Tom sat as close to the door as he could, avoiding contact with his mother. He felt the threat of her suspended tears. If she began to cry, he knew his own throat would go dry, and he would have to swallow and swallow to keep something down. Not sadness but rage, he thought. He glanced at her. She seemed to be in control.

They spun down the winding road, through the cemetery and out through the gates. His father was relieved, in flight; he began to talk about buying Christmas presents. He had a long list to go over with his wife, and all the names were familiar to Tom; the dim associations of sympathy or dislike filled his mind, replacing the anguish he had felt when he saw his brother's grave. How easy it was, now, to shift his focus.

For months after the funeral, he had been tortured by the physical sense of his brother's decay. He had woken, stifling, in the middle of the night, breathing a hot, rotting stench, his eyes branded with images of his brother's long legs, the flesh falling from the bones. He had screamed at the touch of the tiny light feet of the maggots that were infesting his brother's body. Finally he had devised a kind of magic, a ritual to ward off that agony: he would leap out of bed and turn on all the lights and walk up and down the floor of his dormitory sitting room, counting the steps from the wall to the windows and adding up the numbers at each turn. The numbers, the plain, bare numbers, heavy as iron bars, had purged his mind by filling it; he could still feel their weight. Dead weight.

"It should be finished by now," he said aloud.

"What should be finished?" his mother asked.

Turning his face slowly, with a conscious effort, he looked at her.

"What's the matter with you, Tom?" she asked sharply.

"Why, I was thinking about Paul."

She opened her mouth to speak, then thought better of it. "We all think about him all the time," she said after a while.

Chapter Twelve

Louise had made Scottish shortbread for tea. It had been some time since she had made it—out of consideration, mainly, for Shelby's weight—and she mistimed the baking. The shortbread was dry and dark around the edges, and Louise was humiliated. "I don't know what came over me," she explained to her guest. "I never have burnt it before."

"It's not burnt," the nun said. "It's just a little dark." She took an appreciative bite, balancing the square of shortbread on the ends of her short fingers. "Why, it's delicious," she said, wiping the crumbs off her skirt.

"I used to make it for Shelby every Sunday before she got so fat."

"Yes, I remember. I believe it was last March when I was out here and Shelby had herself a tantrum because there wasn't any shortbread." The nun laughed. "You know, you can say a lot of things about Shelby, but she certainly managed to get her way."

"She never heard a word I said when she was in one of

those states. And she knew perfectly well I was scared it might lead to something worse."

"How is she doing?" Sister Mary-Ann asked. She looked at Louise carefully.

"She's doing fine—much better, really—but that place is a mess."

"Oh, I know." Sister Mary-Ann shook her head. "Those public places—well, I guess they do the best they can."

"This one is private," Louise explained. "Big Tom insisted on that. Private or not, it's a mess. They don't seem to know what to do for her."

"Well," the nun said judiciously, "I guess you have to give them a chance. She hasn't been out there so long. But it's true it didn't seem to make a whole lot of difference last time. I mean, she came out pretty near the way she went in, as far as I could see."

"If they don't make her worse this time, I'll be relieved. She's determined to come home. She cried when I had to leave last Sunday. Sitting there without a stitch on"—Sister Mary-Ann did not seem to register this detail—"crying to come home. It almost broke my heart."

The nun said, "Everybody makes such a fuss about keeping clothes on them . . . You remember there was that piece awhile back in the paper. I was thinking the other day: Why, they're just as innocent as babies. And those wards are always overheated, I know."

"It's subhuman," Louise said sharply.

"Easier, though. When you think of all those clothes to wash. Why, some of them aren't even toilet-trained." Sister Mary-Ann shook her head. "It's not surprising, when you come to think of it, that they can't get people to work out there."

"That's the truth. The people they have for nurses are the

lowest type. Foulmouthed is the least of it. They're in it for the money, what there is of it, and that's all. It's certainly not the right place for Shelby. You know she's always loved clothes, and getting fixed up. She never could get enough of the department-store windows; we used to stand there by the hour. It doesn't seem like much in itself, but it kept her in touch—kept her in touch with the world, I mean. Now she's just drifting, just at sea, in limbo." She tried to keep her voice calm. "I can't stand to leave her out there, Mary-Ann."

The nun patted her dark skirt flat over her knees. "Well, Louise, I don't see that you have much choice. You can't have her living here anymore." Her voice, which was high and nasal, irritated Louise. She was not used to disagreement from that quarter. Mary-Ann had grown up out in Elizaville, one of seven children in a tar-paper shack, and it was Louise who had listened to her talk about her dreams and Louise who had agreed that she might have a vocation and Louise who had helped her out with money and who had come, finally, in the place of family, to watch the curious ceremony when she took orders.

"Shelby has lived here with me all her life," Louise said. "If I've put up with her this long . . ." Then, sighing, she added, "Anyway, it was never putting up with her. You know that. That's the way people talk, and I get into the habit. Big Tom, for instance. He can't understand why I want to make the 'sacrifice.' Sacrifice!" She laughed. "Shelby's all I've got. All I've ever had. Now I don't know why I should get up in the morning."

"It's no life for you," the nun said briskly. "Your cousin knows that."

"Why, you of all people—you at least should understand what I'm trying to say. I don't want to make it out that I'm some kind of holy martyr; sometimes I think I'm just plain selfish. Because the only thing that makes me feel good is to do something for Shelby. Something to make her smile, or make her more comfortable. Buy her a pair of shoes that fit. Find a way to get her to eat a vegetable. You know what I mean," she pleaded. "Then, at night, when I go to bed bone-tired, I can lie in the darkness and feel good; I can feel that the day wasn't wasted."

The nun's face had softened. "Maybe you should talk to Tom," she said gently. "He's the one who sent her there."

"He won't have anything to do with it. He's even stopped answering my letters. He told me it's all up to Dick Harris— you know he's Shelby's doctor—but that's just a lie. Dick won't do a thing unless he hears from Tom. And there's no use talking to Tom. You don't understand; you haven't seen him for fifteen years."

"More nearly sixteen."

Louise held up her hand to halt a threatened stream of recollections. "He doesn't want to know anything about Shelby. He's got her fixed, settled, and he wants to forget she exists. That's what he does now when something bothers him. He puts it away somewhere. Out of harm's way, I expect he'd say. Really she's just off his mind. . . . He does believe it's for the best, I grant that. That's how little he knows about it. I can't talk to him about it anymore, I can't even write him. If I do, he's going to quit writing me for once and for all." Tears filled Louise's eyes, and she paused to wipe them away.

She was not crying for Shelby. She was crying because she still could not bear to realize that Big Tom did not understand, that the time when he had understood belonged, implacably, to the time of her childish delusions. She knew now that he had probably never really seen her or heard her, even then, in the old days, when they played their games together. He had already begun, even then, to be distracted by distant sounds, by the faint beginning clamor of his own importance. "Two old ladies, the dearest things, living alone on a hill": she had overheard him describing them that way once. She wondered how long it had been since they had both ceased to exist, for Tom.

"I'm sure the good Lord has a special place in his heart for Shelby," Mary-Ann was saying soothingly. "You know what they say about the sparrow."

Louise would have liked to slap her. Instead she said, "I have to do something for her, Mary-Ann. The good Lord isn't going to be much help."

The nun looked vaguely shocked. Sensing a new threat, she said, "Why, Louise, I don't know what you're aiming at."

Louise leaned towards her. "It would be an act of charity, Mary-Ann. An act of love."

"What would?"

"To help me get her out."

"Oh, help! I couldn't do that," Mary-Ann exclaimed.

"I don't expect you actually to do anything," Louise said with a light touch of scorn. The other woman looked so frail, sitting on her narrow haunches between the arms of Mama's horsehair chair. "All I want you to do is get me one of the habits—one of the old kind, I mean, the full-length ones. They must have them squirreled away somewhere."

Mary-Ann, relieved, almost smiled. "I thought for a minute you meant some kind of kidnapping."

"Never. Never in my life. I just want to get her out of there for a while. She'll be so happy here—you'll see. Maybe Big Tom will agree not to send her back."

Mary-Ann considered, her head on one side, like a robin's. "Still, I don't know if it's right."

Louise studied her. "What would Jesus do?" she asked. "Would He leave her in that horrible place where they let full-grown men and women sit around in the nude?"

"Well, I'm not sure—"

"I'm sure. The things that go on out there. Why, they had a baby born right on the ward a week ago. Deaf and blind, with a head as big as a watermelon, and the poor mother couldn't do anything when she saw it but laugh. Shelby's only forty-three, you know."

Mary-Ann looked startled. "Why, Louise, I can't believe it."

Somberly, abandoning the cause, Louise turned her head away. "I see I should have looked elsewhere."

Mary-Ann stood up hastily. "Now, dear, don't say that. After all you've done for me, why, it doesn't seem like much to ask, does it?" She still seemed uncertain, but as she spoke, her voice began to gather strength. "It isn't as though we were doing something wrong. I mean, poor Shelby has a right to live at home, if that's what the both of you want. I don't see how anybody could say a thing against it."

Louise waited in silence, her face still turned away.

"I suppose I could lay my hand on one of those habits, somewhere," Mary-Ann said.

"You won't regret it," Louise said. Then she leaned forward, and, to Mary-Ann's astonishment, she kissed her.

Chapter Thirteen

Tom sat through the turkey course in silence. At first he used his fork to separate the mounds of food on his plate so that he would appear to be eating; then, thinking that no one was noticing, he laid down his fork and folded his arms tightly across his chest. As the voices around him rose, he bowed his head lower and lower, until his chin touched the knot in his tie.

"I believe Tom is fasting!" his neighbor, a cheerful middle-aged woman, cried after a while.

For a moment Tom did not move; then cautiously, he lifted his head and glanced at her. She had already been distracted by the arrival of the sweet potatoes. "Oh, my diet!" she wailed to Big Tom, on the other side of the table, and she patted her round belly under her napkin.

"Why, May, you've never looked better," Big Tom said. "You know I'm partial to a little flesh." He parted the stems of the chrysanthemums to admire her further, and Tom saw his blue eyes flash.

"I guess you don't eat much at college," his hostess said, leaning across the table to pass Tom the gravy. "I know when my boys come home, they don't eat for a week; their stomachs have shrunk, up there."

"Is that so?" Tom passed the gravy on.

"Well, at least for the first week. You're so quiet," Mary Ellen added compassionately. "I remember when you were a plump little boy. I used to think you were cute. Your father worried a lot about your weight, and I used to tell him, 'Wait till he's twenty, he'll be so skinny you'll be fussing about that.'"

"I guess that was Paul," Tom said.

She peered at him sharply. "Why, no, that wasn't Paul. I never mix you boys up. Or at any rate it wasn't only Paul; you had a fat time, too, when you were eleven or twelve."

Tom did not see any point in arguing with her. He had been confused with his brother so often and for so long that he, too, was sometimes confused; or at least the differences no longer seemed to matter.

Mary Ellen went on, "You haven't said a word the whole meal. I would have put you next to Wright, but I do believe in separating the men."

Tom looked down the long table. Wright was rocking back in his chair while his neighbors argued across him. Tom had been surprised to see him, but after a while he had begun to forget what his parents had always said. After all, Wright was rocking back in his chair, as he had always done, and he seemed to be enjoying himself. The labels that had been hung on him—suicidal, terribly lazy—fell off as soon as Tom saw his friend. Madness, after all, was a matter for dark corridors and strange institutions, not for the lemon-yellow private dining room of a beautiful country inn on a day when the November sunlight streamed as thin and bright as melted butter through the homespun curtains.

"You two be sure to have a good talk after lunch." Mary Ellen concluded the conversation.

"Tom, you haven't touched your meal!" the cheerful woman next to him now complained. "When I think how my Ralph would gobble it up! Dr. Collins warned me rich food might upset his stomach, but he didn't tell me what wonders it would work on his fur. Didn't you ever have one?" she asked, gently reproachful: Tom was not listening.

"One what?"

"Why, a dog, honey. A puppy."

"Paul had an allergy to dog hair."

Paul's name halted her, threw her back. "It must be awfully hard on you," she began, marshaling her sympathies. Forcing himself to look at her, Tom noticed her neck, as pale and plump as a root.

"Why, what's the matter, dear? Did I say something wrong?"

Horrified by his wish—for her neck, after all, would hardly resist him, it would snap as crisply as a stalk of celery—he managed to excuse himself and got up from the table. He had not realized how close he was to rage, and as he stumbled out of the room, he remembered Catherine. He had resisted her all this time. Now he wondered how *her* neck would have felt, if he had tried to punish her.

In the hall, which was papered with some velvety substance, a hidden loudspeaker was piping. "This Can't Be Love."

He went upstairs. The renovation stopped, like an exhausted wave, at the top of the stairs. The second-floor hall was entirely bare. The floorboards, scraped to the nub, was nearly white, and the doors to the bedrooms were green and pink, unchanged since the days when the inn served as a disreputable tavern. A bare light bulb hung at the end of the hall. Going towards it, Tom saw another narrow flight of wooden stairs, and he started up it.

At the top, the attic, which had once been a country ballroom, extended from one end of the building to the other. It was an enormous space, scoured by light from the dormer windows.

The room's dusty smell seemed threatening, unclean; Tom's mother, with the same distaste, would have dubbed it "The smell of the ages." He imagined that servant girls and starving slaves had slept here in the old days, on musty cornhusk mattresses. Clenching his hands, he thought that here, in the cold filth of a hundred years of human poverty, here, on the bare floor between the tiny parcels of mice droppings, he would have been able to force Catherine down and force himself into her. She might have screamed then, or cried, but he would have made her endure, branding her with his revulsion as he had never been able to mark her with his love.

He crossed to the window and looked out at the street. The few trees were bare, and he could see stolid frame houses standing shoulder to shoulder inside their narrow yards. At the edge of town a big shopping center flashed its signs, higher than the trees, higher than the courthouse pinnacle.

All changed, all gone, Tom thought, as though he could have found his place, his strength, in the parched farming village of fifty years before.

All changes were his father's; all new ways were devised to fit his needs. The new highways were his, built to speed his flight from place to place; the new buildings were his monuments. He swam as easily through the intersecting rings of the new developments and the highways as once,

Tom thought, he must have swum through the lukewarm shallows of the French Broad; swam effortlessly, too, through the sessions in Frankfort, where, compared to the real-estate dealers and the used-car men, he would seem as genteel as a block of native granite, although in fact, Tom knew, he was a swimmer with the best of them, a finned and scaled replica of some swift monster of the deep, nosing out his prey on these Midwestern plains. . . . He would never fail. He would never lie stranded on the bare wood floor of a country attic.

Someone crashed up the stairs, and Tom heard a stumble, a heavy fall, and then coughing and strangling.

He turned around. Wright Stillman was crouched against the wall at the top of the stairs. He was holding his head with his hands. His face contorted, and a grinding noise began in his throat. He bent to the floor. Then a clogged whine, inhuman, piercing, began to flow from his mouth.

Tom went to him, bent down, and looked at his twisted face.

Wright's eyes were bulging. He seemed blind. His hand flapped at Tom's arm.

Tom asked, "What's the matter with you?"

Then he saw Wright's hand gesturing towards his throat.

He caught him by the arm and with his other hand struck him hard, two or three times, across the back.

A gobbet of meat shot from Wright's throat. He vomited, gasping, and wiped at his face.

Tom stepped back from the vomit. Sobbing, wiping his face, Wright leaned against the wall.

"What's the matter with you? You choked, didn't you?" Tom asked brusquely.

"That's it, that's what happened," Wright moaned. "You

hit the nail on the head that time, Tom!" He wiped at his face again, then stared at his hands. "I saw you go," he gasped. "I wanted to get away, too. I went into the other room. You know they were having steak?" He laughed, raspingly. "I hate turkey, I always have, Mother knows that. I never have eaten turkey in my life." Beginning again to sob, he turned away.

Maddened by Wright's tears, Tom slapped his shoulder with the flat of his hand. "What's the matter with you?"

"Why—" Wright looked at him, his face smeared with tears, like a child's. "Don't you know? Didn't they tell you?"

"No!" In his revulsion, Tom almost shouted.

"Why, I want to die," Wright said simply.

"Why in hell do you want to do that?" Tom clenched his hands.

"I can't tell you that," Wright said. He was suddenly calm.

"They care about you, don't they? Your mother would do anything for you, I know that. They'd all do anything for you."

"What do you know about it?" Wright asked. "You never have been through anything like what I've been through. You've always lived in a hole."

"Well, I manage. I'm not lying around in a hospital."

"You're hardly alive," Wright said, prissily.

"I keep on moving!" Tom shouted. "I don't just lie down and give up, anyway! I don't keep trying to die and not even do it. Trying and quitting, trying and quitting! I believe it's your way of getting attention!"

"I'll make it one day," Wright said. "Like Paul did. That wasn't his first try."

"Paul fell."

"That's what they say."

"He fell."

"Well, all I know is, I had to call your father, the first time it happened. Paul was over at my place, and I had no way of knowing what he was on. . . . It was a close call, they had to take him straight to Emergency. Your father never would speak to me after that." He grinned. "He thought it was my fault, something I gave him."

"That has nothing to do—"

"I saw him in a fight the night before, at Harry's. You know, that place on Fourth Street. Or maybe you don't know. I keep forgetting how you live in a hole. Well, we've opened up down here, Tom. We've decided to let loose all our pre-versions." He smiled, touching his throat with the tips of his fingers. "So Harry's is where we all go. All of us who didn't make it to college or somehow gave up after a while. All of us who have our special problems. It's a good place, Harry's, but it's a rough neighborhood, and you have to know your way around. I believe that was Paul's first time there," he added thoughtfully. "Or at least I'd never seen him there before, and I go pretty regularly. It's not the kind of place Paul would have liked to be seen in; he tried to keep things proper. No, I don't believe he'd ever been in Harry's before."

"Why are you telling me lies?"

"They're not lies. It's time for you to see what goes on around you, Tom. You want to make some kind of martyr out of your baby brother so you won't have to know what really happened. You want to go all misty-eyed like your Mama every time his name is said."

"Paul fell out of a tree."

"He was drinking and doping, that's what he was doing."

Tom dropped his hands onto Wright's shoulders and began to push him down to the floor.

"Let go of me," Wright hissed, prying at Tom's fingers.

Knocking him off balance with his knee, Tom threw him down heavily and fell on top of him, grinding against him, crushing him into the floor.

Wright's hands flapped against Tom's back. "Hey, Tom, hey . . ."

Tom tore himself away.

The stairs received him and sped him on, the long bare hall raced past, and he did not hear the sound of his own feet as he took the last flight and careened across the front hall to the door. The door resisted him. A colored man with a smile on his face stepped forward to help him. "House afire?" he asked obligingly. The door snapped back and Tom was out, stumbling down the steps, half falling, then catching himself and darting towards the street. "That boy sure can run," the man croaked behind him.

He heard the soles of his shoes slapping the tarmac. The wind was in his face, and he opened his mouth to suck it in, chilling his teeth and drying his tongue as he ran towards the highway.

Later he heard the sound of a car, slowing down, just behind him as he dog-trotted along the shoulder of the road. He did not turn his head. His father's car purred five feet behind him, neither gaining nor losing ground. Tom ran for another hundred feet and then suddenly stopped. His chest was aching, and the raw air burned his throat. He stood looking across the road at a field full of withered corn.

The car pulled up beside him, and his father spoke through the window. "Get in."

Tom opened the door and climbed into the front seat.

Pressing his foot down delicately on the accelerator, his father drove slowly along the highway.

Tom clamped his hands on his knees. It seemed to him that he had never been alone with his father before. Certainly he had never felt the heavy silence that wrapped them together. He knew that he could savage it with a few words. He began to pant like a dog.

"What's the matter with you?" Big Tom asked sharply. "Are you sick?"

"Not sick. No."

His father looked at him. "I can't understand the way you act. You sat there all through lunch like a suffering martyr. I saw you, I was watching you. Not a word, not a bite of food. Not even an effort with Mrs. Dawes, who's always been so fond of you. And then going out before anybody else, and then running out on the road. That colored boy came to tell me, he had sense enough to know something was wrong. I had to tell everybody you were taking a walk." He glared at Tom. "I can't understand you. Nobody can understand you. You don't even bother to talk, you just expect us somehow to catch on. Even your mother tells me she doesn't know what's going on with you. Look, Tom, if there's something wrong"—he tried to control his irritation—"tell us what it is. At least let us try to do something about it." With one hand he whipped a handkerchief out of his pocket, and pressed it against his mouth, clearing his throat with a wrenching sound. "We can't do anything to help you if you won't let us know what's wrong."

"Nothing's wrong," Tom said. He wanted to begin to repeat "Paul jumped, Paul jumped," and continue to repeat it hour after hour.

"You've always done well in school," his father went on. "College shouldn't be a problem for you. You're smart, well organized, mature in your way—you should breeze through.

Lonely, maybe; well, everybody's lonely at first. That's nothing. Your mother wants to make a big deal out of that. Besides, you said you've already made some friends."

"My roommate."

"Why, yes. Well, you've made a start, at least; you're off on your own. Your mother says you're depressed, but I don't believe that. She's the one who's depressed. She's got every right to be. She's all alone now. We're going to Mexico after Christmas, she'll enjoy that, she always has loved to travel. But you—you're off on your own, you've made a good start. 'Depressed'!" He made a bubbling sound with his lips. "All you need is self-confidence."

Tom was suddenly very sleepy. He was overwhelmed by the need to close his eyes. His head buzzed, and his ears burned from the cold. He leaned back against the seat.

"There is one thing I can do for you," his father was saying. "I can get you an invitation to Harold and Jean's dinner party tomorrow. They didn't know you'd be home. All your old friends will be there—Bo, Brian . . ." He racked his memory. "All the ones you knew in school. And there're some new girls in town. I've seen them in church, a little blonde from Connecticut, her father's with the bank . . ."

Tom heard one word out of every four or five.

"You'll have a good time," his father went on earnestly, glancing at Tom from time to time. "You need a chance to enjoy yourself. By Monday you'll be raring to go back."

"I'm not," Tom said, through his buzzing weariness. "Going back," he added.

His father raised his hand. "Now, that's what I mean. You're worn out, discouraged, you've probably been working too hard. Three days here and you'll feel entirely different."

"No."

His father looked at him. "Don't you begin that. That talk. I know better than to listen to that. You talk the way your mother does, to get attention. That doesn't work with me." His voice was rough, panic-stricken; he thrust his face close to Tom's. "Don't make the mistake of thinking you can just do any damn fool thing you want. I'm not going to make that mistake again. Paul started that way, he started talking about coming home from school, and he got your mother on his side. She said he wasn't well. 'Well'!" He laughed. "The last thing he needed was more of her care."

"I don't want to hear," Tom said dully.

"I don't care whether or not you want to hear. I'm not going to let you get away with any more of that foolishness. You never would listen to me, neither one of you would. You were always hanging on to your mother. Or to Bessie, I should say. You'd listen to her when you wouldn't even look at me. You acted like I wasn't there. I was always on the go; that's the way it is with fathers. When I tried to lay aside some time for you, or for Paul, it didn't mean a thing. It was a nuisance, a big bore. I remember one time I asked you to ride up to Frankfort with me; I thought it would be a treat for you. You insisted on sitting in front, next to Amos; you wouldn't even talk to me. You insisted on talking to him the whole time. I let it pass, I didn't make an issue out of it. But what was I supposed to think of that? What was I supposed to do? Your mother keeps telling me I've done too much, she keeps saying it's too much for you boys to live up to. So what was I supposed to do? Stay a hick lawyer, so you boys could grow up?" He seemed to be pleading. "Your mother wouldn't have cared for that, she wouldn't have wanted to limit herself. You haven't said anything to her about not going back to college, have you?"

"No."

"Because it would break her heart. Just break her heart. She might act like she was glad to have you home, but in fact she'd be heartbroken. She went through that with Paul, you can't expect her to start all over. . . . She's awake at four every morning. Tossing and turning. She starts worrying, you know, thinking about things we could have done. Ways we could have acted. Water under the bridge, I tell her. That's brutal, but it's true. Water under the bridge. Then I get her her pills."

"Paul jumped," Tom said.

Calmly, his father replied, "Oh, they've said that, too. I heard it from the start. Slander. Plain slander. You have to expect it when you're in the public eye."

Tom put out his hand and opened the car door. One thought, like a grain of sand, irritated his murky fatigue.

His father stepped on the brakes. "Where are you going?"

Tom got out and closed the door. "To the airport," he said, thinking of Louise's handwriting on the front of a blue envelope.

"Have you lost your mind?"

"I'll hitch a ride." He walked in front of the car.

His father, hunching forward, peered at him through the windshield. "Get back in here, you damn fool."

Tom did not answer. He stood with his right arm rigidly extended towards the traffic, his thumb in the air.

Time passed. The engine of his father's car idled close to Tom's knees.

"What's the matter with you?" his father shouted at last.

A green pickup truck, patched with dried mud, coasted to a stop twenty feet beyond Tom. He turned and began to run towards it.

Behind him, his father pressed the horn.

A farmer with a two-day beard glanced at Tom as he climbed into the front seat. Behind them, the horn blared again.

"Friend of yours?" the farmer asked.

"No," Tom said.

Chapter Fourteen

Driving again; here I go, Louise thought on her way to her car, with the old mixture of panic and glee. She relished, as she went, the memory of the sly way she'd learned to drive, during the last year of her father's life. Every Tuesday she'd slipped out of the house and taken the bus into town to have her lesson. Finally, when she got her license, she'd announced it to her father, expecting a storm. Instead he had said mildly, "You might as well learn to drive, you'll never have a man to take you around," and she had shrilled, "Why, Papa!" He had been mean, that last year.

At the front door she stopped to pour more seed into the bird feeder. A chickadee, glossy and impudent, watched her from the maze of the bare forsythia. "Cheeky," she said, admiring his nerve, and dropped a handful of seed on the ground. Looking back, she saw him swoop down to the feast.

A blue day, clear and cold: beyond the valley, the faint edges of the mountains scalloped the sky. Standing beside the car, Louise could not see the town in the valley or the net of highways that was tightening around her hill or the big cement plant that had taken the place of the park on the French Broad River where they had always gone for a picnic on the Fourth of July. Her hill and her house hung suspended above change, as long as she did not move forward and see the real view. From here it was the same prospect that her mother had seen on her wedding day, with the spire of the church where she had been married pricking through the trees.

Louise pulled on her driving gloves and got into the car. As she went down the drive she saw Tish Loman, the old handyman, plowing along on his flat feet. He carried his shotgun carelessly across the crook of his arm.

Louise stopped the car. "Good morning, Tish."

Too deaf to have heard the car approaching, he started at the sound of her voice and turned his bleached face.

"No more windows now, Tish. I'm not going to put up with it. I thought Herman told you to be more careful with that gun."

"Just looking for a rabbit, Miss Louise," he mumbled. Leaning close to the car, he peered at his old employer's daughter. "Weren't me shot out those windows."

"Never mind that now. I don't have time to listen. Make sure you don't go anywhere near the big house. I did see a rabbit last night, down by the east barracks," she admitted. Then she drove on towards the gate.

"Oh, they are malevolent!" her mother had exclaimed about Tish and his kind, after all her chickens were discovered torn up and thrown like bloody feather dusters around the yard. "Trash; what can you expect?" she had added bitterly. Louise tried to explain that dogs had killed the chickens, but it was all one to her mother: dogs reflected the personalities of their masters, she believed. "Give me a nigger anyday," her mother declared. "At least I know how to deal with them."

The rumbling dislike between her parents had burst into a full-scale storm on that note, the pride of the Tidewater farmer's daughter clashing with the stubborn morality of the old schoolteacher, who hated what he called "Southern truck" and the moonlight and roses of the antebellum myth. "You need to understand these people," he had told his wife. "You're going to be living with them the rest of your life."

Louise had listened calmly, sorting the truth from the lies as rapidly as she sorted the colored threads for her sampler, but Shelby had often chosen those times to throw a fit. Later, calmed down and propped up in her bed, she would begin to giggle, pressing her hand to her mouth.

Their mother, dying alone in her room, with a thermometer and a glass of water on the bedside table, had told Louise (who had not wanted to listen), "He never cared a thing about me. Even at the start, he hardly could make the effort. Not a bad man, but he wanted sons."

Then who had provided the love? Louise had wondered, but by then it was too late to ask. Her parents were both dead, and she was cleaning out the big maple rolltop desk they had somehow managed to share. She had found the shoe box of letters then, but they had not seemed worth reading: old recriminations, faded explanations that could not have been very effective even in their own time. Later, of course, she had realized how useful they could be. At the time of her father's death, though, she was more interested in the drawerful of screwed-up bits of paper, the orders he had dropped every morning on the kitchen table for her mother: "Get Clyde to see to the pump"; "Tell Tish he can't have any more of my kindling"; "Somebody has got to weed the peas." Her mother had obeyed the orders, and then she had saved them, as though they took the place of the love letters she had never received. Louise, too, had tried to take the bits of paper as proof that something had existed between her parents, a powerful bond, a partnership—forged out of hatred, perhaps, but proof against loneliness.

Otherwise, with nothing, Louise still didn't see how people survived, how they managed to get up in the morning.

Big Tom seemed to have found the answer. When she sat at his table in Kentucky and unfolded the linen napkin, the folds always cool, winter or summer, and took a sip of wine from the thin-edged crystal glass, it seemed clear, it seemed obvious, even, what his answer was. "Of course, that's it," she would say to herself, looking around at their calm neutral faces, as alike as pennies, uninscribed by pain. Everything seemed to happen by magic: their food was cooked, their clothes arrived in the mail, their feelings were neat and appropriate to the occasion, as if they, too, had been ordered. No pain, no hysterical crying, even at funerals: she remembered how white and lilylike Mugsie had been when Paul was buried. *Resigned.* Was that the word? No, it was something almost sublime: they knew themselves to be above destruction. She admired that, she loved that with a passion, as she had loved the plaster copy of the Italian Apollo in the Kentucky art museum.

Later, when she tried to remember what it was she had understood, what it was she had loved, it seemed to be only that they had a great deal of money; but that was not it, that was not all, she knew.

She reached the turnoff for Sand Hill Road and the church, and a pinch of excitement, sharp as red pepper, made her draw her breath in sharply. She drove up to the church and sprang out of the car with the vigorous, nearly violent energy that had made her father call her "strong as a posthole digger." She darted into the church, and then, flustered by her own vitality, she paused, smoothing her face with her fingertips and peering into the gloom.

Her mother's memorial window was flashing greens and blues. She gazed at the white figure with the lilies. It had never been clear to her whether it was meant to be a picture of her mother or of the angel who had taken her away. In any event, the figure was beautiful and scarcely sad.

Hastening down the aisle, Louise saw Mary-Ann kneeling in a pew. She slipped in beside her and dropped down on the wooden kneeler. The loud thump resounded in the nave, and Mary-Ann looked startled; she put a finger to her lips and, with a crafty movement, shoved a bulging paper sack towards Louise. "Not a word," she hissed, and then she glanced around the empty church. Louise patted her wrist, seized the bag, and stood up. She was out in the sunlight again and locked in her car in less than two minutes.

No time to spare, she thought with the same peppery excitement as she drove through the slanting streets to reach the highway. Dingy clapboard houses with double-decker verandas screened the view of the mountains. She drove down Catalpa Street and saw that the Hendersons' old carriage house had finally been pulled down by kudzu vine. Then she turned onto the highway.

Now and then she reached across to pat the bulging paper

bag. It sat solidly on the seat beside her, chock-full, its open top revealing a tongue of black material.

Driving, looking at the bag, Louise began to chuckle; then she sang a snatch of a tune and clapped one hand lightly on the steering wheel. It was suddenly clear to her that nothing else would matter once she had Shelby home. Nothing would ever be able to bother her again. The roof could cave in; they'd abandon the place and go to live at the Sunset View Motel. Two ladies together. Or Big Tom might stop sending the monthly checks, to punish her. Well, what would it matter? They could go and stand in line for welfare; they could start a garden. It would be like the old days. They would weed together, and she would make Shelby wear Mama's straw sunhat; they would put up rhubarb and tomatoes in the kitchen at night.

Finally, they might be entirely alone. Big Tom might use this escapade as an excuse to make a final break. "And the train is so filthy!" Mugsie would say. Well, and then? She'd take Shelby to Herman's store for company, and they'd sit on the upturned crates and talk about the days when every adult in Elizaville had worked for the school. Why, yes. Why, surely. They could come at her with fire and havoc, rainstorms, desolation, but she would be beyond their reach. With Shelby, big as a cow, fixing a scene for both of them, a foaming fit, whenever things got too dull. Shelby like a white turnip in the bathtub, hollering for Louise to scrub her back, Shelby with her head in her plate, sucking up spaghetti, Shelby holding up her foot for Louise to tie her shoe, Shelby padding in, in the middle of the night, to crowd into Louise's bed.

Speaking out loud, in the pearly light and silence, Louise began to string the old phrases together gleefully.

"Why, you can't!"

"Simply unbelievable."

"The sheer sacrifice!"

"All her life with a human vegetable."

She shaped her long, mobile face into the acquired expressions of outrage and dislike.

"All her life."

She laughed and turned off the highway. After driving fast to the hospital parking lot, she left the car and went towards the outside stairs, carrying the brown paper bag in her arms.

She started up the stairs, not hurrying but marching steadily until she was out of breath and had to stop and look at the hills, lavender this time of year, their outlines smudged. Why, they never have meant anything to me at all, she thought, discarding the piety. Hateful things! She remembered her father's standing on the hill with his hands clasped behind his back, admiring the view; Big Tom, too, was always transfixed by the mountains. Why, they're just plain hills, she thought triumphantly. We'll get a back room at the Sunset View and be shet of them at last.

She climbed another flight and knocked at the locked door. Through the grilled window she saw a disorderly procession of patients herding down the ward, some of them purposeful, hurrying along, one woman nearly running, her arms spread out as if she might fly. Two other women shuffled side by side, sharing a green sweater. Louise knocked again. She had never seen the ward in so much motion; only one patient, a young girl, was sitting on the floor with her face pressed against her knees.

At last the familiar nurse, flushed, coarse, oxlike, came and put her face to the glass. Then, with pursed lips, she unlocked the door. "Bright and early as always!" she said.

"Did you bring her more candy? Doctor won't be pleased. She's commenced to gain again."

"Where is she?"

The nurse was locking the door behind her. "Honey, it's Thanksgiving, I'm all alone here, Dolores has the flu. And they're carrying on something awful today, up and down and everywhere, it must be the weather. Last time I saw her she was sitting on the john."

Louise started off in that direction. The bathroom was empty except for a large woman who was swabbing a sink with a bit of rag. The stench, corrosive, ammoniac, made Louise hurry away. She remembered how Shelby had always kept sticks of incense on the pink commode at home, calling Louise in to light them: "Eau de Pine."

She joined the procession of patients and walked towards the far end of the ward. Glancing at the women on either side, she tried to imagine them combed and washed, restored to the appearance, at least, of normality. They did not seem to notice her or care that she was among them, and with a subdued chuckle she remembered her mother wading through her chicken yard, surrounded by the rustling, bickering Rhode Island Reds.

When they got to the end, she watched the other women turn and drift off; the procession had lost its drive. One frail elderly woman hesitantly touched the wall, then jerked her hand back. As she moved on, Louise saw Shelby sitting on the floor in the alcove with another woman. They were both huddling over their arms; their knees were drawn up, and Louise could see Shelby's pink underpants.

"Sister!" she cried, and leaned down to kiss her, at the same time pulling Shelby's skirt down over her knees.

Shelby drew her lips back, baring her teeth, and spat.

"Why, Sister," Louise gasped, wiping the saliva off her

cheek. Shelby stared at her moodily; then, hitching her knees up higher, she turned to look at the other woman. After a while she smiled and reached out to touch her arm. The woman was nearly as fat as Shelby, though younger; her round calves bulged over pink angora socks, and she cradled a patent leather purse in her arms. Her hair curled tightly around her face, which was fixed like a searchlight on Shelby's. When Shelby touched her, the woman slowly released her purse and with a careful, almost trembling movement, took Shelby's hand.

Louise stared. She felt something rise in her throat, rage and tears combined. For a moment she did not know what she was going to do. Then she looked more closely at Shelby's friend. She had pierced ears with gold hoops in them—a gypsy, a wild woman. Her smile was as sickly sweet as a taffy apple, and her teeth were bad.

Louise crouched down in front of them and began to speak, distinctly, to get Shelby's attention. "I want you to listen to me now, Sister. This is important." The other woman rubbed her thumb across the back of Shelby's hand. "Now listen to me, please. We don't have all the time in the world. I haven't come here today to fool, Shelby, I've come to take you home." She waited. Shelby did not look at her; she was watching the other woman's thumb trace the back of her hand. "I've got the plan all made, and it's a good one," Louise went on. "I've got something in this bag you can wear so those fools won't stop us." She pushed the bag towards Shelby, who glanced at it.

"Candy?" Shelby asked languidly.

"No, not candy this time, Shelby. We'll have plenty of that when we get home. This is something for you to wear, something I brought for you."

Shelby looked away. Slowly her eyes returned to the

woman sitting beside her, and the same smirk of satisfied
affection moved across her face. Then, slowly and languidly,
she reached out and took hold of the other woman's breast,
pressing the nipple between her thumb and forefinger.

Louise did not try to stop her. Instead she seized Shelby's
chin and turned her face. "I've got you a whole box at
home," she whispered. "Barton's Autumn Gold. Two
pounds, three layers." Shelby stared at her sister. "The top
layer is plain sweet chocolate, solid. Some of it is wrapped up
in gold paper. Underneath is the fruit-filled. There are
cherries—your favorites. The bottom layer is the nut clusters."

She stood up and grasped Shelby's arm and began to hoist
her up. The other woman fell away like an empty sack. "At
the bottom are those peanut balls with the marshmallow
insides; I counted eight of them. You know how you like the
cashews, the chocolate-covered ones. I counted nine." She
had Shelby on her feet now. Putting her arm around her
waist, she started her towards the bathroom. "It even has
that picture inside the lid so you can tell from the shapes
what the fillings are." They were at the bathroom door.

"What do you want in there?" the nurse called, hurrying
by with a tray of plastic medicine cups.

"My sister has diarrhea," Louise said haughtily.

The nurse hurried on.

"Then, of course, there's the marzipan." After checking to
make sure it was empty, she guided Shelby into the bathroom, propelling her to the far corner, by the sinks. Still
talking, she bent down and pulled the black habit out of the
bag. It was intricately hooked and zippered, and Shelby
began to shift from one foot to the other while Louise tore
at the fastenings. Finally she got the thing open and pulled
it over Shelby's head, forcing her arms into the narrow

sleeves. It wouldn't fasten up the back, but nothing could be done about that, she decided. She placed the large white coif, its wings crumpled and slightly soiled, on top of Shelby's short hair. "There're some of those almonds, too, the nice fat ones with the chocolate outsides. Now stay there, don't move an inch," she whispered savagely, and darted to the bathroom door.

The nurse was unlocking the door to the stairs for a man who had his arms full of laundry.

Louise tore open her purse. Pulling out her wallet, she snapped it open, upended it, and poured a shower of change onto the ward floor.

An old woman in a pink bathrobe crouched down and began to gather up the coins.

With a little cry, another woman swooped down, followed by two more. The first woman began to scream, piercingly.

The nurse rushed over.

Louise looked at the outside door. It was still open; the orderly was setting down his stack of laundry.

In one step Louise seized her sister's arm and began to propel her past the squabbling women. "Caramel centers," Louise said. "Dates with coconut covers. Brandy creams."

They reached the door as the orderly turned back to close it. Louise pushed him aside. "Just passing through," she said, tightening her grasp on Shelby's arm. "Sister has to get back." They swept through, and the man closed the door behind them.

As Louise bundled her down the iron steps, Shelby began to moan. "Hold on to the railing, or you'll give us both a fall," Louise warned. But Shelby was moaning loudly now, a windy sound, infuriating. "Modjeskas," Louise said, although she knew they were never included in an assortment. "Bourbon beauties! And I won't set any limit this time, it won't be three a day; it won't even have to be after meals."

The moaning stopped, and Shelby floated, almost free, down the remaining stairs.

Chapter Fifteen

In the glassed-in porch, the hanging ferns were swaying and dripping. Louise had just gone around with the long-nosed zinc watering can. Tom, sitting in his great-aunt's horsehair armchair, watched her closely. "I don't know why you do it that way. There must be another way to do it so they won't drip," he said.

Louise smiled. "If there is another way, I have yet to discover it."

"But the floor is being ruined."

"Has been ruined already. Was already ruined when I was a little girl. Mama used to water the ferns with this same can, and I used to sit there and criticize, just the way you're doing."

She put down the can and stood with her hands on her hips, gazing at the largest fern. After a while she reached out and stopped its swaying. Then she wiped her hand slowly across her apron. "It's not that I believe the old way's best, or even the only way. I never have learned anything else."

"Don't you want to get away from here?" Tom asked.

She considered. "I counted once. It came to forty-one days somewhere else. Mostly in Kentucky," she added.

"Father said that was why he put Shelby in. He said you wanted to go to Florida."

She shrugged, studying the fern.

"At least that's what he told me," Tom said. He was still speaking cautiously, feeling the edges of the words. After a week of eating, sitting, walking, driving, and occasionally talking with Louise, he was beginning to get the hang of it. Half of what he said sank into her silence; hours later she would give him her response. The other half seemed to clear the top of her head and float off into the far distance— anything that he told her about college, for instance. When he had tried to describe Catherine to her, Louise had said, with a vagueness that he had already learned was not vague in intent at all, "Well, times have changed. Times have certainly changed. When I was nineteen, I wasn't allowed to walk around the parade ground with a boy. Never even thought of it or wanted to, as far as I can remember."

One day she had launched into a description of what it had been like to grow up in the old school. Tom was surprised because he had never heard her talk about herself before. Something was hidden there that might be helpful to him, he knew, but he was too restless to listen carefully. He ate five baking-powder biscuits, loaded with butter and honey, before she was finished.

Finally he had realized, from her smile, that she had intended only to shut him up. There were sections of his life that she simply refused to acknowledge. "I'm no safe harbor," she had warned him the first evening. She had rushed to the airport to meet him, Thanksgiving night, responding fast to his telephone call, but she had been as shocked as his mother would have been that he had made the trip without a suitcase.

"He may have told you I wanted to go to Florida," Louise said now. "He may even have believed it, too, and still he may have had something else entirely in mind." She sat down in her rocker and took her knitting out of its basket. She was trying to finish the last sleeve of a pink sweater for Shelby, but she was an inexpert knitter and spent most evenings unraveling the day's dropped stitches. "One thing you never have understood about your father: he never tells lies."

Before Tom could protest, she went on, "He has this way, has always had it, of holding two separate things in his mind at once. They may have no connection at all, or they may contradict each other. But he believes both of them. You have to find out what both of them are before you know what he feels about anything. One simple answer just isn't his way." She seemed proud of her conclusion, and Tom saw that she had learned never to be disappointed by his father's changes. "Why, I remember the first time Shelby was in, your daddy himself told me we ought to get her out. He told me it wasn't a fit place, though how he knew . . . He's never been there to this day. Then when I went to Dr. Harris for the papers, he told me your daddy had called and said under no condition was he to sign to get her out. I was fit to be tied. When I called him on the telephone, there was simply no way to fight him. No way at all." She smiled, stroking the heavy pink yarn, her face luminous and remote. "Oh, I tried to fight him, I screamed and yelled, I even ended up crying over the telephone, which was one thing I never had done. I felt like dirt about that afterward. He told me that he felt it was too great a burden for me to take care of Shelby. He said he's seen it in my eyes when he brought up the subject of getting her out. How was I going to tell him what he had or hadn't seen in my eyes? He's always been so *bright*. That's your daddy for you," she said affectionately.

The door to the living room was shoved open, and Shelby came out onto the porch. She hurried past Louise, her eyes on the floor, her hands intently working themselves into white cotton gloves. A large leather bag was pressed under her arm, and she was wearing what Tom had come to think of as her traveling clothes. Her slippers slapped across the floor, and she went out the door and hurried across the gravel to the car.

"There she goes," Tom said.

Louise did not look up from her knitting. She was slipping a heavy loop from one needle to the other. "Why, yes," she said.

"Yesterday she sat in that car for four hours."

"Yes, well." Louise sighed, sliding the stitch down the needle. "She always did like riding in cars."

Tom stood up, crossed to the door, and stood looking out at the car. In the front seat, Shelby was sitting bolt upright, staring straight ahead. She looked as fixed and serene as a monument, but Tom knew that if he went out he would see tears on her cheeks. Putting his hands in his pockets, he rocked back and forth, wondering why he felt tempted to whistle. He had been close to tunes for the last three days, ever since he found himself actually humming when he was loading the garbage into the car for the weekly trip to the dump.

"Shelby's crying out there," he told Louise.

She sighed again, lightly. "Yes."

"I believe she wants to go back to that place."

"Yes, I believe she does."

It was a statement of fact, nothing more. Tom rocked and watched Shelby's profile. He was tempted to plunge in, demand, ask questions that Louise would be forced to answer. But his curiosity was diluted; he was willing to wait for an answer, even to acknowledge that there might never be any answer at all.

As though gratified by his patience, Louise said, "I want her here with me. I want Sister here with me." It sounded soft and firm, like a closing door.

"Yeah," Tom said, "but she doesn't like it."

"Oh, she gets these ideas, it helps her to pass the time. Now she's gotten the idea she wants to go back out there. I believe it's mainly the car ride she wants."

"She told me she loves somebody out there," Tom said.

"When did she say that?"

"Yesterday, when she was in her garden. She was out there looking at the dead squash; she had one in her hands that was two feet long. She saw me coming and screwed her face up and had tears in her eyes by the time I was close enough to see. 'Gladys, Gladys,' she said. 'Gladys, Gladys, Gladys.' She kept saying it and patting that squash. I asked her finally what in the world was the matter. 'Why, they've taken her away, my darling Nellie Grey,' she said, and then she really started to carry on. I had to hold the squash for her while she just stood there and cried."

Louise said, judiciously, "Don't go out in the garden, next time you see her there. That's her private place. If she wants to carry on, that's the place she's been taught to go."

"Has she told you about Gladys?"

Louise looked at him sharply. "Young man, I saw Gladys."

"I wasn't sure she was real."

"She's as real as a car or a dog or a bird, even. Last spring a barn swallow got into Shelby's room and she wouldn't let me drive it out; she sat there for hours, watching it and singing to it and holding out her hands. There's always something for Shelby, or somebody; that's where she's lucky."

"I guess she misses Gladys."

"Oh, she'll get over that. She'll have the memory, though, and that's what counts."

"How do you know that?"

"I don't know it," Louise said.

She had a way of bringing things to an end which Tom didn't think of disputing. Still, he felt concerned about Shelby, and he said, "Why don't we take her for a drive, if that's what she wants?"

"I'll have to get back in time to start those chicken croquettes for lunch. All right." She stuffed her knitting into the basket. "If you'll let me drive."

Tom had hurt her feelings by insisting on driving the first few days. He had thought it was the only thing he could contribute, and it had taken him awhile to notice her pressed lips and her silence, in the car. Now he bowed to her with a gallantry that was not ironic. Responding to his courtesy, she swept past his toes with a flick of her old gray skirt that amazed him. Parched and dim as she was, she still retained, at times, the powerful magnetism of a beautiful girl. Glancing back over her shoulder, she smiled at him, and he wondered how he had been lucky enough to find her.

"Why did you write me those letters?" he asked when she was putting on her coat.

"Why, I don't know for sure," she said slowly.

"You never had written anything before."

"Up till then it wouldn't have been worth it. I mean, there was no point in writing you more blather, you didn't need that. There was no use in writing you about the cardinals around the feeder."

"No."

She climbed into the driver's seat and reached across to pat Shelby's arm. "All right, Sister, we're going to take you for a drive." Shelby did not respond.

Tom climbed into the backseat. "Why did you do it?" he asked.

She started the car with a jerk, and they crawled slowly down the drive. Shelby turned her head to watch her garden as it passed. Louise said, "Now, I don't know if I can tell you so you'll understand. When you were here in September, when they took Shelby away, I thought you were sorry. That's the first time I knew anything could bother you—I mean, anything that was not to do with yourself. I thought you were bothered when we were eating lunch at the hotel that day. Then later, when we talked, you didn't seem to understand, and I knew there wasn't a thing in the world you could do to help me. So I guess I wrote those letters in a fit of spite. The first ones, anyway."

"I didn't like them."

"That's neither here nor there. I enjoyed writing them. I enjoyed dropping a pebble in your little pool."

"I remember the first one. The one about your mother."

"I was trying to tell you the truth."

"She drowned herself."

"Right here in the French Broad River."

Tom looked down the bluff and saw the narrow, muddy stream. "It doesn't look like enough water."

"Where there's a will there's a way. Nobody would say, for a long time, what had happened. Nobody would admit that was what it was. I knew if I died without telling somebody, nobody would ever know the truth. So I told you. It means something to me to keep the past the way it was."

"I hated that letter."

"I didn't write it to please you."

"I hated the one about Paul, too."

She looked at him with some kindness. "That's the way it was, Tom."

"That's not the way they told me."

"Well, your mother had to change it. She felt like it was all her fault. That was the first thing she said after it happened. So your father, to spare her, said it had been an accident. That's the way the past gets changed, mostly," she added. "People blame themselves."

"It was Mother's fault," Tom said. "Her fault and mine."

Louise struck the steering wheel lightly with her palm. "Now, that's what I can't stand. It's pride, nothing but pride. How you two can believe that somebody like Paul, somebody who had so many different things in him, could be driven to jump out of a tree by anything you said or did . . ." She shook her head. "Why, you couldn't have made him buy firecrackers on the Fourth of July."

"I used to make him feel like dirt. I used to tell him he was dumb. He was dumb, too," Tom said.

"Listen, the best way to know nothing is to think that way. I used to think I made Shelby the way she is by letting her fall downstairs when she was a baby. I used to think it was me who'd rearranged her brain. It's taken me all this time to realize I had nothing to do with it. Shelby's like a million pieces of broken glass, arranging and rearranging themselves according to some rule of their own. About all I can do is throw shade on them when I make her get dressed in the morning." She looked across at her dozing sister. "Shelby's herself," she said.

"Paul didn't get that way by himself. He was locking himself up in his room last Christmas. He was staying twenty-four hours at a time in his room. He didn't get that way in a vacuum."

"That part was built into him, the way his blond hair was. I saw it when he was little. He had some weak part in him, some connection that would break if too much weight was put on it. That's the reason he was such a cute little fellow. It always seemed like he wouldn't last."

"Louise!"

She looked at him. "I can't afford too many tears."

"I can't forget him," Tom said gloomily.

"The truth is, you've already forgotten him. You forgot him the day of the funeral, when you started to blame yourself. That's all you've been thinking about."

"I've got to live," he said grumpily.

"There's only one way to live, Tom, and that's to get out."

"I did get out. I went to college."

"And came home last summer like a sick dog and came home again a week ago. What are you after, Tom?"

"I have this feeling like I'm being starved," he said slowly. "When I'm up there in my room trying to study, I have this feeling like there's a hole in my stomach."

"Too late," she said.

"I can't believe that."

Louise sighed. "Your mother never did like babies. If she could have, she'd have said they made her sick to her stomach. She couldn't say that, so she had to act like she loved you two all to pieces. That made things confusing. And then that old Bessie"—she laughed—"why, she never liked anything except babies."

"She told me she'd quit if I came back home."

"Well, I guess she finally got her fill."

"She told me she'd done all she could."

"I guess that's so. Your mother doesn't like her much, I guess you know that. She won't let her go now till they're both dead." She patted Shelby's knee. "Wake up, Sister, and look out. That's where they're building the new department store."

Shelby grunted but did not open her eyes. A thread of saliva dangled from her lip.

"How she can get so worn out, and it isn't even eleven," Louise marveled.

"What about Father?" Tom asked.

"Oh, I can't tell you anything more about him."

Tom sank back into a corner of the seat. "I thought you knew him better than anybody else."

"Nobody knows Big Tom," Louise said dryly.

She turned the car through the cemetery gates. Looking out, Tom saw the gravestones standing thick on the hills. "What are we doing here?"

"I want to check on the ivy. Herman's cousin told me he was going to prune it last week. I'm ready to swear he hasn't done a thing all fall, and here it is December already." She swung the car expertly along the curving road. "I must know half the people here."

She pulled up near the family plot and hopped out. A few bare trees fenced the valley; the view of the mountains was pierced by an obelisk.

Tom, following more slowly, turned back to look at Shelby. She had opened her eyes and was watching him through the window. "What about Shelby?" he called to Louise. "Do you want her out?"

"Yes, get her out." She was hurrying briskly down the hill towards the graves.

Tom opened the door and reached in to grasp Shelby's

arm. She came along, sliding heavily across the seat. He thought she might fall when her feet touched the ground, and he threw his other arm around her waist. She leaned against his shoulder, her head bobbing, her big body airy and warm. "Honey," she said, under her breath. "I love you, honey." She shaped her lips to kiss his cheek, and Tom found himself bending down to let her do it.

"Hello, Shelby." Her lips were cushy and moist, and he expected to feel repulsed, but in fact he could not help smiling, and he pressed her fat arm.

As they walked slowly downhill to the graves, Shelby's face suddenly wrinkled and she began to cry.

"What's wrong?" Tom asked.

Louise, kneeling beside her father's grave, explained without looking around, "She remembers when we buried Mama."

"Oh, God," Tom said. "You mean she remembers all that?"

Louise did not reply. With a pair of shears, she was nipping off the fringes of the ivy.

"Don't cry," Tom pleaded with Shelby. He put both arms around her and stood, weighed down, while she sobbed and sobbed.

"Give her some candy," Louise suggested after a while. She dug a roll of mints out of her coat pocket and tossed it in Tom's direction.

Bending down to pick it up, Tom nearly fell under Shelby's sliding weight. He righted her with difficulty and with his free hand began to peel off a mint. "Here," he said, holding it out flat on his palm. She shuffled it up and into her mouth.

"Sit here," he said, lowering her onto a tombstone shaped like a table. She sat on the edge, delicately, her feet barely touching the ground. Tom stayed beside her, afraid that she might topple.

"He hasn't done a darn thing to this ivy," Louise complained. "I'm glad I brought shears." She was piling the cut ivy at her side.

"Is that your father's grave?" Tom asked. He was too far away to make out the words.

"Yes. Mama's over there." She stood up stiffly and went to the next stone. She stood for a while, staring at the inscription. "I never have understood why he put that."

Tom craned to see. "What does it say?"

"'Loveliest and Most Beloved.'"

Tom waited.

"I don't believe she was either one of those," Louise said quietly.

"Well, maybe he thought she was."

"Not he." She leaned down and began to snip off more ivy.

"Well, you never know," Tom said. He handed Shelby another mint. "I mean, you never can tell. I used to think it was a habit or something between Mother and Father. Something that had to do with time."

"It is that, I guess, as well as some other things."

"One time when she was sick—oh, this was years ago—he was lost. I was surprised. It never seemed to me Father needed anybody."

"I guess he needs what she shows him. What she reflects."

"That's not much," Tom said.

Louise went around to the other side of her mother's marker. She stood with her hands on her hips, looking across at Tom. "It may not be much, but it's something. It's more than spending your life on a dog, or a bird. I used to think I'd have more, too. It wasn't the opportunity I lacked;

there was opportunity aplenty." She said it flatly, without pride. "I couldn't have stood it. I found that out in time."

"How did you find out?" Tom asked, alarmed.

"The only people I could put up with were the people who didn't need much. Those were always my kind. My father, he hardly would let me pass him a biscuit. Your father, the year he spent here, he used to let me read to him at night. And, then, of course, Shelby. I've been lucky," she said.

"My God."

"It's better than trying too much and having to give it all up."

Shelby wanted another mint. She pinched Tom's arm to get his attention. Absently he peeled off another candy and laid it in her warm palm.

"Your father most of all," Louise was saying.

"Him?"

"I mean, that was the closest I came. Can you imagine the disaster? I mean, I couldn't have kept it up, I couldn't have done what he wanted; I would have wanted to do too much, or not the right thing. He would have drowned in all that. You know what I like?" She turned to Tom quickly, frowning. "I like to sit by myself in my kitchen and let it get dark. I like not even turning on the light."

Tom stared at her. At a loss, he said, "Father always used to worry about your getting lonely."

"Lonely! I've never been lonely in my life."

"Well, you have Shelby."

She darted to her sister and kissed her on the cheek. "Yes, I have Sister. I'm always going to have Sister now." She was almost singing. "He agreed to that, you know. Your daddy agreed."

"I know. He said he'd done all he could." Hesitantly,

Tom added, "I don't know if that would be enough. For me."

Louise closed the shears and dropped them into her pocket. "I only hope you'll be as lucky."

A cold breeze sifted through the bare trees, and, shivering, Tom hugged his arms.

Louise came close to him. "I told you it wasn't inherited. In my letters. Nothing is passed on like that. What is inherited is the way we all have to stop, quit . . . give up. I don't know how to put it. There isn't much sap in this family anymore. There isn't much juice. You have to accept that, Tom. That's the way you are, too."

He stared at her, chilled. "I don't believe that."

"Then you'll get yourself into a lot of trouble, trying to do things you can't do. Trying to get married, for all I know, and trying to raise children. Going through the motions, to be like everybody else. That's all they'll be: motions. You'll be as dried up inside as I am, and you won't even have the satisfaction of taking care of Shelby."

"You can't decide those things like that. You can't tell me what I can't do."

She started briskly towards the car, without answering. Tom hoisted up Shelby and followed behind.

"You can't expect me to accept that," he said.

She looked at him over the roof of the car. "Why, Tom, I was trying to tell you about your family. Three suicides. In three generations." She slid into the driver's seat. "Not to speak of the small miseries. The drinking, the crying in the night."

Tom pushed Shelby into the front seat and crowded in beside her, shoving her against Louise. "I don't know what you mean. I don't even know if you mean anything."

"Maybe I don't," Louise said. "You go ahead and try."

Rapidly, he insisted, "Tell me what you think."

"I think you're a fool," she said calmly. She started the car and swung slowly around the circle. "Look at that view," she said, edging the bluff. "I've been trying to tell you we don't work in this family the way other people do. That's all I mean."

"You're telling me a riddle."

"Look at your grandparents. Look at my mother and father. Look at your own parents. They learned to get along on little or nothing, the ones who survived. I don't want to use worn-out words, but you know what I mean. A kiss in the morning. A polite word at night. 'My, these corncakes are delicious.' A good feeling for good manners. It's something; it's not nothing," she said.

"It's not enough."

Shelby turned, beaming. "Honey," she crooned. Tom hastily handed her the last mint.

"Well, I don't have a parakeet, and I've never had a dog," Louise said. "It's enough for me." Her voice was low. Looking out the window, she said, "It looks like winter now. There're no leaves left, except the oak."

"I don't want to be like that," Tom said. His voice failed, and he cleared his throat and coughed.

"Then you'd better get out of here," Louise said.

"I like it here." He heard the whine in his voice, petulant, like a child's.

"Then stay and be like the rest of us."

"No. There was a girl, at college . . ."

She raised her hand. "Don't tell me any more about that. If you stay here, it won't ever matter. It won't ever come up again. You can go on here with me and Shelby and cut our firewood in the winter. You can go down to Herman's on Saturday mornings to pick up some doughnuts for breakfast. You can take us to the movies now and then. You can go on here forever, Tom. We'd be grateful."

"I'm not going home," he said.

"No, never. There's nothing for you there."

"I'm not going back to college, either," he said stubbornly.

"All right. Stay here. We'd love it. Wouldn't we, Shelby?"

Shelby was feeling in Tom's jacket pocket for another mint. Tom caught her hand and placed it firmly back in her lap. "All right," he said.

"All right what?"

"I'm going back up there," he said.

"Hallelujah. Go back and beat your brains out against a stone wall."

"Maybe."

"Well, if you're going, you might as well go." She swung sharply onto the highway, heading north. "You don't have anything to get at the house. I'll take you right to the airport."

Tom sucked in his breath.

"You might as well start now," Louise said.

Shelby, clasping her hands, began to whimper.

"Be quiet, Sister," Louise said.

Tom reached out and stroked Shelby's knee. "I'll be back, Shelby," he promised.

Louise turned her head to look at him. Her eyes glittered suddenly, and Tom was reminded of his father. "No you won't," she said.

They drove in silence to the airport. Pulling up before the entrance, Louise stopped the car. "Have you got enough money?"

He felt for his wallet and counted out twenty dollars.

"Here." She thrust her hand into her purse and brought out a wad of bills. "I don't know how much it'll cost."

"Aren't you going to get out?" Tom asked.

She hesitated. "No, I don't believe I will. I have to get home to start those chicken croquettes."